What Draws Us Apart

Isis Chandler

WHAT DRAWS US APART

ISBN: 979-8-218-78530-7

The author, Isis Chandler, created the original artwork seen on the easel on the book's cover.

CONTENT WARNINGS

This book contains underage drinking and a consensual love-making scene involving a seventeen-year-old.

To my husband, Adam, who taught me everything I know about writing.

Table of Contents

Chapter One………………………………………………… 1
Chapter Two………………………………………………… 9
Chapter Three…………………………………………..... 29
Chapter Four………………………………………….. 35
Chapter Five………………………………………………….. 45
Chapter Six…………………………………………… 61
Chapter Seven…………………………………………… 73
Chapter Eight…………………………………………. 83
Chapter Nine…………………………………………… 89
Chapter Ten………………………………………… 93
Chapter Eleven……………………………………….… 101
Chapter Twelve……………………………………………. 105
Chapter Thirteen……………………………………….. 111
Chapter Fourteen………………………………………. 121
Chapter Fifteen…………………………………………. 131
Chapter Sixteen………………………………………..... 139
Chapter Seventeen…………………………………….. 149
Chapter Eighteen………………………………………. 155
Chapter Nineteen…………………………………….… 169
Chapter Twenty……………………………………….... 179
Chapter Twenty One………………………………….. 205
Chapter Twenty Two…………………………………….. 233
Chapter Twenty Three………………………………….. 245
Chapter Twenty Four…………………………………..... 259
Chapter Twenty Five……………………………………. 265
Chapter Twenty Six…………………………………….. 271
Chapter Twenty Seven………………………………….. 275
Chapter Twenty Eight………………………………….. 279
About the Author………………………………………. 287

Chapter One

Saturday, July 8, 2023

The sound of screeching tires causes me to make a black smudge with my charcoal stick. I look at my drawing and frown at the mistake. Headlights pour into my bedroom window. "Bad Romance" blasts from the car's stereo. A blur of grey and white fur leaps to the floor, scurries under my bed, and hides behind my dust ruffle. I guess my cat, Alma, isn't a Lady Gaga fan.

"That was awwesoooome," my sister's idiot friend Kimber shrieks. Her voice is as shrill as her tires. A group of girls compete to be as obnoxious as Kimber. I can't tell if the girls are singing along to the lyrics, "Rah, rah-ah-ah-ah," or all shouting random words. "Roma, roma-ma. Best night eeeevvverrr. Chloe Wells is a whore!"

Houses in Marblehead are built close together. I'm sure our neighbors on Ruby Avenue want to murder the obnoxious clique of teenage girls. How many bimbos did Kimber cram into her sedan? I bet it looks like a clown car.

I try to ignore them and go back to drawing my cat. Kimber's antics made me draw a deep scratch through Alma's green eyes. I erase the line, but the textured charcoal paper makes it almost impossible to fully remove. Now I have another reason to dislike my sister's moronic friend.

I was trying to capture the exact details that make Alma unique. The tiny flecks of yellow in her green eyes. The way her little pink nose is darker in the center. The gray markings that frame her eyes. When I finish this drawing, I'll start portraits of my sister and my parents. That way, if I lose my vision, their faces will be burned into my memory.

I refuse to tell my parents my vision is getting worse. They will rush me to the ophthalmologist, who will tell us, yet again, nothing can be done to improve my eyesight. All the eye doctor will do is prescribe even thicker glasses. The frames I have now

1

are heavy and uncomfortable enough. Why put my parents under stress? My sister gives them enough to worry about.

The sound of babbling teenagers slowly disappears as Kimber drives off. My body relaxes for a moment. The silence is wonderful.

My phone buzzes on the bathroom countertop. I pay it no mind. Instead, I look towards my bed. "You can come out now," I say to Alma.

A blurry grey head pokes out from under my bed.

"It's alright. Come on out."

Alma takes a few steps forward.

Our front door bangs shut. "Do you have any idea what time it is?" my mother yells.

Alma darts back under my bed.

"Oh God, here we go," I whisper. My crap vision makes my other senses excellent. I'd hide under my bed too, if I thought it could muffle the sounds of the argument.

"You're an hour late!" my father yells.

"Whaaateeeever," my sister Tonya slurs.

"And you're drunk!" Mom shouts. "Was Kimber drunk when she dropped you off?"

"No, she was the deeesignated—driiiiver." Tonya slurs and giggles.

Anybody in earshot of Kimber's voice could tell she was drunk tonight. "She could've killed somebody!" Mom yells.

"Don't be so dramatic." Tonya never takes anything seriously.

My phone buzzes three more times. Who is that? My friends never message me this late.

"Your mother and I aren't going to put up with any more of this, Tonya. You're grounded!"

"Whaaat-EVVVEEER!" Tonya sounds like a banshee. "Like there's anything fun in this shit town to do anyway!" She thumps up our stairs. Her bedroom door slams so hard that everything on my easel rattles.

I'm too annoyed to keep drawing. I drop my charcoal stick, put my glasses back on, and go wash my hands in the bathroom I share with my sister.

I reach into the dark bathroom and switch the light on while keeping my eyes closed. Sudden changes in light can cause huge white glares in my vision. It's scary not being able to see anything in those flashes.

Our bathroom still smells of the jasmine perfume Tonya sprayed on before she went out. The scent is intense, and it lingers long after Tonya leaves a room. It's a perfect scent for her. People often talk about her long after she's left a room. Mostly about how freaking beautiful she is.

I wash the charcoal off my hands, and I look at my reflection in the mirror, making sure I have no black dust smudged across my face or in my brown hair. Nobody would say anything about my appearance after I've exited a room, except maybe how thick my glasses are.

I pick up my phone and see several new Instagram notifications. Someone with the username jdrakos likes a few photos of me from my cousin Mike's Instagram. A photo of me, Mike, and our friend Seth dressed up as Harry, Ron, and Hermione for Halloween when we were young. A photo of Mike and me at my middle school graduation. My glasses are in one hand; my diploma is in the other. Mike's arm is around me. A photo from last week of Mike and me at the beach. My glasses are in my hand again. I hate this photo. I look like a stick in my bikini. I wish Mike hadn't posted this one. Thank God my top has some padding, and I have a cover-up wrapped around my hips. The beach attire helps create the illusion of curves.

Alma meows, flops down on the bathmat, and shows me her belly. She needs some love to relieve the stress Tonya caused tonight. I bow down to my furry overlord and pet her fluffy tummy.

Another notification telling me that jdrakos has commented on a post I'm tagged in. I click on it. This person wrote, "pretty girl," in the comments under a photo of me in a bikini. I blush.

Who the hell is this person? I click on their profile. Their profile picture is a drawing of a dragon. "This Account is Private." I have to send a follow request and have it approved before I can even see who they are. Screw that. I'll ask Mike who this is the next time I see him.

3

I head downstairs. Most of the lights are off in the living room because Mom and Dad were gazing out the window, waiting for Tonya to come home. They always do that when she turns off her phone and breaks curfew. The only light source comes from one standing lamp next to our couch.

"Tonya is going to be an adult in a few months," Mom says. "Then what are we going to do?"

"I don't care if she's legally an adult." My father pushes his glasses up his nose. "As long as she's under *my* roof, she'll do things *my* way."

"That is brilliant, Doug," Mom says. "Treating her like a child will make her flee to New York before she has enough money to take care of herself."

I walk past our couch close enough to see that my parents look older than usual. Maybe it's the overhead lighting showing off their laugh lines and other wrinkles. Even in bad lighting, my mom still looks beautiful. She's only thirty-nine years old. She looks like an older version of my sister. They're both tall with thick straight hair that hangs down to their perfect C cups. They both have light brown hair, although Tonya bleaches her hair light blonde. They both have striking green eyes. My mother is two decades older than me, and she's still one hundred times prettier.

I head to the kitchen for water and painkillers.

"If she'd apply to colleges, we wouldn't have these problems," Dad says for the hundredth time.

"We can't force her to go. She insists she doesn't want to, 'waste her best modeling career years trapped on a dumb campus," Mom says in Tonya's voice. "Duh, Mom. Everyone knows if you're not booking major fashion magazines by twenty, your career is over."

Dad yanks his glasses off and starts cleaning them on his shirt. He always does that when he's frustrated. He thinks if he could clean his glasses enough, he'd be able to see a solution to all his problems.

I rattle the bottle of aspirin in my hands to get their attention. "Is that for your sister?" Dad asks.

"Yes."

"Good idea," Dad says. "Make sure she drinks a lot of water."

Mom smiles at me. "Thanks, Kira. You're such a good sister." She looks back at Dad. "Isn't there some scary documentary about abuse in the modeling industry we can make Tonya watch?"

I hate it when Mom belittles our dreams. "Maybe there's some *scary documentary* about artists *stabbed to death* with their own pencils you can make *me* watch."

Dad laughs until Mom gives him a disapproving look. He stifles his laughter. "Nobody likes a smart ass, sweetie."

"Yes, they do, they just don't admit it. Good night."

"Night, Kira," Dad says.

I tuck the aspirin bottle under my arm so I have a free hand to grip the banister. I count the steps in my head so I don't trip. I always walk up and down stairs like a careful old lady. I pass family photos hanging on the wall. I have an eyepatch on in every photo from early childhood. In the photo of my second Halloween, the whole family dressed up in pirate costumes to match my look.

When I'm almost back in my room, Mom says, "I'm sure we could find a scary documentary about how many artists *starve to death*."

My body tenses up. My mother's mind is narrower than her waistline.

Our bathroom connects my room and my sister's room. I walk through it and knock on Tonya's door.

"Come in."

Her room is so girly compared to mine. She loves light pink bedspreads and curtains. I love plum purple walls covered with prints of my favorite artists.

"Mom and Dad are freaking out," I scold.

Tonya holds out her hand. "Because I came home buzzed or because I refuse to budge on the college discussion?"

"Both." I drop two tablets into my sister's hand.

"Whatever. Mom can nag us about our goals being unrealistic when she's brave enough to get a goal herself."

God, I love my sister.

She pops the tablets into her mouth and chugs them down with water.

I sit on the edge of Tonya's bed. I get close enough to see that even with smudged eye makeup and bedhead, she looks gorgeous.

"What happened tonight?"

"Don't ask."

"That bad? What did Scott do?"

She looks at me, surprised. "Nothing. Scott and I broke up last month. Remember?"

"Then who did you go to the dance with last week?"

"Steve."

"Right, Steve. I got him confused with Scott. What'd Steve do wrong tonight?"

"I wasn't with Steve tonight. I dumped him the night of the dance."

I shake my head. "Jesus. I can't keep up with all your boyfriends. Who the hell were you with tonight, and what did he do wrong?"

"It wasn't one of my boyfriends. I'm single. Eric Lawndale spent the whole night flirting with me. He's too boring and stupid to date. I don't think there is a single boy left in my school that I'm interested in."

"So, why'd you get drunk? What caused all the drama?"

"Kimber's asshole boyfriend got caught kissing Chloe Wells. Kimber was pissed. She needed a good drinking buddy, so I…"

"Got really drunk, turned off your phone, and came home an hour past curfew." I give her a disapproving stare.

"That's not true." She pauses and picks up her phone. "I didn't turn off my phone. It broke." She hands it to me. "See. That's why I lost track of time. That and Kimber told me it was an hour earlier than it was to keep me partying."

It won't power on. "Maybe the battery died."

"No, I—well, I may have *accidentally* dropped it in the toilet." Tonya giggles.

I throw it across the room. "Gross." I wipe my hands on my jeans. "Yuck. It's covered in the ass germs of a hundred teenagers."

She laughs. "You know, you could've come with me to the party tonight."

Eric Lawndale's huge house seems like a scary maze. That house is so big, I could get lost stone-cold sober. With my bad vision, the possibilities of humiliating myself at a party are endless. I don't mention any of these concerns to my sister. I don't want her to feel sorry for me. Instead, I say, "Then I'd have to hang out with Kimber. No, thank you. Besides, Mom and Dad would be furious if they knew where you really went to party. If they found out you took me, you'd be grounded until you're ninety."

Chapter Two

Saturday, July 15, 2023

"Morning, birthday girl," my mother says. I open my eyes to see her blurry outline standing over my bed.

I reach for my glasses and slide them on. My mother's hazy form becomes her familiar slender figure. I blink. Two slender figures are standing over my bed. I blink a few times.

"What's wrong?" my mother asks.

The double vision morphs back into one image. "Nothing. I saw double. It's fine now."

My mother sits down on my bed and looks at my eyes. "They're looking straight, but we should still do the test."

The eyepatch I wore until age six did not fix my inward-turning eye. I had to have an operation to correct the problem. My ophthalmologist told my parents that the esotropia could return at any time.

Every time my parents see me so much as squint, they make me do this. My mother holds her hand up. She moves it left, right, up, down, and in a circle, making sure my right eye doesn't turn inward at any point.

"They're fine. No crossed eyes. Your vision was probably blurry for a second because you just woke up. Now get up and get dressed."

An hour later, Tonya and I are rushing to finish getting ready. "Where's the blush?" I ask her as I rummage through our makeup kit.

"It's under the bronzer." Tonya takes the steam rollers out of her hair.

I never have to buy makeup because Tonya always lets me use whatever she has in stock. We have the same round facial features and the same skin tone. I find the blush and apply it to my cheeks.

"I don't know why I even bother to put curls in my hair," Tonya complains as she separates her ringlets with a wide-tooth comb. "The humidity is gonna make them fall out in twenty minutes. I'd give anything for your natural waves." She fluffs the end of my high ponytail.

"Yeah, well, I'd give anything to have your *everything*." I think Tonya's biological father must have been a male model. She fills out her pink sundress perfectly. I barely fill out my similar green dress.

"I'd give anything for your thin figure," Tonya insists. "Today you're gonna pig out on pizza and birthday cake. You won't gain a pound. I'm gonna eat half as much as you and I'll have to work it off at the gym later this week."

"I guess the grass is always greener." I put my thick glasses back on to see my appearance. "How does my makeup look?"

She zooms in closer. "Great, but you need eye makeup."

"Why? My glasses are so thick nobody can tell I'm wearing any."

She takes off my glasses and starts working on my eye makeup. "They can. It's your birthday, you need eyes that pop. You're gonna look beautiful today. Are you sure you don't want to try contacts again?"

"No way. They gave me pounding headaches. I'm never putting those things in my eyes again."

She blends the shadow. "Your eyes look great in this shade. Take off your glasses when we take pictures. She finishes my shadow, liner, and mascara. "You look beautiful."

"Girls, come on," Mom yells from the hall. "Melony's here. We've got to go."

"Coming," Tonya and I say in unison.

We head downstairs and see my best friend Melony dressed in a pretty blouse and a short skirt. She's holding balloons and a birthday gift. Her super curly blonde hair is pulled into a high bun. The poor girl has bad acne. She layers foundation to try and cover it. "Happy birthday." She scans my outfit. "Oh my God, that is the cutest dress."

I hug her hello.

"Your boobs *actually* look full in it, too," she whispers.

10

"Really?" I glance down. The Empire waist shows off what little I have. I guess they grew a little when I wasn't looking. "Maybe I should buy a B cup bra."

"If you think it'll help," Melony says.

"You're gonna be late to your own funeral." Mom yells into her phone as she crosses behind us to the coat closet. "Are you leaving now?"

"Yes," Aunt Ginny insists on the other end of the phone.

"I mean, right *now*! Not twenty minutes from now. I mean this minute!" Mom rushes to add her sunglasses to her purse.

"God, you're uptight. Yes, we're leaving *now!*" Aunt Ginny makes fun of the way Mom said it. "We'll be there as soon as humanly possible. We're driving to Boston in my car because I'm not gonna put up with your bitching all the way there." She hangs up.

"Oh, you little bit—" Mom stops herself when she sees all of us staring at her. She shoves her phone in her purse and rushes us all out the door. "Come on, everyone. There are three floors and over twenty rooms to see before the museum closes at five." We rush out to our minivan with gifts and balloons in everyone's hands.

It is a beautiful summer day in Boston. The city's streets are lined with lush, green trees. We turn onto Evans Way. I'm so excited to finally be at The Gardner Museum. I rush ahead of everyone.

"Kira, don't go too far." Mom treats me like I'm still five years old. I hate it when my mother says things like that around my friends.

Aunt Ginny's old Toyota comes barreling down the one-way street. Shakira's "Whenever, Wherever" is blasting out of her speakers.

"Does constantly blasting music from your teenage years keep you mentally a teenager forever?" Tonya asks.

Before I can answer, Aunt Ginny's brakes squeak. She drove past an empty space. Her engine rattles as she shifts into reverse and backs up way too fast.

"Isn't it a bad idea to back up that fast on a one-way street?' Melony asks Tonya.

"Yeah," Tonya says. "Aunt Ginny is such a masshole." Asshole Massachusetts drivers think road rules are only suggestions.

Ginny aligns her car to parallel park.

Our mother rushes over, yelling, "You shouldn't park here. You should drive to the paid lot the way we did."

Ginny's car isn't at a good angle. She pulls out.

"The lot is that way," Mom points towards the garage.

Ginny starts the parallel parking process over again.

Our mother realizes she's being ignored. "Hello. Did you hear me? I said, you shouldn't—"

Ginny turns up her stereo, drowning out everything Mom is saying. She finishes parking as slowly as she can. She turns off her engine and gets out of her car. I can't see her clearly from this distance, but I know exactly how she looks today. She's dressed in jeans and a t-shirt. Her long, obviously dyed red hair is in a high ponytail. She dresses like she's still in her early twenties.

"Hi, Doug," Ginny says to Dad, before turning to Mom. "Sorry, did you say something?" She rushes over to the meter and starts putting in quarters.

"Are you crazy? If you park here, you have to come outside every few hours and put quarters in," Mom insists.

"Better that than walking half a mile to the lot," Ginny says.

Tonya sighs. "Here we go again." She pulls a small thermos out of her purse and sips.

A car door slams. My cousin Mike and his best friend Seth step closer to us. I recognize Mike's light brown hair color. I can tell it's Seth from the bright yellow and orange shirt he has on. Seth always wears colors as loud as his personality. He walks with an extra spring in his step. It makes his blonde hair flop.

"We're going in one group," Mom insists. "If you have to leave the group every hour to come out here to put quarters in, we're not gonna wait for you."

"Cindy, let your sister do what she wants," Dad says.

"Thank you, Doug," Ginny says.

My sister drinks more from her thermos.

"No, Doug, Ginny always messes things up," Mom snaps at Dad.

An unfamiliar person in a green shirt gets out of my aunt's car. I can't recognize any of their mannerism, so I know it's someone I've never met before. Did Mike bring a date to my birthday? I smile. It's about time he got a girlfriend. The mystery person steps closer. They're too tall and their shoulders are too broad to be a girl. My hopes of Mike having a date are dashed.

"Who's the hottie?" Melony asks.

"I've no idea." I don't mention that I can't see him clearly at this distance. Nobody wants to be friends with someone they feel sorry for.

As he comes closer, I can tell he has wavy black hair.

"What about the time we got stranded outside of that dive bar at two in the morning because you parked in a space marked tenants only," Mom reminds Ginny. "Your car got towed, and we had to call Dad to pick us up. Of course, he found a way to blame me for that!"

"That was twenty years ago, Cindy. Let it go already." Ginny finishes dropping in quarters. "Who am I kidding? You never let go of anything. You're probably going to die of constipation."

My cheeks feel like they're turning red. My aunt did not say that in front of a stranger. Tonya and I exchange glances.

"Could you be any more immature and inappropriate?" Mom yells.

"Could you be any more of a control freak?" Ginny yells back.

Tonya takes a big gulp.

Mike walks up to me. He looks as uncomfortable as I do. "Happy birthday, Kira." He hugs me.

"Thanks," I whisper.

"Yeah, happy birthday," Seth says. He tries to ruffle my hair.

I move my head to the side. *Screw you, Seth.* I backstep and—*Oh shit.* My foot hits an uneven surface, and I brace myself for the impact of my butt slamming on cement.

I fall into someone's arms.

"Whoa, careful," a concerned voice says.

I grip onto the warm arms wrapped around me. I attempt to steady myself. I look up at the most beautiful face I've ever seen, inches away from mine. Perfect round lips. Cut cheekbones. The green eyes I wish I'd been born with.

"Are you alright?"

"Huh?"

He helps me regain my balance.

I look away from his perfect face so I can regain the ability to speak.

He keeps one hand on my lower back, making sure I don't lose my balance again.

"I'm fine – thank you." I look down and notice the uneven surface where the cement sidewalk becomes a brick walkway. Any normal person with decent peripheral vision would have seen that. "I'm so sorry."

He smiles. "For what? Trying to avoid Seth's crap. I've lived next to the guy for three weeks. I'm ready to put up a fence the size of the Great Wall of China."

I smile.

Mike finally introduces us. "Girls, this is our new friend, Jason Drakos."

This is the guy who said I looked pretty in a bikini. My heart pounds.

"Jason, these are my cousins Kira and Tonya, and that's Kira's friend Melony," Mike says.

Melony smiles and gives a breathy, "Hi."

My sister pops a breath mint. "Did you move into the same apartment complex Mike lives in?"

"Yeah," Jason says, "My aunt rented one of the units."

"Cool. So, I guess you'll be at Marblehead High with us next fall?" Tonya asks. "You look too old to be an underclassman. Are you a senior like Mike, Seth, and me?"

"Yeah."

"It must suck having to move your senior year." My sister never feels intimidated by anyone. She'd be able to saunter up to Timothée Chalamet and start a conversation. "So, where'd you move here from and what are you into?" she asks Jason before he has a chance to respond to her last sentence.

"A small town in Connecticut," Jason says.

"Did you do that on purpose?" Melony whispers in my ear.

"Do what?"

"Fall so that hottie would catch you?" She giggles.

"What? No. I lost my balance again because I'm clumsy."

Tonya continues her friendly interrogation of Jason. "And what do you do for fun?"

"Jason's into art, sci-fi, and fantasy," Mike answers for him. "That's why I invited him today. He heard we were going to an art museum with a gelfling, and he just had to come."

Everyone glances at me, including Jason. He knows I'm named after a rubber puppet. I'm so lame. "My Dad's a fantasy geek."

"Of course. Of course, you forgot your debit card," Mom bellows at Aunt Ginny.

I'm almost grateful for the distraction.

"You never carry cash, and you always conveniently forget your card when we go out."

My face blushes. "I'm so sorry about all the family drama." I apologize to Jason.

"You call this drama?" he asks, smiling. "Trust me. You haven't seen drama until you've seen my aunt yell at my dad. This is so mild."

He makes me feel a little less embarrassed.

"I guess you expect me to pay for you and your kid again." Mom fumes.

Tonya takes my arm. "You don't need to listen to this crap on your birthday." She leads all the teens inside the museum lobby.

Tonya has agreed to use her phone for the guided audio tour of each room. I'm grateful because as long as Mom and Aunt Ginny have to listen to the information, they can't fight.

"Artists are invited to stay in the Museum, now in apartments located in the New Wing," the audio recording says.

Aunt Ginny smiles at me. "Maybe you can get a place here when you're older. After you graduate from art school."

I smile, somewhat excited. Until my mother makes a disapproving huffing sound.

"That would be amazing," Jason says.

I turn and see him staring at the portrait of *Mrs. Gardner in White*. Jason takes the time to look at each piece of art carefully. Unlike my cousin and his idiot friend. Mike and Seth's way of appreciating the art in this room is to laugh as they point out the small breasts on the statue of the goddess Diana.

Everyone moves around the room, looking at all the pieces one at a time. I've seen everything in here, and I'm excited for the next room. I studied a map of the museum yesterday, so I don't get lost walking around this huge place.

I head into the narrow gallery called the Vatichino room. It used to be a coat closet before they turned it into a gallery. I'm guessing most of the pieces in this room are meant to be viewed close up.

This is where they house one of the paintings I've been dying to see. *Pergola, Green Hill*. The painting is only sixteen by twelve inches, but it stands out from the other pieces in the room. It has the perspective of a Renaissance painting and the blurry brush strokes of the Impressionist period. I hope to recapture these lighting and shading techniques myself in a future art project.

"You wanna paint something similar, don't you?"

I turn to see Jason. "How'd you know?"

"Mike told me you're an artist."

"Yeah." I look back at the painting. If I look at him, I'll stammer again. "The problem is, I have the hardest time drawing or painting perspective. That's why artists who do it well amaze me," I point to the center of the canvas. "I love how the shrubs in the distance look as in focus as the plants in the front."

Jason leans in to see what I'm pointing at. He's close enough for me to smell his woody-herbal scent.

My cheeks blush, and my body temperature spikes. "My eyes can't see like that." *What the hell is wrong with me? Why did I say that?*

"Sorry, that must be frustrating."

"Very," I agree. I move to the side to look at another portrait of Mrs. Gardner. I hope he can't see how flushed I am. "I got a C in art when I had to do a painting using perspective. I never get C's. I usually get A's in art class."

He follows me around the tiny room, looking at the same pieces I look at.

"Is the art teacher hard to please? Do I have to worry about her giving me bad grades?"

"You take art classes?" I look at him, surprised.

"I wanna start this year. Things were kind of crazy back in my hometown. I didn't have time for electives, but I will now."

"I take it you're the jdrakos who blew up my phone. Did you do that dragon drawing in your profile picture?"

"I wish," he scoffs. "I can't draw that well. Do I have to worry about the art teacher being critical of my mediocre skills?"

"Yeah. Miss Coleman can be demanding."

He steps closer and stands in front of me. "So, what do you create that gets you A's in such a demanding teacher's class?"

"Uh, I, um." *My god, he's beautiful. Boys shouldn't get to be this pretty. It's not fair.* I move to the side and look into a display case. "Close-up, detailed images of small objects." I look into the case. "You see that knife?"

Jason leans down and reads the description, "A Sudanese dagger purchased on a trip to Egypt."

I bend over to get a better look. "Well, do you see all the stitching on the hilt? And all the lines and ridges in the crocodile skin?"

"Yeah."

"And the way the light reflects off the metal, skin, and leather?"

He doesn't answer.

I look back at him and notice that his eyes aren't examining the dagger. Is he looking down my sundress? I stand up quickly. I'm not used to having anything to look at. Melony is right about this dress showing off what little I have. *Why are all guys obsessed with breasts?*

"Well, I could, um." I cross my arms over my chest. "I could draw that dagger close up and re-create all those small details."

"Really? You've gotta show me how you draw. I can't draw details for shit. That's why I'm more of a photographer and cartoonist than an artist. I'm awful at realism. What medium do you use?"

"Charcoal and pastel mostly."

"Let me see your right hand."

I look at him, surprised, and hold up my hand.

He takes it in his. "How'd you get this scar?" he asks, looking at my palm.

"My parents said I cut it on broken glass. I must have been really young because I can't remember."

"I'm sorry." He examines my hand more closely.

"Are you into palmistry? You could work at my Aunt Ginny's store in Salem, giving readings."

"No. I'm seeing how dedicated you are to your craft. It's hard to see the fingerprints of artists who use a lot of charcoal." He uses his right hand to trace his fingertips over mine.

I jump.

"Super smooth. You draw constantly."

"Uh-huh," I stammer. I'm blushing so hard. I can't look at him. I stare at our linked hands. I can't think of a thing to say. My heart pounds in my ears.

"Any naked people in here?" Seth invades our small space.

I jump back and pull my hand away. I'll be teased to death if Seth finds out how hard I'm crushing on Jason.

I turn and face the artifacts cabinet again.

Seth takes a glance around the small room. "None. I'll see if there are any naked boobs in the Yellow Room or the Blue Room." He looks at me before he leaves. "Why are all the rooms named after colors, Kira?"

Jason's too close to me. I can't think straight. "I don't know." I move to the side and pretend to be interested in a painting I've already seen.

"I think it has to do with the color of the walls," Jason explains.

"I've only seen like one or two naked paintings so far," Seth complains. "This museum is a tease. Why don't they have a red room? That could be where they hung all the naked pics."

"Oh, my god," I whisper.

"Why don't you go make that suggestion to the receptionist, Seth?" Jason says.

"Good idea," Seth heads out. "See you two later. I'll be in the Blue Balls Room."

Jason laughs.

"He must be the most obnoxious person in Massachusetts," I complain.

"Yeah, but he has his good qualities."

"Like what?"

"Well, for one thing, he adores you," Jason says. "He talked about how awesome your art is. He also mentioned in the car that he can't believe you're sixteen already. He said when you were kids, you were the cutest little girl he's ever seen."

I smile. "He was so different when we were kids. As soon as he hit puberty, he got so, well, obnoxious."

"I can't wait to check out your art to see if he's right about how awesome it is." He steps closer.

"Well, um, we should, uh, probably catch up with the rest of the group. I mean, there's a lot of art to see." I exit the room. I need to find an air conditioning vent to stand under.

My sister is standing in the hallway. "Can I have some water?" I reach for the thermos in the pocket of her purse.

"I already drank it all." She pulls her purse closer. She makes the mistake of breathing too close to me.

I can smell the alcohol on her breath. "What the hell, Tonya. What's in your thermos?"

"Orange juice."

"Don't lie."

"Relax. It's a little vodka. I made a Screwdriver."

"Are you insane? Mom and Dad will kill you if they find out."

"So don't tell them. It's a special occasion. A birthday party. At least it should be. I'm so bored in this museum. I wanted something about today to be fun. I poured a tiny bit into my thermos. Mom and Dad will never miss it, trust me. Don't tell them. Mom has already done enough yelling today, don't you think?" She pops another breath mint.

"Kira," my mother says, rushing around the corner. "Where did you go? I was worried."

Jason comes out of the Vatichino room just in time to hear my mother's overprotective rant.

Mom takes my arm. "You shouldn't go off like that." Her hand squeezes my arm. "You could get lost on your own."

I cringe.

"Would you stop treating her like an invalid?" Tonya says to our mother. "It's a museum, not a nightclub. What do you think is going to happen? Is Kira going to get trapped in one of the paintings like people in that stupid Roald Dahl book?"

I'm grateful my sister points out how ridiculous my mother is. My Dad's voice comes from the Blue room. I walk towards him.

I guess my mother's master plan for everyone to stay together at all times isn't working out the way she expected.

By the time we get to the restaurant, everyone's starving. Mom and Dad sit at one end of the table.

"Sit down here with me so we can catch up." Tonya leads Aunt Ginny to the far end of the table away from our mother. Tonya keeps Aunt Ginny busy, talking about all the crazy people she meets while giving psychic readings in Salem.

Melony waits for Seth to sit down and then takes the seat right next to him. She motions for me to sit next to her, so I'm right between her and Tonya.

We order all our food without the adults arguing over whether everyone should order individual pies or large pies for

20

the table to share. Once our order is placed, Tonya insists I open my presents. I get a pink rose quartz pendant on a silver chain from Aunt Ginny and Mike.

"It promotes self-love and stimulates the heart chakra," my aunt explains.

I have no idea what she is talking about. "Okay, cool, thanks. It's really pretty," I tell her. I think it will look great with my pink tops, but I have no plans to use it to stimulate my heart chakra, whatever the hell that means.

I get a pair of earrings from Melony. My sister gives me a new set of charcoal drawing pencils and a set of pastels. Seth hands me another small box. I assume I'm getting a bracelet to go with all my other new jewelry. I open it and pull out a silver key ring with a car decal.

"For the car you'll get this year," Seth says.

Everyone at the table goes silent.

Seth looks at me. "Aren't you gonna get your license this year? Your parents got Tonya a car when she got her license. So, I figured you'd get one too."

"Dude. Kira's vision might prevent her from getting her license," Mike reminds Seth.

"Oh, right, shit." Seth looks so uncomfortable. "Sorry, Kira. I didn't realize—"

"It's okay, Seth," I assure him. He might be the only person who looks at me and doesn't think about how thick my glasses are. I don't want him to feel bad about this. "I can still use it for my house keys. Mom, Dad? Should I open your gift next?" I'm hoping this will be the end of this conversation.

"I was so bummed when Kira couldn't take driver's ed with me," Melony tells Seth.

My stomach tightens. "Nobody needs to worry about it. I've already prepared myself for a life of taking Ubers."

"Why can't Kira take driver's ed class?" Seth asks, confused. "Most of it is memorizing boring crap." He looks at me. "In a few years, doctors will have some new turbocharged micro laser tool to correct all vision problems. You'd be closer to getting your license after they fix your eyes if you pass the written part of the test."

21

"The driver's ed programs costs like eight hundred bucks," Melony reminds him. "That's a lot of money to pay for something you won't use for a few years." Melony is so delighted to be having a conversation with Seth that she isn't considering my feelings.

"Besides," Melony says, leaning into Seth, "Kira's glasses are thick. I'm sure her prescription is, like, way too bad to qualify for the—"

I kick her under the table.

"Ow." She looks at me, shocked.

"Shut up," I whisper.

"Kira can get laser eye surgery in two years. Then she'll take driver's ed and do anything else she wants," Tonya insists.

"Let's not get ahead of ourselves," Mom says. "Kira's doctor said that everyone should wait until they're twenty-five to get LASIK."

I sink into my seat.

"Whatever. If Kira's an adult at eighteen, then she should be able to get LASIK no matter what the doctor says," Tonya insists. "Her eyes, her decision. Waiting seven years for an operation you need *now*, that's just stupid."

"Tonya, human eyes develop and change until age twenty-four. Having that procedure too early can cause complications later in life," Mom reminds her.

"I'll take it," Melony announces and picks up my new key ring. I guess that is her attempt to get everyone to drop the subject. "I'll get my license soon, and then I can drive Kira around."

Tonya makes a disapproving huff.

Dad is the one who notices how uncomfortable I am. "Why don't you open our gift next?"

I take it from him. "Thanks, Dad."

Tonya looks frustrated. She picks up Aunt Ginny's wine glass and gulps some down before any of the adults see.

I tear at the wrapping paper and see a Wacom drawing tablet. "Cool. Thanks." I rush to get the rest of the paper off and tear open the box. I turn it on and see that Adobe Creative Cloud is already installed. "This is amazing."

"Now you can create digital art too," Mom says. "I hope that leads to fewer pencil and charcoal shavings to vacuum up each week."

"A car would've been cooler," Seth mumbles.

I open Adobe Illustrator and use the stylus to practice painting. There are so many different brushes and colors to paint with. So many different features to practice using.

I begin a drawing of the dagger I saw in the display case. I'm so intrigued by my new toy that I'm unaware of any of the conversations happening around me.

Jason walks around the table and stands by my chair. "Happy birthday, Kira." He hands me a rolled-up poster of *Pergola, Green Hill.* "Sorry, I didn't have time to wrap it. It's from the museum's gift shop."

"Thank you. I'm going to get a frame for this. I really love it."

He pulls his phone out of his back pocket. "I followed your Instagram today. The details you draw are sick. I can't draw like this."

"Is 'sick' a good thing?" Aunt Ginny asks, confused.

Melony looks at my aunt like she's stupid. "Uh, yeah."

"Do you think you could teach me to draw the way you do?" Jason asks me.

I look at him, surprised. "I don't know. I could try if you want."

"I'd really appreciate it. I looked up Miss Coleman online. I don't think she has half your talent."

I smile. "Really?"

"Yeah. So can I come over for a drawing class?"

"Okay. Yeah. Sure. I'll, uh, let you know, um, when I have time." Why can't I speak a normal sentence around him?

"Happy birthday, Kira." He heads back to his seat at the other end of the table.

Tonya smiles at me and raises her eyebrows. She thinks she knows a secret, and we'll talk about it later. I notice that Aunt Ginny's wine glass is empty. Tonya's eyes look glazed over, and her smile is a little too happy for someone who was so frustrated a moment ago.

Melony gets my attention by poking me in the ribs. "Maybe you could pose for him naked."

I blush. "Mel."

"Or you could draw him naked. I'd buy that one from you," Melony teases.

"So would I," Aunt Ginny says.

We all look at her, shocked.

"What? I assure you, girls, when you're my age, you'll still notice beautiful people."

Mike grunts in disgust and pinches the bridge of his nose.

It's late, but I'm too wired to sleep. I can't get Jason's face out of my head. He approved my follow request. I scrolled through his Instagram photos until I found a clear image of his face. I've been drawing his portrait for over an hour.

I've got his facial features down. It's time to add shading. I should be drawing with my new tablet. I started playing around with all the features in Adobe Illustrator, but digital art doesn't feel like the right medium for this drawing. You can't smudge digital art like charcoal. Using your fingers is more intimate.

I put my headphones on and listen to "Daylight." I use my ring finger to blend the pastel colors as I draw Jason's lips and cheekbones. I grab my flesh-colored pastel stick and blend it in with a pink stick to recreate lip color. Then I blend with my fingertips.

My super smooth fingertips.

The memory of his hand on mine makes me blush again. My hand stills on the paper. I imagine his fingertips running down my neck, down my shoulders. Unzipping the back of my dress. Running down my...

My sister's standing five feet away from my easel.

"Jesus Christ!" I yell and yank off my headphones. I grab a new sheet of paper and cover my drawing. I lock it in place with a drawing clamp.

"Jeez, you're jumpy. What's with you tonight?"

"Nothing." I rush to close Jason's Instagram on my phone.

"Did you have fun today?" Tonya asks. "Was it a good birthday?"

"Yep." *She didn't see my drawing.* I take a deep breath. Then I start drawing random black lines on the new paper.

"Why are you so spastic right now?"

"I'm not." I scratch my charcoal stick in clumsy strokes so she will think I'm really into what I'm working on. "I'm fine."

"So, Jason is a hottie, isn't he?"

My charcoal stick snaps.

Tonya laughs at me. "He's so hot, just the sound of his name gets to you."

"Shut up." I grab another stick from my art bin. "I don't even think he's hot. He looked kind of blurry to me."

"Oh, please. You looked so *enamored* with him today."

I stop drawing and stare at her. "I wasn't enamored."

"You blushed every time he looked at you."

"I did not."

"And when he broke your fall, you stayed in his arms way longer than you needed to." She puts her hand on her forehead and pretends to swoon.

"I did not. I was just finding my balance."

"And the two of you were alone in that tiny gallery room forever. What happened in there?"

I hide behind my easel so she can't see me blush. How can someone's fingertips touching mine for a split second have such an effect on me?

"Hello, Earth to Kira. What happened in there?"

"Nothing. We talked about art."

"*Just* art, huh?"

"Yes, Tonya. Believe it or not, some people actually like visiting museums."

"Some people, like you and Jason. You two have so much in common. We should start planning your wedding."

"Would you shut up already?" I yell at her. "You're acting so stupid."

"Why don't you admit that you like him?"

"I've known him for five minutes. He could have a girlfriend back home. I don't even know him." I go back to randomly adding lines to a page.

25

"Yeah, but you want to. That is why you're attacking your canvas in frustration."

I stop drawing. "This is *not* a canvas. It's an eighty-pound sheet of charcoal paper. You don't know everything, Tonya."

"So, are you trying to tell me that you have *no interest* in Jason?"

"Not at the moment."

"*Liar.* Why do you always lie when you like someone? It's normal to have crushes. The cops aren't gonna arrest you for having one. Would you at least admit that you think he's hot?"

"I guess he could be considered good-looking."

"That's it? That's all you have to say about him?"

"Yep." I go back to my fake drawing.

"Why are you such a liar?" Tonya asks. "I tell you everything about my boyfriends. You can't even tell me when you think someone's hot."

"If and when I think someone's hot, I'll tell you. Everyone looks blurry to me, so I rarely see a blur that I think is hotter than another blur."

"Bullshit. You can see fine close-up. If everything and everyone's a blur, then why the hell did we spend your birthday in an art museum? If you can see paintings close-up, you can see people close-up too. And I know you saw how hot he is. Especially when he caught you. Your face was inches from his. Stop using your eyes as an excuse to hide away from the world."

"I don't hide from the world. Get out and let me draw." My hand scrubs the charcoal stick into the paper.

"Yeah, right. What's that a drawing of? Your huge black void of insecurity?"

She knows me too well. I give up the farce. I drop the charcoal stick and glare at her.

"Tell me how hard you're crushing on Jason so we can figure out how you can get him."

"*Get* him? Are you insane? He's not an object you can pick up at the store."

"He's into everything you're into. He wants you to teach him how to draw. Why don't you text him and invite him over?"

26

"I will. When I get to know him better."

"Do it now."

"No way. Hanging out and drawing with someone is really personal. I always draw in my room. I'm not ready to invite someone I barely know into my personal space." I need to wait until I know him well enough not to act like a stammering mess around him. I'll hang out with Jason a few more times when Mike invites me to join them. Then I'll be ready.

"So, draw in the living room."

"You know Mom won't let me."

"So, teach him in the backyard. It's summer."

"Too windy."

"Oh, my God. Stop making excuses. That guy is gonna have every girl in school after him. Go for it before someone else does."

"Are you crazy?" I ask her. "Jason's a senior. He's not gonna date an inexperienced sophomore in Coke-bottle glasses."

I've only been kissed once. It was during a game of Spin the Bottle at Melony's thirteenth birthday party. Kenny Cramer's spin pointed right at me. He's four inches shorter than me. He's known for having bad dandruff and acne. He had Dorito chunks in his braces, and his kiss had an aftertaste. It wasn't the first kiss I dreamed about.

"Jason is so far out of my league it's ridiculous. I'm not gonna make a fool out of myself by trying to 'get' him," I yell.

"You're so insecure, it's pathetic! So, you're telling me you're not gonna go for him then."

"No way."

"So, you don't mind if I do?"

My hands ball into fists. I'm too horrified to speak.

"Don't look so shocked. He's gorgeous. Mom and Dad like him. Mike and Aunt Ginny adore him. He saved you from falling on your ass, offered to help pay for your birthday dinner, and bought you an awesome gift. Most guys our age are *major assholes*. If you're too stupid and insecure to go for Jason, I will."

The idea of Jason dating Tonya makes my stomach turn. "Fine, go for it. I don't care." I lie through clenched teeth.

Tonya pulls her phone out of her pocket and starts typing a DM. She reads what she's typing to torture me. "Hi, Jason. Want to come to a party with me and my friends next Saturday? If you come, I can introduce you to a lot of people from school." She hits send.

My stomach is in knots.

Her phone buzzes a second later. She reads his message, "Sure, that sounds fun." She glares at me. "See how easy that is? He's way too nice for you anyway. You prefer people who treat you like crap. Like Melony. Who gives backhanded compliments and takes other people's birthday gifts without asking. I don't wanna hear another word about how you don't like Kimber. Your BFF is way worse than mine."

"What's going on in here?" Our mother steps into my room wearing her pajamas. "It's almost midnight. What are you girls fighting about?"

"Sorry, Mom." Tonya snaps. "I guess a public street is a better location to fight with your sister than the privacy of your own bedroom. It's too bad you couldn't get Kira some self-esteem for her birthday." She slams her bedroom door.

"What in the world was that all about?" Mom asks.

I want to tell my mother that the idea of Tonya and Jason together turns my stomach. I want to tell her that I know Melony was rude for taking the gift Seth gave me. I want to tell her I'm worried my eyes are getting worse.

But all I say is, "Don't worry about it. Tonya and I will sort it out in the morning."

Chapter Three

Saturday, July 22, 2023

I shove clothes into an overnight bag for a sleepover at Melony's. Tonya is in our bathroom getting ready for her night out with Jason. We haven't spoken much since our fight last week. I step into our bathroom to grab my toothbrush. She's putting lipstick on, and she's dressed in a sexy red dress.

She catches me staring. "What?"

You look sluttier than usual. "I just need my toothbrush."

Tonya steps back and lets me collect my toiletries. She looks at my makeup-free face, grubby jeans, and messy bun. "*Another* sleepover at Melony's?"

"Another drunken party?" I ask, sounding just as bitchy. "Why don't you drive tonight? Kimber drinks like a fish. Don't go with her."

"Jason's picking me up and driving me home."

My hands clench my toothbrush so hard that my nails dig into my palm. What the hell is wrong with me? I don't even know this guy. "Well, hopefully, he doesn't drink as much as Kimber." I exit the bathroom and shove my stuff into my bag.

"Seth and Mike are coming with us," Tonya tells me. "We're going in a group."

Relief washes over me. It's not a date if everyone's going together. I smile to myself.

"The guys will be here any minute to pick me up," she says.

I want to get out of here before Jason arrives and sees me looking so grubby. I shove the rest of my stuff into my backpack and swing it over my shoulder.

"You could come too, you know," my sister reminds me.

I'm not having this conversation with her again. "Have fun tonight." I leave my room and head downstairs. "Mom, Dad. I'm heading to Melony's."

"Text me as soon as you get there," Mom yells from Dad's office.

"Have a good time. We'll see you tomorrow," Dad adds.

I grab my jacket out of our front closet, then exit our house, put my headphones on, and cue up "Brutal."

A black sedan pulls into our driveway.

Why the hell didn't I rush out of here before they arrived? I look so gross right now. Now I have to say hello.

Seth steps out of the back seat, takes a big swig of his soda, and burps.

Jason gets out of the driver's seat. "Dude, there's a girl right there." He motions towards me and waves. "Hi."

"That's not a girl. That's Kira." Seth takes another swig.

I wave at them as I rush down our porch stairs. "Hi, guys. Bye, guys. I'm headed to Melony's. You all have fun tonight." I make a beeline for our front gate.

Jason steps around the car. "You're not coming with us tonight?" He sounds disappointed.

"Um, no. Parties aren't my cup of tea." I push my glasses up my face and rub my nose, trying to cover my makeup-free face. I turn to Mike. "If you can, please don't let Tonya get too drunk tonight."

"I'll try, but you know what she's like," Mike says.

"Baby, I'm drunk, and I don't wanna go home," Seth sings and then burps again.

"Please don't let her get in the car with Kimber. That girl drinks like a fish," I tell Mike.

"We'll make sure she gets home safe," Jason says.

I'm relieved. "Thanks." I push my glasses up my nose and adjust my headphones. "See you guys later." I turn to leave again.

"Do you want a lift to your friend's house?" Jason asks.

I turn to face him again. "Thanks, but no need. She's only a few blocks away, and it's a nice day. Bye, guys." I hit the play button, and angry drumbeats fill my ears. I rush out of our gate and shut it behind me.

I turn right and walk past the house next to ours. Then I turn right onto West Street. I come to a corner house with a long fence with ten main support beams. My fingers tap each one as I walk by. There's a pool behind this fence. I can always smell the chlorine as I pass by. When I reach the tenth post, I know it's time to turn right onto Tedesco Street. I follow the fence, and it leads me directly to Melony's big white house on my right.

I turn off the music and hear Melony's mom ordering her gardener to do a better job ripping up weeds. He's hunched over, scrabbling to spray every weed growing between the cracks of their stone walkway.

"Hi, Mrs. Blackwell." I wave. I wish Melony's parents would let me call them by their first names. Melony calls my parents Doug and Cindy. Mr. and Mrs. Blackwell keep everything so formal.

"Hi, Kira. Go on in."

I go in through their front door. Melony's house always smells like lemon-scented Pledge and glass cleaner. It is twice the size of my house. I never touch anything because I'm afraid my clumsiness will cause me to break something.

I grip their banister as I head up the stairs to Melony's bedroom. There are thirteen steps on our front staircase at home. Mel's house is so big that her staircase has eighteen steps. I walk into Mel's room.

"Hi, Kira," my friend Liz says.

I step close enough to see that Liz is sitting on the floor painting Melony's toenails.

Liz flips her long black hair back. "Guess what?"

"What?"

"I lost ten pounds."

I smile. That's wonderful news. I worry about the stress Liz's weight puts on her heart. "That's great. You look a little thinner."

"Really?" She smiles.

"Pay attention, please," Melony says, shaking her foot. "Try not to smudge it again. I'm running out of nail polish remover."

"Sorry, Mel," Liz says and gets back to work. "You want me to paint your toenails next, Kira? I'm done with mine." She slides her foot out to show me.

"Sure. Thanks." I drop my bag next to the guest bed.

31

"So, Kira, have you done a naked drawing of that hottie yet?" Melony asks.

Liz looks at me. "What hottie?"

I blush. "He didn't ask me to draw him naked. He asked me to teach him how to draw."

"And have you invited him over for art class yet?" Melony asks.

"No."

"Why the hell not?" Melony asks. "When a guy that hot wants to hang out, you don't hesitate. Everybody knows that."

"Who are you talking about?" Liz asks, confused.

Melony uses her phone to pull up Jason's Instagram. She starts to tell Liz the whole story about our trip to Boston.

I cringe and shake my head at Melony, trying to tell her to stop talking.

"You all went to Boston without me?" Liz sounds hurt.

I did want Liz to come. The problem is that her parents are so poor. Whenever Liz joins us, my parents end up paying for her. "Sorry, Liz. My dad's been having a difficult year. Houses are so expensive that nobody can afford to buy one right now. They told me I could only bring one friend."

"Also, there's limited space in Kira's dad's minivan," Melony adds.

I cringe again. Liz is sensitive about her size.

"It only holds nine, and we thought Ginny, Mike, and Seth were driving with us," I explain.

"Then why'd this new guy get to come?" Liz sounds offended. I don't blame her.

"Because my aunt took her own car, so there was room for more passengers. Also, because he, um, paid for himself," I whisper.

"Oh." Liz drops her eyes and goes back to finishing Melony's toenails.

"So why haven't you hung out with him yet?" Melony asks.

"I don't know. I've been busy working on my portfolio. Miss Coleman told me to spend the summer adding pieces so I have a vast amount of work when I apply for colleges and scholarships."

Liz caps the bottle of polish and sits on Melony's bed.

"You have two years to do that," Melony insists. "Invite him over before I hack into your phone and do it for you." She waves her foot up and down, drying the polish.

"If you're so brave, why don't you ask Seth to do something?" I ask.

She frowns and crosses her arms. "I would. If I could think of something we have in common."

Liz comes up behind me and pulls my phone out of my back pocket. "Let's slide into this guy's DMs."

"Liz!" I shriek, trying to grab it back.

"Oh, hell yes," Melony agrees and hobbles over to us, trying to keep her wet toenails elevated.

"Are you two crazy? Give me my phone back." I reach for it, but Liz is much taller than I am and holds it too high for me to get it. She's still pissed off and using this to torture me.

"Come on, just say a harmless hello to get the ball rolling," Mel says.

"There's no point doing that now. He's at a party with Tonya," I insist.

Both my friends frown at me. "You let Tonya get to him first? Are you crazy?" Melony asks.

"What's the big deal? They are just at a party. It's not like they ran away to elope or anything."

Liz uses my phone to check Tonya's Instagram. "There are already photos of the cute couple."

"What? No way." I grab my phone out of her hand. Sure enough, Tonya has posted a photo with Jason. His arm is wrapped around her, and they are both smiling. It's a multi-photo post. I scroll through the pictures of all her friends together. Kimber, Seth, and Mike are also in the photos. "See? It's photos of all her friends." The last one is of Seth with his mouth hanging open. It looks like Tonya caught him in the middle of a burp. His greasy blonde hair is plastered to his forehead, and his face looks red and sweaty. I show that one to Melony. "Look, it's the heartthrob of the millennium."

Liz laughs at how bad Seth looks.

"Oh, whatever." Melony takes my phone and scrolls back to the first photo. "Point is, I think you blew it. Why'd you let Tonya move in on him?"

My phone buzzes with an annoyed text from my mother. I was supposed to text her when I got to Melony's house. I roll my eyes. It's a few blocks away.

"I didn't," I insist. "I just wanted to wait and get to know him better before I invited him over," I say while writing my mother back. I let her know that I managed to get here without getting abducted by aliens.

"You snooze, you lose," Liz says.

"I didn't snooze."

Melony takes my phone and opens Tonya's Instagram. "Yeah, well, it looks like Tonya pounced, like a typical Leo." She zooms in on Tonya's photo. "Your sister's annoyingly pretty, you know."

What is she resentful for? I'm the one who is going to be in Tonya's shadow for the rest of my life.

"Whatever." Melony hands me back my phone. "She'll go off to college. Then we'll be upperclassmen and I'll be the hottest girl in the school."

Chapter Four

Thursday, August 17, 2023

I wake up with a throbbing headache. It feels like someone is pressing on the backs of my eyes from the inside of my skull. I sit up in bed and hope the pressure will go away once the blood drains out of my head. I take two painkillers. Alma meows at me for disturbing her, so I pet her until she lies back down next to me. Supposedly, a cat's purr has healing properties. I pet her until my headache goes away.

I get dressed and go down to the kitchen. Tonya's birthday is tomorrow, and I've agreed to make the cake. It's dark in here. The house is empty and the blinds are closed. I open the refrigerator door.

The fridge light becomes a million shining pieces. I'm blinded by a huge white glare. I close my eyes.

I slam the fridge. It finally happened. *I'm blind.* I'm so dizzy, I need to cling to the door handle. *My shitty eyes finally broke.*

I take a deep breath and force myself to open my eyes. The kitchen looks normal. I rush to turn on the kitchen's overhead lamp and open the blinds. I give my eyes a chance to adjust to the light. *Everything looks fine. It was just a glare.*

I go back to the fridge and grab the handle again. I slowly pull the door open. Everything looks normal. There's no huge white flare, no growling stone gargoyle, no creepy voice saying "Zool." I suddenly feel silly for being so scared. I just needed a second to adjust to the light. I take out several boxes of butter and set them on the counter to warm.

Tonya invited most of her class to this party. I've decided to bake three batches of cupcakes so nobody at the party has to spend time slicing and plating cake.

I'm a perfectionist when it comes to baking. I measure and level off all the ingredients carefully. Then I sift all the dry ingredients. It takes forever, but it is worth it. It makes the batter so light and fluffy.

I'm spooning the last batch into the cupcake tray when the front door opens. I look at the clock. How is it five already? I'm a little too particular about all the steps, and I take way too long to do this, but these will be the best cupcakes ever.

"Can we shoot in here?" Tonya asks.

"Sure," Jason says. "I can take photos of you on the couch and the chairs."

I freeze. I drop a big blob of batter onto the middle of the tray. It drips between the paper cupcake molds and the metal of the tray.

What the hell is wrong with me?

I look down at my t-shirt and jeans. I have flour and melted chocolate on my clothes. My hair is up in a messy ponytail. I have no makeup on. I resist the urge to run up the stairs to my bedroom and make myself look presentable before Jason sees me. Since I'd have to pass him on the way to the stairs, that would be impossible.

"I can't believe how beautiful your house is. Did you guys hire an interior decorator?" Jason asks.

"No. My mom and Kira did this together," Tonya says.

I pull out the dirty molds and toss them. I grab a paper towel and clean up my mess on the cupcake tray.

"Please let me introduce them to my aunt," Jason says. "Our apartment looks so ugly compared to your place. My aunt has no artistic abilities."

"Will the light in here be okay?" Tonya asks.

I frown. She ignored what he said.

"Uh, yeah, sure. We'll be closing the blinds anyway. Most of the light will be coming from my LEDs," he explains.

A moment later, Tonya and Jason head into the kitchen. "God, it smells so good in here," Jason says. Then he looks at me and smiles. "Hi, Kira."

I look up and see them on the other side of our center island. "Hi. What are you guys doing in the living room?" I carefully spoon the batter.

"Jason's gonna take photos of me for my modeling portfolio," Tonya explains. She has a stack of magazines in her hands. They have a ton of Post-its sticking out of the pages. "It's his birthday gift to me. Isn't that cool?"

I force a smile. "That's a perfect gift for my sister. Thanks."

Jason looks at my cupcakes, cooling on the table. "These look delicious."

"Kira should open up her own bakery," Tonya says proudly. "She bakes birthday cakes for everyone in the family."

"I wish I had a little sister like you," Jason says.

I force another smile. I'm always the cute little sister or little cousin. He thinks of me the same way Seth and Mike do. I'm never an equal.

"I need to go get ready," Tonya announces and hands Jason the stack of magazines. "I've marked the pictures I wanna create. Can you look through them and set up your equipment as I do my hair and makeup?"

"Sure."

"This is so exciting," Tonya squeals. "New York City, here I come." She leans in and gives him a quick kiss on the mouth before she leaves.

Every muscle in my body tightens. I turn around and shove the last batch in the oven. I set my timer for twenty-five minutes. I grab all the dirty mixing cups, bowls, and pans and toss them into the sink. Then I grab the kitchen cleaner and start attacking the dirty island.

"Is something wrong, Kira?" Jason asks.

"No. I'm just tired from being on my feet all day. Baking is tiring."

"I'm jealous," he says.

"Of what?"

"Nobody has ever baked me a homemade birthday cake."

"Not even your mom?" I ask while scrubbing a blob of batter.

"She passed away."

I freeze in place. My gaze travels up to his face. I'm such an asshole for bringing it up. "Sorry."

"It's okay. It was a long time ago."

"How long ago?" I ask before considering if it's an appropriate question.

"She died in childbirth."

My eyes widen. He hasn't mentioned having any siblings. I haven't seen any pictures of brothers or sisters on his Instagram. "With you?"

"Yeah. There was a complication when amniotic fluid entered her bloodstream," he says. "That's how my aunt explained it to me."

"Jesus." I lean against the counter. I suddenly feel like all the energy has been sucked out of my body.

"It's okay, Kira."

"No, it's not. That's terrible. I'm so sorry." An alternative reality plays in my mind, where my mom died having me. It's a horrifying thought. "I can't even imagine growing up without my mom."

"I have one," he assures me. "My aunt raised me."

"What about your dad?"

Jason's face drops. "He's as cold as ice. Raging egomaniac. That's why my aunt had to take care of me."

"So, you and your dad—"

"Have no relationship," he says sharply. Then he looks at me, and his eyes soften. "Sorry. Talking about that guy puts me on edge."

"And your aunt never baked you a birthday cake?" I ask, trying to lighten the conversation again.

He snickers at the idea. "No. She's not much of a baker. She's also a nurse and works crazy long hours. She's bought birthday cakes for all my parties."

I toss a bunch of used paper towels in the can. "I heard what you said about our living room. Why don't you invite your aunt to Tonya's birthday party tomorrow? I'm sure my parents would like to meet her. Maybe my mom and I can give her decorating advice."

He smiles. "Thanks. I will."

I turn my back so I can start washing everything I'll need to make the frosting.

He comes closer. "So why didn't you come with us to the party at Lawndale's?"

"I don't like big parties." I pick up a pot and sponge off the melted chocolate.

"Why?" He stands next to me. "Do loud places give you sensory overload?"

I look at him, shocked. "How'd you know?"

"You could hear what I said to your sister all the way in the living room," he explains. "People with bad vision usually have excellent hearing."

"How the hell do you know all this?"

"My aunt's a nurse," he reminds me. "So, am I right?"

I go back to washing the pot. "Yes. Everything more than five feet away is a blur to me. I guess that is why I have excellent hearing." I rinse the pot and put it on the drainboard.

He picks up the dish towel and starts drying. "Is that why your mom won't let you out of her sight?"

I can't tell him that he's wrong. "Probably." This conversation is making me so anxious. I scrub a mixing bowl hard with steel wool.

He places the dry pot on the counter. "Kira, I think your mom is way too overprotective of you."

I stop scrubbing. I turn to look at him.

He looks guilty. "Sorry. It's just…Mike told me about your psycho grandfather. Your mom and her sister had messed-up childhoods. That's why they fight all the time."

"I know. Believe me, I wish my mom and aunt could work out their issues." I place a bowl on the drainboard.

He dries it. "I think your mom has a ton of anxiety, and it makes her crazy overprotective," he says, frustrated. "I mean, you should be allowed to walk around a museum by yourself without your mom worrying where you are." He places the dry bowl down. "She treats you like a five-year-old."

My hands still. "You think I'm a closed-off freak, don't you?"

"What? No. I didn't say that."

I turn to look at him again.

"I think you use your vision as an excuse to hide yourself away from the world."

"I don't hide myself away."

"Prove it. Come to the next party with us."

I'm horrified at the thought. "No way. Tonya and Mike will spend the whole night babysitting me. I don't want to ruin their good time. Plus, I don't like Eric Lawndale. Something about the guy gives me the creeps. I wish my sister would find a different place to party."

"Why didn't you set up the equipment while I was getting ready?" My sister yells from the living room.

"Sorry, I felt like I should help your sister clean up," he yells back. "See ya later, Kira." He rushes out of our kitchen.

"Well, did you look at the magazine pages I marked?"

"Shit," he murmurs and rushes back to grab the stack of magazines off the kitchen table. "No, sorry." He heads towards the living room.

"Why not?" Tonya sounds annoyed. "We have less than two hours to take these pictures before my parents get home with dinner."

I start the frosting. I put butter into a bowl and turn on my hand mixer. I beat the butter until it is soft, so I don't have to listen to Tonya complain.

Jason's been thinking about me, my eyes, my family, and my relationship with my mother since the day I met him. He might think I'm a closed-off freak, but I'm a freak who's been on his mind.

When the mixer stops, I put on my headphones and listen to "You Belong with Me" on repeat.

My parents come home around seven. My mom comes in carrying Chinese take-out. "Hi, honey." She looks at my creation. I used the pastry bags to write "Happy Birthday, Tonya." Then I drew a bunch of balloons and gifts all over the cupcakes in various colors. Mom says she's impressed.

Dad insists we have plenty to share and invites Jason to stay for dinner. Tonya, Mom, and I discuss the party. Dad and Jason are engrossed in a discussion about the Patriots. Dad seems delighted to have a guy here to talk about sports with. Mom even lets Dad skip helping with the cleanup because he's so engrossed in his conversation.

After dinner, Alma's in the kitchen by herself, devouring the chicken and beef I cut up for her. Tonya is sitting on the couch, showing Mom all the photos Jason took. Jason packs up all his equipment and takes it out to his car, and comes back in to say goodnight.

"I have to show you something." I motion for Jason to follow me into the kitchen. "It's about the birthday party, so nobody else can see."

He looks puzzled but follows me to the kitchen. I go to the fridge and pull out the small container I hid in the back. I hand it to him. He opens the top to reveal a cupcake with his name written in green frosting.

He looks touched. Big green eyes look at me for an explanation.

"I, um, figured it was about time you had a birthday cake from scratch."

He smiles. "My birthday's not 'til October."

"Well, um, I'll bake you a cake in October then," I say, looking down at the small cupcake.

He puts the container on the counter.

"In the meantime, this will have to hold you over until—"

His arms wrap around my waist. He pulls me into a tight hug.

My heart skips a beat. My arms end up around his shoulders. My nose ends up tucked into the bend of his neck. His skin is smooth with a hint of stubble. I close my eyes and savor his woody herbal scent.

"You're amazing," he whispers in my ear.

The raspy sound of his voice sends a chill through me.

My sister's laughter from the living room shatters the moment. I back up and look at Jason, shocked. "Maybe you should try it now."

He smiles and unwraps his cupcake. He takes a bite. "Mmm," he murmurs with a mouth full of cake. "Oh, this is so good. Wow."

"Really?" I'm so happy they came out as well as I'd hoped.

41

"Yeah. Delicious." He finishes the whole thing. "Best birthday cake I've ever had."

We walk back into the living room. Jason says goodnight to our parents and heads towards the door. Tonya walks Jason out. She wraps her arms around him.

I have to walk by them to get up the stairs. *Don't look.* But I have to. The way you have to look to see how bad a car accident is as you pass the crash on the highway. I have to watch as they kiss each other goodnight. I hate how long they stay pressed up against each other. It's way longer than the hug he gave me.

I rush upstairs to my room.

I get in bed and turn off my light. All I want to do is turn my brain off and go to sleep.

"I love you for making me those cupcakes today," Tonya says from our bathroom. "Tomorrow is gonna be so much fun."

"I love you, too, but I'm exhausted from baking. Goodnight."

She ignores what I said and comes into my room. She sits on my bed. "Promise me you'll have fun tomorrow. I invited all the cutest guys from school. Promise me you won't spend the entire night only talking to Melony, Seth, and Mike."

"I promise I won't spend the whole night only talking to them. Liz is coming too. Good night, Tonya." I can't hide the annoyance in my voice.

"It's too bad Jason doesn't have a little brother."

"That would be impossible since his mom died giving birth to him."

"What?" Tonya asks, shocked. "That's terrible."

I roll towards her. "He didn't tell you?"

"No. He only told me that he lives with his aunt because he and his dad don't get along. Why did he tell you all of this?"

Maybe because I actually listen to people when they talk. "I don't know. It just came up." I roll away again and close my eyes. "I'm sure he'll tell you all about it, too. You're his girlfriend, aren't you?"

"Well, we haven't officially labeled it yet," she says.

Yes.

"But we've already had sex."

My eyes snap open.

"So, I guess I should probably have that conversation with him."

I roll over and look at her. "Already? When?"

"The night of the party. In one of the bedrooms."

"Oh, my god. You move faster than a speeding bullet. Superman has nothing on you," I pull my covers up.

She laughs. "And, Kira. He is so good at it. Seriously. I mean his di—"

"I'm exhausted, Tonya!"

"Oh, right. Sorry." She gets off my bed. "Don't worry. We'll find you a great guy, and then you'll be telling me all about him soon." She walks to our bathroom. "Love you, Kira." She shuts the door.

I am not going to cry. Why the hell did I give him that cupcake tonight? Why the hell did I let him hug me? I never would have done that if I knew he slept with my sister.

I'm pathetic for replaying moments in my mind. The moment Jason caught me in his arms. When he touched my hand when we were alone. *His hand in mine the day we met obviously meant nothing because soon after, his penis was inside of my sister's vagina.* I curl into a ball. My tears start falling.

Chapter Five

Friday, August 18, 2023

I wake up with the worst headache I've ever had. The morning light coming into my windows hurts my eyes. My head feels like it's going to explode with pressure. I guzzle down three painkillers and pull my covers up over my head. I'm such an idiot. I made myself sick over a guy I never had a chance of getting.

I force myself to ignore the pain and get out of bed. I make a game plan as I get ready for the party. From now on, when I'm around Jason, we will have brief, meaningless encounters. If he wants to have deep conversations, he can have them with his girlfriend.

I do my makeup, and I put my hair up into a French twist on account of it being a humid summer day. I put on a black sundress, a pair of low black heels, and black jewelry. The color matches my mood.

"Are you kidding me?" Mom yells from downstairs.

I guess I'm not the only one in a bad mood today. I go out into the hall to hear what's going on. I stand at the top of our stairs.

"You and Mike aren't coming? It's her eighteenth birthday!" Mom must be on the phone with Aunt Ginny. Nobody else makes Mom yell like this. "He's manipulating you! He always pulls this crap on special occasions to drive a wedge between us!" Mom pauses to listen to Aunt Ginny's excuses. "I don't wanna hear it, Ginny! I'm done listening to your bullshit!" Mom hangs up and goes outside to get some fresh air.

I take a deep breath. I have a feeling it is going to be a bad night.

The party guests start to arrive. Most of them are seniors. Mom, Dad, and Tonya are in the backyard making sure everyone has snacks and drinks. I busy myself with tasks in the kitchen so I don't have to socialize. Our doorbell rings again. I'm the only one in the house, so I rush to the living room to open the door.

Jason is standing in my doorway. He looks gorgeous. He's dressed in a pair of black dress pants and a green button-down shirt. "Hi, Kira."

"Uh, hi." I focus on the woman with him. "Hello, you must be Jason's aunt." She has dark hair, dark eyes, and olive complexion. Her straight hair has been cut into a bob.

"I'm Dimitra, but you can call me Mimi," she says.

"Hi Mimi, I'm—"

She surprises me by giving me a hug. "Kira. The beautiful, talented artist I've heard so much about."

Jason described me as beautiful and talented. I smile. *He slept with my sister.* My smile drops.

"It's nice to meet you,' I tell Mimi. "My parents are in the backyard," I say to Jason while trying not to look at him. "Why don't you go introduce your aunt to your girlfriend's parents. Excuse me."

I go outside to find a task. The chip bowl is low. I rush to the kitchen for more and take the bowl back outside. Then I go back to the kitchen to get more dip. I purposely get only one item at a time.

The garbage cans are getting full of paper plates and cups. I haul the full bags to our garage and refill the cans with new bags. Then I have to go wash my hands. It's amazing how many people you can avoid talking to by staying busy.

Melony and Liz finally arrive together. We grab our pizza slices and soda and find three empty seats to enjoy our dinner. The sun is going down. That means the party is about to gear up. "Raise Your Glass" by P!nk starts playing. That's everyone's cue to get on the dance floor.

"Excuse me," Melony says. "I'm gonna ask Seth for a dance." She gets up and walks away. Liz and I are impressed by her courage until she comes back a few minutes later looking miserable. She flops down in her seat.

"What happened?" I ask.

"Halfway through the song, Mike arrived. Suddenly, I was invisible," Mel complains. "Your cousin looks really upset. Seth left me alone on the dance floor to go see what was going on. They went into your house together. Couldn't Mike wait 'til the end of the song to come in looking miserable? I mean, did he—"

I stand up and go off to find my cousin. I walk into our living room. Tonya and Mike are sitting together on the couch. His eyes are red and swollen.

"He's such a fucking bastard," Mike says.

"I know," Tonya agrees. There is no way my sister would leave her own party to console Mike unless something really bad happened.

"When he said that about her, I wanted to punch his fucking lights out." Mike balls his hand into a fist. "You're so lucky you never have to see him."

I step closer. "What happened?"

They finally notice me. "Nothing, Kira. Don't worry about it," Tonya says. "I've got this."

Mike looks at me with big, sad, blue eyes. "You look really pretty tonight." Saying it seems to make him sadder.

"Thanks," I say, confused.

"I'm fine," Mike insists. "You should go back to the party, Kira."

They both sit looking at me, waiting for me to leave before they finish their conversation. Tonya and Mike always do this when he's upset. For as long as I can remember, they have gone off into their own world.

"Who are you guys talking about?" I ask.

"I told you not to worry about it," Tonya says.

I walk away feeling annoyed. I'm old enough to bake their birthday cakes and cook feasts for them on the holidays, but I'm too young to hear their problems. I go back to my seat and flop down. Is this party over yet? I'm calling it an early night as soon as my sister blows out the candles.

Liz and Mel spend their time checking out guys at the party. "Tony Jarvis is really cute," Melony says. She waves at him.

"I guess," Liz says. "He's a bit too muscular for my taste."

"He's a football player," Mel says. "He must get a lot of exercise."

"You don't even like football, Mel," I remind her.

"I'd like it if I could watch him play every day." She waves at him again.

"If you say so," Liz says. "I think it's better to find someone you already—"

"Oh, my god, he's coming over," Melony squeals.

Liz and I exchange glances and smile. I hope Tony asks Melony to dance. I hope he's nice to her and she starts crushing on him. It's obvious Seth isn't interested in Melony.

Melony jumps up and stands in front of him. "Hi. I'm Melony." She holds her hand out.

He shakes it. "I'm Tony. Excuse me, Melony." He walks right past her, comes around our table, and sits next to me. He has sandy brown hair and brown eyes. Mel is right. He's cute. He looks like a nice person too.

"Hey, you're Tonya's little sister, Kira, right?" he asks.

"Yeah."

"I'm Tony."

"It's nice to meet you." I shake his hand.

"I figured you were her sister," Tony says to me. "You look a lot like her."

I smile. "Thank you." I love it when people say that.

I look over at Melony. She looks ready to spit nails. She flops down in her seat and crosses her arms.

The DJ is playing a slow song.

"You wanna dance?" Tony asks me.

I look at him, shocked. "Oh, um. I'm a terrible dancer."

"That's okay. I'll lead."

"Um. I don't…uh…usually feel comfortable…slow dancing with someone I don't know."

"Fair enough," Tony says. "We can wait for a fast song."

"If I dance, I'll end up bumping into, stepping on, or tripping over someone and embarrassing both of us," I tell him.

"My peripheral vision sucks." I push my glasses up my nose. "I was planning on sitting here all night."

"What a shame. You're way too pretty to be a wallflower," Tony says.

I giggle.

"Is there any reason why a guy can't sit next to you?"

"No, of course not."

"Good." Tony smiles at me.

Melony stands up and storms off.

"So, what are you into?" Tony asks.

I pull out my phone to show him photos of my art.

"Wow. You're talented. I can't do that, but I'm on the football team. Do you go to the games?

"No, sorry," I tell him. "If I were sitting in the bleachers, I wouldn't be able to see anything happening on the field."

"Kira," Liz interrupts me.

"What?" I turn around and look at her.

"Jason is glaring at you and Tony," she whispers in my ear. *"Glaring.* He's slow dancing with your sister. She has her head on his shoulder. She looks like she's in seventh heaven. He looks way more interested in what's happening over here with you."

"Really? Are you sure?"

Liz looks back at Jason and Tonya.

"Is he still looking?" I ask.

"No. Kimber just walked up to them. She looks so drunk. She's wobbling in her heels," Liz explains.

"Figures," I say.

"Now she's holding up a flask. Asking Tonya to get drunk with her."

"Oh, shit," I murmur and stand up. "Would you excuse me, Tony? I have some family drama to deal with."

"Sure. I'll see you later, I hope," he says.

Liz and I rush over to my sister.

Tonya takes the flask and gulps some down.

"That's not a good idea." Jason takes it away from Tonya.

"Don't beee soooo lame," Kimber slurs. She snatches the flask out of Jason's hand and takes a big gulp.

"This isn't Eric's Lawndale's house," Jason says. "Tonya's parents are here. So is my aunt." He looks at Tonya. "I'd rather my aunt not see you drunk tonight."

"You're soooo boring," Kimber says, pointing a finger in his face. "It's a good thing you're hot and you have a big one."

Everyone's too shocked to speak.

"Tonya would lose interest if your face and dick weren't—" Kimber pauses and looks at my sister, "How'd you put it? Sculpted by God." She giggles.

"Okay," Tonya says and wraps her arm around her friend. "Did I show you my new boots? They're in my room. You'd love them, and you can borrow them whenever you want." She tries to lead Kimber upstairs to lie down.

"Really? You're such a good friend." She wraps her arms around my sister. "You're my best friend."

"I know Kimber. Let's go upstairs."

"But you're so boring since you started seeing *him.*" She points at Jason. "He's so boring."

"Tell me how boring he is upstairs." She leads her friend into our living room and heads for the stairs.

"But he has the best dick ever," Kimber shouts. "Maybe we should all get a turn. Then we'd all be less bored by him."

Tonya manages to get Kimber up the stairs.

I think my face is turning red from secondhand embarrassment. "I'm so sorry," I say to Jason.

"Don't worry about it. I'm just glad your sister didn't get drunk again," he says.

"Kimber's a lush. I'm sure you're not actually boring," Liz says.

"Thanks, Liz." Jason looks at me. "So, what's going on with you and *the tight end*?"

"Nothing. I met the guy five minutes ago."

"Kira?" my mom calls.

"It must be time to light the candles. Excuse me." I walk away from him.

Liz follows me. "*The tight end,*" Liz imitated the way Jason said it. "He sounded so jealous."

"I'm sure he was just being protective."

50

"I don't know," Liz says. "I saw his face. It looked jealous to me. If I was you, I might not give up on Jason yet. He didn't seem at all into your sister when he was dancing with her. "

"He's into her enough to sleep with her. Even if they break up one day, I'm not gonna go creeping after my sister's ex. That's messed up. The best thing I can do is avoid him."

"Kira," my mom calls again from inside the house.

"Coming." I walk faster.

"That's a bad way to get over a major crush. The harder you try not to think about them, the more your brain rebels. It's so hard dealing with—" Liz follows me into our kitchen and sees all the cupcakes, "temptation."

I laugh at her big eyes and goofy expression.

"Hi, girls," Mom says. "I wasn't sure how you wanted to arrange the cupcakes and place the candles, Kira. I wouldn't dream of messing up your art." She hands me the box of candles.

"You did a beautiful job," Mimi says. She's seated at our kitchen table with a glass of wine. Mom sits back down at the table with her.

"I do *not* want to devour all of them," Liz says. "I'm gonna go back outside. When it's time to eat them, give me one."

"Okay," I agree.

"Just one," she insists and rushes away. She closes the kitchen door, and the music from the party is muffled enough for me to hear Mom's conversation.

"How long has it been since you've seen your brother?" Mom asks Mimi.

That's Jason's father. I look in their direction.

"About three years," Mimi answers.

I shouldn't care. I don't care. I focus on my task. I get out Mom's biggest platter and arrange the cupcakes.

"Does Jason keep in touch with his father?" Mom asks.

"Not anymore. The truth is, my brother never wanted to be a father. It was Niamh, my brother's wife, who wanted kids." Mimi sips her wine. "What about you? How long has it been since you've seen your father?"

My head pops up. Mom never talks about this. I move closer.

51

"Since Kira was five years old," Mom finishes her glass of wine and pours another. "My whole life, my father treated my sister like gold and me like dirt." She raises her glass high in the air. "He projected all his good qualities onto Ginny," she lowers her glass down to her lap, "and all his insecurities on me." She takes a big drink.

"That's called the golden child and the scapegoat," Mimi explains. "What's your relationship with your sister like now?"

"Awful. All we do is fight. Every time I have to see her, I tell myself, 'This time I'm gonna get along with her.' But as soon as she opens her mouth, I wanna punch her lights out." Mom makes a punching motion with her free hand.

"Let me guess. Your sister won't admit that anything was wrong with your upbringing."

"Exactly." Mom slams her hand down on the table. "My sister comes up with an excuse for every psycho thing my father has ever done. My father found out Tonya's party was tonight. Ginny isn't here tonight because my father *insisted* that he needed to be driven to Boston today for a Red Sox game. Out of all the games played this season," she slurs and leans forward, "he just *had* to go to *this one*." She slams the table again. "It's pathetic the way my sister lets him manipulate her."

I know all of this already, so I interrupt. "Mom, the cupcakes are ready."

She looks at me like she forgot I was in the room. "Right, good." Mom stands up and steadies herself by holding onto the table.

Tonya blows out the candles, and everyone takes a cupcake.

"I'll only eat one tonight, too," I tell Liz.

"Cheers," she says, and we pretend to toast by mushing the cupcakes together.

Melony walks up to us. "Where have you guys been?" she asks with a mouth full of cupcake. "I've had a lousy night. I haven't found anyone new to crush on." She reaches for a second cupcake and starts unwrapping it. "Nobody has asked me to dance." She gobbles it down in a frustrated eating frenzy. "Also, we're like the only sophomores here. I wish your sister had invited some people from our grade, too."

Liz looks tense with frustration as she watches Melony.

"I mean, really," Melony says, annoyed. "Would it have killed your sister to invite a few sophomores?"

"Oh, please. If you had a party, you'd never invite students younger than us," I tell her. "And slow down before you get diabetes."

Melony looks at me, surprised. "I'm not gonna get diabetes, or fat. My metabolism will burn this off in a day." She reaches for a third cupcake.

Liz walks away.

I slap the cupcake out of Melony's hand.

"Ouch! What's your problem?" Her eyes are wide with shock.

"Liz is desperately trying to lose weight. You'd notice if you ever thought of anyone but yourself!"

She stares at me with a shocked expression. "I felt like pigging out for a minute. What's the problem? It's not my fault she has a slow metabolism."

"Mel! God!" I'm exasperated. "You never notice how anyone around you is feeling. You always act like a spoiled, selfish brat. I'm sick of it."

"*I* never notice how anyone is feeling? What about you? You attracted Tony's attention and then acted like you didn't want it."

"I didn't want it. He's too old for me. I was trying to be nice."

Her voice deepens. "You think you're so cool. You think you can swat hot guys away like flies, and another one will start buzzing around you. I'm sick of you thinking you're so cool because Tonya's your sister."

"I don't think I'm cool because I'm her sister."

"Like hell! If you were a random sophomore, no guy would've given you a second glance tonight. You're like the discount bargain basement Tonya knockoff."

I step back like I've been kicked in the chest. "It doesn't matter how much makeup you layer onto your face. Seth can

53

still see how nasty you are on the inside. That is why he doesn't like you."

She looks like she's been kicked in the chest, too. "I'm going home." She storms off.

"Nobody here will miss you." I pinch the bridge of my nose. I'm getting a headache again. My feet are killing me from being in heels. I go to the kitchen for a glass of water.

Jason and Mike's voices are coming from our living room.

I pour a glass and take the heels off my throbbing feet.

"I told my mom I'm done with that asshole. I never wanna see him again," Mike says.

I sigh. Mike is like my mom. They're both filled with so much anger and bitterness.

"I don't blame you," Jason says. "I feel the exact same way about my dad. Just because someone shares your DNA, that doesn't make them family. Your grandfather sounds like an asshole. Everyone's born with an asshole. Nobody needs a second one."

Mike laughs. "He is, believe me. I almost jumped into moving traffic to get out of the car with him."

Whoa. What the hell happened between Mike and our grandfather today? I want to go into the living room and ask him, but I know he won't tell me. He'll talk to Tonya and Jason about his problems, but not me. He's known Jason for five minutes.

Listening to Mike is making my headache worse. I need to get upstairs, take my glasses off, and lie down. I tiptoe across our living room. Jason and Mike are sitting on our couch, talking. They don't notice me.

"What he said tonight about Seth and Kira was the last straw," Mike says.

I freeze in my tracks.

"He never uses Kira's name," Mike complains. "He calls her 'The Other One,' 'The Cross-Eyed One,' or 'The Cross-Eyed Freak.' It makes me sick the way he talks about her."

That is what my own grandfather thinks of me.

"He's resented her since the day she was born."

I take one more step, and the floor creaks under my feet.

The boys turn and see me. Mike's face drains of all color. "Kira."

I cannot look at Jason. My grandfather thinks I'm a freak. Jason must think I'm such a loser. "Good night, guys," I manage to whisper. I rush past them to the stairs. Thirteen steps up. Twenty steps to my room. I drop my shoes on the ground and burst into tears.

Why did Mike have to say that to Jason of all people? I set my glasses down on my nightstand, grab a tissue, and try to stifle my tears. *My grandfather thinks I'm a freak. If my own family thinks that, how bad do I look to everyone else? Like a bargain basement Tonya knockoff?*

A soft knock on my door. "Are you alright?" Jason asks.

I inhale a sharp breath. Why is it him instead of Mike? Why the hell won't my cousin talk to me? "Not really."

"Mike went to get your mom," Jason explains. "I'm sorry you had to hear that."

"I'm not crying because of what Mike said. Melony and I had an awful fight. I think our friendship is over." I wipe my face with a tissue.

"I'm sorry, Kira." His voice sounds closer. "It sucks to lose a friend. Although it doesn't seem like Melony was much of a friend. Liz is, though. I bet she'll be up here to check on you as soon as she hears you're upset."

I smile. "Yeah, you're right." I put on my glasses and see him standing in my room by my desk. The button-down shirt has been replaced with a green t-shirt. Probably because it was a hot, humid night. His wavy hair has a slight frizz from the humidity, but he still looks like a Greek god to me.

I look away from him. I must look like a raccoon with mascara smudged all over my face. I open the jar of painkillers. "I have another headache." I take the medicine. I take my glasses off again and put them on my dresser. The updo I put my hair in is making my head feel worse. I pull the bobby pins out of my hair and rake my fingers through it. Now I probably look like a raccoon with a rat's nest hair. "Thanks for checking on me. I'm okay now. You should go back to the party."

"Okay, but first," he steps closer, "I need you to know that nobody thinks any less of you because of what your grandfather said. Tonya and Mike don't." He's a foot away. Close enough for me to see him without my glasses. He looks me in the eyes. "And I'd never think less of you because of what he said."

That's a huge relief. I know it shouldn't be, but it is. My tears start falling again. "Okay. Thank you." My voice cracks. I close my eyes and try to stifle my emotions again.

His hand strokes my cheek. "Kira," he whispers my name.

I burst into tears.

His arms wrap around me.

I drop my head onto his shoulder.

"Toxic people project their toxic crap onto us," he says and holds me tighter. "Your grandfather said that Seth wasn't good enough to be Mike's friend. He said that Seth is a loser for not knowing what he wants to do with the rest of his life. He said that Mike should find more motivated friends. Do you think any of that is true?"

I shake my head.

"Does what your grandfather said make you think less of Seth?"

I shake my head again.

"None of us think any less of you, Kira." His finger thread through the back of my hair. "You have big, brown doe eyes. They look straight ahead. They see details that most people overlook."

I breathe a sigh of relief and hold him tighter. "Thank you."

A few sets of footsteps come up our stairs. I pull away from Jason and grab another tissue. I wipe my eyes and put on my glasses.

"Kira," my mother says. "Mike told me what happened." She hugs me.

"I'm okay, Mom," I tell her.

"Jason, I think Tonya's looking for you," Mike says.

"Oh. Right. I should get back, I guess. I'll see you later, Kira." He exits my room.

My mom sits me down on my bed. Mike sits next to me.

"Do you know why your grandfather resents you so much?" Mom asks.

I shake my head.

"In his mind, all of us, his children and grandchildren, are extensions of him," Mom says. "Not individuals with our own needs and wants. He thinks we were all put on this earth to serve him."

Mike takes my hand. "That's why he got so mad at me today. I told him there was no way in the world I was joining the military after high school. He's been telling me I had to join the Marine Corps for years. Just like him, his father, and his grandfather."

"My father was always disappointed that he had daughters," my mom explains. "Mike, when you were born, my father decided he wanted you to be his carbon copy."

Mike scoffs. "There was no way in hell that was gonna happen. I never wanted to be anything like him. I could tell there was something wrong with him when we were kids. You don't remember him, do you?" Mike asks me. "You don't remember how awful he was to us?"

"No."

"Good. I'm glad," Mike says. "That's why I don't talk to you when I'm upset about him. Tonya can remember how sick and twisted he is. I don't want to dump all that negativity on you, Kira. I'm glad you can't remember him."

"I hate it when you don't talk to me. It makes me feel bad. You looked so miserable today, and I couldn't help you."

Mike hugs me. "I'm sorry."

"What the hell happened today that got you so upset?" I ask.

Mike pulls back and looks at me. "We were all in my mom's car, headed to Boston. Grandpa was already angry at me because I kept insisting that Mom and I should be here today for Tonya's party. That pissed him off.

"He started nagging me about my future. I told him there was no chance in hell of me joining the military. I made it clear that nothing he could say would change my mind. Then I told him it was none of his business what I decide to do with my life because I'll never take a penny from him.

"He lost his mind and started screaming at me at the top of his lungs. When I didn't react to anything he said about me, he started talking shit about Seth and you." Mike squeezes my hand. "I told my mom to pull over and let me out of the car. She refused. I told her if she didn't pull over, I was gonna jump out into moving traffic.

"She pulled off at the next exit. I told Grandpa he was never going to see me again and got out of the car. My mom rushed after me, making excuses for his bad behavior. She started crying and laying on a guilt trip. Mike imitates Aunt Ginny's voice. 'He's your grandfather. He's getting old. He won't be here soon.' I told her 'Good. The sooner he's dead, the better off we'll all be!'"

I gasp, "Oh, my god."

"I agree," Mom says.

"How'd you get here?" I ask.

"I took an Uber to the closest train station, the train to Salem, and another Uber to your house. I'm sorry I came over here like a tornado of toxic energy."

"Mike, it's understandable," Mom says. "My father makes everyone crazy."

"I still don't understand why he hates me so much," I say.

"Mike was born, the perfect, healthy grandson," Mom explains. "Tonya was born the perfect, healthy granddaughter. Our father didn't want Ginny or me to have any more children. If we only had one child each, he thought we'd still have time to serve him.

"When I decided to divorce Tonya's biological father, my father didn't support me. He said that I should have stayed with my first husband. The alcoholic who wanted no part in raising his own daughter. But he made a lot of money and was really good-looking. That's all my father cared about.

"My father was angry at me for getting a divorce. He was angry at me for marrying your father. He said that Doug was too short. That he didn't make enough money. That he wasn't good enough for me."

I frown. I want to kick my grandfather's ass for saying that about my dad.

"I married Doug anyway. Then you came along. Your grandfather considered you a byproduct of all my bad decisions. Then, when he found out about your vision problems, it was a blow to his ego. Nobody with his superior DNA could be born with any type of disease or deformity."

I start crying again.

Mom pulls me into a hug. "Kira, he's a crazy, sick, and twisted old man. He's not part of your family. His opinion doesn't matter."

"Agreed," Mike says.

I know they are right, but it still hurts like hell.

Liz comes upstairs to check on me. I'm already showered and in my pajamas. I tell Liz the whole sordid tale. "I think I'm done being friends with Melony."

"Me, too," Liz says. "I'm sick of being her best friend, her hairdresser, her manicurist, and her therapist. She never does anything for me."

We hug. Liz agrees to sleep over because we are both upset about Melony. I tell her the rest of the story.

"You ended up crying in Jason's arms?" Liz asks, shocked.

I sigh.

Liz giggles. "Tell me again about your plan to avoid him entirely."

I flop down on my bed in frustration.

Chapter Six

Tuesday, September 5, 2023

"Just one more." Dad snaps a picture. Capturing us on the first day of school is a yearly tradition. "This time, pick up your backpacks and put them over your shoulders."

"Come on, Dad," Tonya complains. "We aren't in elementary school anymore."

"Humor us. It's your last, first day of school," Mom reminds her. "I remember doing this on Tonya's first day of kindergarten. She looked so cute. That seems like five minutes ago," Mom says to Dad.

"It seems like a lifetime ago," Tonya grumbles.

Our drive to school is miserable. Tonya has no interest in talking about my hopes or goals for the year.

"I seriously thought about taking the GED so I could work full-time and save more money," Tonya says. "The only reason I don't is because I don't wanna miss out on prom." She gulps down the juice in her thermos, then she slams it back into the cup holder in her car door.

By the time we get to school, the lot is filled up with cars. "I hate this overcrowded prison," she says.

"I'm sure inmates in actual prisons would sympathize with your problems," I tell her.

We have to drive to the extra lot, furthest away from the school. There are a few spaces left in the last row. "We'd have been here earlier and gotten a better space if Mom and Dad didn't hold us up taking all those stupid pictures," she complains as she parks her Honda. She rolls the windows up, turns off the engine, and gulps down more of her drink.

I get a whiff of what she's really drinking. I couldn't smell it with the windows open, but now I can. "Jesus Christ, Tonya! It's seven thirty in the morning!"

She looks at me and frowns. She knows she's been caught.

"Thanks for drinking and driving me to school."

"Oh, calm down. It's a ten-minute drive. It takes longer than ten minutes for alcohol to affect me."

"I'm glad you have such a high tolerance from drinking so much."

"Relax, I needed a little to help me deal with coming back to this hellhole." She gets out of the car.

I get out too and slam the car door.

"What's your problem?"

"You're drunk!"

"I'm slightly buzzed. Calm down." She pulls on her rear door handle, but it's locked. She fumbles with the unlock button on her keychain. She keeps pushing the wrong button.

"Would you mind opening it this century?" I complain, "I'd like to get to class on time."

She finally hits the right button. I open the rear door and get my backpack. Tonya picks hers up without realizing she left it unzipped. Some of her books fall out. "Oops," she says with a giggle.

I roll my eyes, slam the door, and walk away.

"I'll see you at lunch," she says.

"Yeah, hopefully by then you'll be sober."

I follow behind dozens of other students like they are my seeing-eye dogs. They lead me to the entrance.

I told Liz I'd meet her by the stone circle at the front of the school.

"Kira," Liz shouts my name.

She waves her arm to get my attention. As I get closer, I notice that her blurry outline looks thinner than usual.

"Seven more pounds gone," Liz announces proudly. She's in a new sundress and a jean jacket. She looks really pretty.

"That's great," I tell her and give her a hug. She almost helps me forget how angry I am at my sister. "You look amazing."

"So do you." She checks out my skirt and top. "I love that outfit." Liz's face drops. "Oh, shit. Here she comes."

I turn around and see Melony's familiar blurry strut. She always walks like she's better than everyone around her. She walks past us with her nose in the air. Nobody speaks a word.

"She still hasn't apologized to you?" I ask Liz.

"No."

"Well, until she apologizes to you, I don't feel like I should apologize to her."

"Agreed," Liz says as we head inside together.

I'm counting down the minutes until the third period when I can show my art teacher all the work I completed this summer. The bell finally rings. I jump out of my chair and rush to the door before any other students in my algebra class get in my way. I speed down the hall to my art class.

I yank the door to the art classroom open and run inside, bumping into a chair somebody forgot to push in when they stood up. It goes sliding across the floor.

Miss Coleman looks up from her desk. "Kira, slow down before you hurt yourself or someone else."

"Sorry, Miss Coleman." I put the chair back. "I just really wanted to show you all the work I did this summer." I pull my tablet out of my bag.

She holds out her hand, making all the bangles on her arm jingle. She looks nothing like the other teachers. She is dressed in a floral print dress and a pair of leggings. Her long, wavy hair is down around her shoulders. She's always adorned with dangling jewelry decorated with large stones. She always looks like an artistic hippy.

I take a deep breath and hand her my tablet. The first drawing is a portrait of my sister. I captured her smiling with her hair flowing all around her. "Very impressive. Excellent proportions," Miss Coleman says. The second one is of Tonya looking like a sexy goddess. "I get the sense from this portrait that your sister is a wild child. Is she?"

"Yes."

"You've managed to capture your subject's personality as well as her features. It takes an experienced artist to do that."

I smile with pride.

Miss Coleman swipes to see my next piece. I drew Liz with her head down so I could focus on the way the light reflects off her shiny, dark hair. "Excellent use of shading and blending. I love the way you capture all the highlights."

The next ones are all the close-up drawings of objects I did. A pair of scissors, a pencil, a glass of water, and a leaf with drops of rain on it.

"Your ability to capture detail is incredible, and it's clear that you're mastering charcoal and pastel."

I can't remember the last time I smiled this much. "Thanks."

"However, last June, when I told you to create a wide variety of work, I meant that you needed to use different mediums. All these are close-up charcoal drawings."

My smile fades.

"You should focus on painting or sculpture more this year. How about focusing on more abstract work?"

I cringe. "Everything looks like a blur to me. Why would I wanna paint an unrecognizable blurry shape?"

"I know. You're a realist. So, I guess you'll need to capture something realistic at a distance. You should work on developing perspective techniques."

I frown. "I can't see anything in the distance because I'm legally blind."

"I'm sorry about that, Kira. But the truth is, when you apply for art colleges and scholarships, you'll be competing with students all around the country with two good eyes. If you're going to stick to your goals, you need to step up your game and find a way to capture subjects at a distance."

I'm so deflated. I'll never be able to do that.

Students start to fill up the classroom. I move to take a seat near the front.

"Kira," Miss Coleman says.

I turn around and look at her.

"Half those students with two good eyes aren't nearly as driven or as skilled as you. I know you can find a way to do it. Have you ever tried using a pair of binoculars to see things at a distance?"

"No," I perk up a little. "That's a good idea. I'll try that."

"I suggest you get a pair as soon as possible. The first homework assignment this week will be a perspective painting of your own street. This could be a good opportunity for you to build a different piece for your portfolio."

"Okay. Thanks, Miss Coleman." I take a seat in the front row.

As soon as I get home from school, I pull a chair and my easel outside and set them up on the sidewalk in front of my house. Miss Coleman taught the history of Renaissance paintings, vanishing points, and perspective. My homework assignment is to paint the street I live on using the same techniques.

I take my glasses off. I always do when I draw because I can't see close-up details on the canvas with glasses needed to see distance.

Thank God, Dad had a pair of binoculars in his office. I hold them up to my eyes and adjust the settings. Miss Coleman was right. This was a great idea.

I plan to get the basic outline of the street done in pencil and then use paint. "Okay. I can do this. Find the vanishing point." I put on my headphones and cue up some relaxing music to keep me calm. I look through the binoculars, then I put a small dot in the center of my paper where I assume the vanishing point will be. I use my ruler to draw the line of the sidewalk disappearing. I look through the binoculars and see that the vanishing point needs to be lower. The sidewalk angle is off. I erase it and try again. Now the vanishing point is too high. Then it is too far to the left. Then too far to the right. There are so many erased lines now that my paper is a mess. I flip the paper over and try again. This time, I know where the point goes. I finally got it right. I take a deep breath. I start drawing the lines of the sidewalk. I raise and lower my binoculars so many times that my left hand is getting pins and needles from being elevated. I drop my hand and wait until the numb feeling goes away. I look at my drawing and see I've got the basic outline of the sidewalks and street down. I smile.

I start sketching where I want all the houses to go. There are three houses on the right side of the street and one on the left. I'm feeling great until I look through my binoculars again and see I've drawn all the houses way too big and close together. I didn't leave room for driveways and yards.

My hand balls into a fist. If I could see the whole street at once like a normal person, this wouldn't be so frustrating. I can't look through the binoculars and draw at the same time. This is like doing a million-piece jigsaw puzzle of a blurry picture.

I erase the houses. I decide I am going to focus on just one house. The closest one to me is on the right. I draw the steps leading up to the front door. I use the ruler to make sure each horizontal line goes back to the vanishing point. I get the entire stoop drawn. Then I realize that the stairs I drew don't lead to the sidewalk. They lead to the street. I have to erase the whole damn thing and start again. I grab the eraser and start scrubbing. I can't get the lines light enough because I was frustrated, and I pushed too hard with the pencil. I need to use a new sheet of paper and start the whole process over again. I just wasted almost two hours of my life.

"Fuck this!" I throw my pencil and eraser down and yank my headphones off. I rub my tired eyes in frustration.

"Are you alright?"

I pick my glasses up off my easel and shove them on my face. I turn around and see Jason standing in our driveway by his black Toyota.

"Not really," I tell him. I start gathering up my art supplies. "Trying to draw perspective is impossible for me."

He comes over and looks. "It's really not that bad."

"It's awful. I have steps leading down into the middle of the road. It looks like a death trap." I gather up all my pencils and shove them into my art bin. "Where's my eraser?" I move my chair and look down at the ground. It's not there. "Whatever. I'll buy a new one." I shove all my supplies back into my art bin. "Or I won't. I won't need a new eraser because I should forget about being an artist." I slam my bin shut and secure the lid.

Jason picks up my eraser off the ground by our front gate. He hands it to me. "I think you're being way too hard on yourself. It's one bad drawing."

"It's not one bad drawing. It's my crap vision. It's gonna be crap tomorrow, the day after that, and every day of my life. I'll never be able to draw perspective. I wish I could just get into art school, doing what works for me."

"Isn't the whole point of going to art school to learn new techniques that make you a better artist? Won't *always* doing what works for you hold you back creatively?"

I hate how right he is. I open my art bin. "Forget it. Even if I get into an art school, and that's a big if, once I'm there, I'll never be able to keep up with all the assignments. There's no way I can compete with the other students." I drop the eraser into the bin and slam the container shut.

"Kira, take a deep breath. It's not the end of the world. It's one failed drawing."

"Yes, but my eyes will still suck tomorrow."

"That doesn't mean that tomorrow won't also come with a solution to your problem." He helps me pick up my easel and chair and bring everything back into my house.

"A solution. Right. Can you give me a ride to the hardware store? I want to pick up a new pair of eyes."

Wednesday, September 6, 2023

I felt relieved not to have art class today. Not having to think about perspective feels like a mental vacation. I flop down on the couch, open my book bag, and start my algebra homework.

I'm on the second-to-last problem when our doorbell rings.

I get up to answer the door. I'm surprised to see Jason standing in my doorway.

"Hi, Kira."

"Hi," I say, shocked. "Tonya's not here."

"I know. I came to see you. I've got an idea how to solve your perspective problem." He holds up his camera. It has a super-long lens attached to the front.

"Really?" I move to the side and let him in.

"I couldn't stop thinking about how upset you were yesterday. As I was falling asleep last night, I had a great idea." He looks around. "Where's that chair you had yesterday?"

I point to the wooden chair we keep in the corner of our living room. Alma is sleeping on it. I pick her up and move her to the couch. She meows at us like we've wronged her.

"Sorry, little furball," Jason says.

She meows again and runs upstairs.

Jason laughs, picks up the chair, and carries it outside to where I was seated yesterday. He sits in it, takes his lens case off, and starts adjusting his lens.

"I've tried drawing perspective using pictures before. It doesn't work," I insist.

"Let me guess. You used the camera on your phone. If you take a photo of the whole scene, the images in the background are too blurry. And if you take zoomed-in photos of sections of the scene, you can't piece them together afterward. Am I right?"

"Yes."

"That's because you didn't use a long-range lens." He holds up his camera. "This is a telephoto lens."

My eyes aren't on the camera. His biceps are visible in his short-sleeved t-shirt.

"Wait until you see the difference."

I can see the difference. Most teenage boys are so skinny. Mike and Seth look like sticks. I can't help noticing the muscle definition Jason already has. No wonder his arms always feel so good around me.

He adjusts the lens again. He's so focused on what he's doing that he doesn't notice me staring at him. I want to draw his shiny, dark hair. I want to capture the way the sunlight reflects off it.

What the hell is wrong with me? I look away. *Get a grip, Kira.*

"Why'd you pick the name Alma for your cat?" he asks.

"Lawrence Alma-Tadema is one of my favorite artists. Him and John Williams Waterhouse. Alma seemed like a better name for a girl kitten than John, Lawrence, Williams, or Waterhouse."

"I should've guessed. When I was in your room the night of your sister's party, I saw a framed print of Alma-Tadema's *Spring* on your bedroom walls. Along with the poster I gave you for your birthday." He looks at me. "You framed it."

"I told you I would."

He smiles. "I'm glad you liked it so much." He goes back to taking pictures. "Have you ever been to the Getty Museum in Los Angeles?"

"No. Why?"

"That's where *Spring* is housed. It's incredible when you see it in person. The details Alma-Tadema captured are amazing. The people and buildings look so realistic. It looks like a window into ancient Rome. You have to go there someday and see it in person."

"To Los Angeles? My parents get nervous when I go to Liz's house."

"You won't always be a kid, Kira."

"I know, but I'm not sure I'll ever travel. Not unless my eyes are better after an operation, and who knows if that's ever going to happen."

He looks at me and frowns. "Why didn't you dance at your sister's party?"

"Because I'd have tripped over something or bumped into someone."

"Or you might have ended up having fun." He adjusts the lens and takes more photos. "Yesterday, you were convinced you had to give up on dreams because of one bad drawing. I'm beginning to think you're a bit of a pessimist."

I can't tell him he's wrong. "I know."

"If you're able to create a decent perspective painting from these photographs, will you stop being so closed-minded?"

"I doubt it."

69

"I suggest you start thinking about places you wanna travel to and things you wanna accomplish. There are always ways to find solutions to problems." He stands and closes his lens case.

I cross my arms. "And if your photos don't help me, does that mean I get to keep being closed-minded?"

"They'll help." He picks up the chair and carries it back into our house. "I've gotta go do my homework. I'll be back later once I get these photos printed and organized." He sets the chair down in our living room.

"Thanks. I hope this isn't too much work for you." I'm guilty about taking up too much of his time.

"Don't worry about it. I'll see you later, Kira." He heads out our front door.

At eight o'clock, the doorbell rings again. My parents and I are finishing up dinner. "Who in the world could that be at this time of night?" Mom asks.

Dad gets up to open the door. "Hi, Jason."

"Hi, sir. I hope it's not too late. This will just take a minute."

"Tonya's not home. She's working tonight," Dad explains.

"I know. This isn't for Tonya." Jason comes into our living room with a large piece of posterboard and a rolled-up sheet of paper. He sees me seated at the dining room table with my mom and walks towards us. "Hi, Kira." He puts the posterboard on my lap.

This is perfect. He printed all the pictures he took and collaged them together. I can see the whole street in detail. "This is amazing. This is exactly what I need. Thank you."

"It was pretty easy. Photographs never line up perfectly next to each other, but I did my best to give you a panoramic view of the street." He unrolls the sheet of paper he's holding. "Here's a large black and white view of the entire street. It doesn't have as much detail as the small pictures, but it'll give you a full view of the street if you need it." He points to the center of the large poster. "Oh, and I marked the vanishing point for you, too. That should help."

"You're awesome," I say.

"I hope this didn't take up too much of your time," Mom says.

"The whole thing only took two hours. Most of that was time spent waiting for the printer. I did my homework as the photos printed."

"Can we reimburse you for the ink and paper?" Dad asks. "You'll need that ink for school this year."

"I don't want money. I want," he pulls on the ends of my hair playfully, "the art classes I asked Kira for back in June. It's September, and you've never invited me over to teach me how to draw the way you do."

I'm such an asshole. "Does Saturday afternoon work for you?"

He smiles. "Great. See you then. Goodnight."

"Night, Jason," Mom says, sounding a bit stunned by this whole interaction.

He exits our house and closes the door.

"That boy is amazing," Mom says.

"He sure is," Dad agrees. "Tonya hit the jackpot this time."

My smile drops.

Chapter Seven

Saturday, September 9, 2023

The desk I use for my homework can be converted into a drafting table. I move everything off the flat surface so I can set up an area for Jason to draw. All the drawings I did over the summer were scanned and loaded onto my tablet. I have yet to put them in the plastic sheets of my portfolio. I move them to the top of my dresser.

Our doorbell rings. I rush to check my hair and makeup in the mirror. I managed to make myself look cute in a blouse, cardigan, and a pair of skinny pants.

Dad lets Jason in and tells him to go up to my room.

I rush back to my easel and pretend to be engrossed in my painting. I don't want to look like I've been waiting around for him. I squeeze a little black paint onto my palette and dip a small brush. I use it to add some detail work to my neighbor's windows.

I wait for him to knock on my door before I turn around and look at him. "Hi, Jason. Come on in." I drop my paintbrush in my water bucket and stand up.

"Hi. I wasn't sure if I needed to bring anything. All my art supplies are still packed."

"I have everything you'll need already set up." I point to the paper and art supplies I have set up on my drafting table. I borrowed my sister's desk chair for Jason to sit in.

"Oh, good." He steps closer and looks at my painting. "Well, it seems as if I was right. The photo collage worked. That's coming out great. I guess your pessimistic brain was wrong," he teases.

"Don't gloat." I cross my arms and try to hide my smile.

"I wonder what other lies your brain tells you. That you'll *never* dance or travel."

"You're gloating."

"I was right. I deserve to gloat a little." He takes off his leather jacket and hangs it on the desk chair. "So, where do you want to travel to?"

I look at him, surprised. "I don't know. I haven't thought about it. Where do you want to travel?" I sit back down in my chair.

He sits next to me. "Ireland. My mom's family lives there."

"Really? Have you ever met them?"

"No. But I'm dying to. My grandmother in Ireland offered to get me an airline gift card with enough money for an international flight for graduation. That way, I can come meet her whenever I want."

"You'd really get on a plane and go to a different country all by yourself?"

"Sure"

"Even if I had perfect vision, that would scare me. You're braver than me."

"We'll just see about that." He rolls his chair closer to mine. "I'm gonna make sure you dance the next time there's a special occasion, Kira."

I back up a little. "Don't hold your breath." The back of my chair touches my easel. There is limited space here for two people to work.

He rolls closer. "And you're going to get on an airplane someday." His leg brushes mine.

"You'll suffocate waiting for that," I tease him, and pick up my tablet. "We should probably get started. I've put a whole lesson plan together to teach you. I think we should start with this picture you took." I show him a photo I pulled off his Instagram. I opened it in Photoshop. It's a close-up of a fall leaf. I desaturated the photo until it became black and white and put a grid over it. "I want you to pick one square of the grid to draw." I point to the paper I've set up on the drafting table. I used artist tape to mark a large square on the paper.

"One square. How will anyone even tell what it's a drawing of if I do it that close up?"

"Nobody needs to tell. Don't worry about drawing anything another person would recognize. I want you to draw only the light and dark variations you see in the zoomed-in picture. Pick a square."

"Three down and four from the left."

I zoom in and place my tablet down in front of Jason. "Start by drawing the largest veins in the leaf. Make them really dark with the charcoal stick."

He picks up a charcoal stick and begins to sketch. "I'd never think of drawing like this. The idea of not seeing the whole object in the frame is so foreign to me."

"I guess you're gonna have to trust me."

He draws a line he's going to regret later. I point out his mistake. He erases it and draws it correctly the second time. We sit in silence as he draws. I keep my eyes glued to his paper. Watching to see if he needs help again.

"Can you please talk about something?" he asks.

"Like what?"

"I don't care. Anything. Just talk. The silence is making me self-conscious. You're a way better artist than me. If we talk, this will feel like we're hanging out. If you're silent, I feel like I'm being scrutinized."

I giggle at the idea of Jason being insecure and intimidated by me. That's ridiculous.

He looks at me, surprised. "What's so funny?"

"*You* being insecure. I didn't think guys like you got insecure about anything."

"What do you mean 'guys like me'?"

"You just moved here. It takes most new kids a few weeks to make friends, but you had a bunch of friends and a beautiful girlfriend even before the first day of school. You'd be hot at the North Pole and cool at the equator."

He raises his eyebrows at my compliment. "Really?" A cocky smirk appears on his face.

Heat rises to my cheeks. "Can you please forget what I just said?"

"No." He laughs at my embarrassment. "I'm gonna tease you about that statement for the rest of your life."

"That won't help your art skills." I point at his paper. "Focus."

He stifles his laughter and goes back to his drawing. He still has a smug smile on his face. "I'm sorry. I feel less insecure about my mediocre drawing abilities when you're blushing."

I lean in to get a better look. He has most of the largest veins drawn. "Let's not label you as mediocre. That's coming along nicely." He's almost done sketching the largest veins in the leaf. "Now use the charcoal pencils to add the smaller veins."

He picks up a pencil and starts sketching again on the top left corner of his paper.

"Wait," I say. "Charcoal smudges easily. If you turn the paper upside-down, you can work on the left side of the paper without your right-hand smudging what you've already drawn." I bend over and adjust his paper.

He leans closer. "Lavender."

"What?" I ask, confused, and look at him. God, his eyes are gorgeous. They are so green they look like emeralds.

"You smell of lavender."

And his lashes. There isn't a mascara in the world that could make my lashes look that dark and long.

"Are you wearing perfume?"

I look away so I can regain my ability to talk. "No. It's just my shampoo. I don't wear perfume. Tonya is the extra girly one." I sit back in my chair. "That should help you avoid smudging."

"Thanks," he says and starts drawing again. "I don't wanna use up all your art supplies, so I'll bring over my paper and pencils next time. Once I actually unpack them."

"So, why'd you and your aunt move here anyway?"

His hand stills on the paper. "My aunt and I both decided a move would be the best thing for us."

"You agreed to move your senior year? Most teenagers would've protested like hell."

He looks at me. "Most teenagers don't have a ton of toxic ex-relatives to escape from. I actually wish we'd moved out of that area years ago."

"So, what did your ex-family do that was so bad you had to leave the state?"

"That's a long, complicated story," he warns.

"We have time. Draw and talk, like you wanted."

He smiles at me. "Okay. My ex-father, who I like to call Sperm Donor, is named Damien. He was the pride and joy of his mother, who I like to call Grand Mommy Dearest. Sperm Donor became a lawyer, moved to New York City, got married to a beautiful woman, and had a baby on the way. Grand Mommy Dearest was so proud and loved to brag nonstop about her successful son.

"My mom's death shattered the illusion my grandmother was so proud of. When Mimi rescued me from Damien, she brought me back to the town where she grew up. She talked to her friends about how neglectful Sperm Donor was with me. How he'd left me hungry and in dirty diapers, crying for hours. Mimi was not being a gossip. She talked to her friends because she was upset and needed help learning how to raise a baby.

"Once the truth was out, more people started talking about what a narcissist Damien was and how he'd mistreated people in the past. It's weird how when one person speaks up about an asshole, tons of other people speak up too.

"He'd been a bully in high school. His grades were always crap. His parents practically paid his way into college. He'd been a nightmare customer when visiting every business in town. This shattered Grand Mommy Dearest's illusion of being the perfect matriarch, leading her perfect family. She never forgave Mimi for letting others know about our family business."

"Mimi didn't ruin anything. Your Dad did. Your grandmother needs a therapist."

"I think we should put cameras in a small room, lock your grandfather in there with my grandmother, and have a Hunger Games," Jason jokes.

I giggle. "That's a bit extreme."

"Come on. Tell me you wouldn't enjoy watching those assholes fight to the death. I can see the commercial now." His voice deepens. "Tune in, Sunday, Sunday, Sunday. Two assholes fight to the death. Sponsored by Preparation H."

I laugh uncontrollably.

"Charmin Ultra Soft and Ex-Lax."

"Everything assholes need," I say between giggles.

"Exactly." He looks at me. "Thank you for having a sense of humor about all this. I love that you and Mike, both understand me."

"Tonya gets it, too, right? I mean, she doesn't want anything to do with our grandfather."

He looks back at his drawing. "I don't really talk to her about this."

I'm beginning to think he doesn't talk to my sister about anything important. His answer makes me happy. Then guilt begins gnawing at me. I shouldn't be glad that he opens up to me instead of her.

"I'm really glad I met you and Mike."

I giggle. "Kimber was *so wrong* about you. You're not boring at all."

"Yeah. But she *was so right* about me having a huge penis, though."

"Oh, my God." I blush, cover my face, and try to stifle my giggles.

He laughs at my red face.

I try to regain my composure by checking the progress of his drawing. "Good. You've got the outline down. Now for the fun part." I lean in and use the tablet to zoom in even closer on the square he's drawing. "Now I want you to focus on the creases. Do you see the way the light reflects off the leaf? How it makes dark, medium, and light creases?"

"Yeah."

"Good. Go section by section. Draw the dark parts and medium parts with the softest charcoal pencil. Use your fingers and the kneaded eraser to lighten the medium sections and leave the paper white for the lightest sections."

"This is the fun part?" he asks. "It seems like the nerve-racking part to me. This is like drawing pixels."

"You'll do fine. Go section by section and focus on every detail you see."

He looks closely at the tablet. Then he takes a deep breath and starts shading with the pencil by the largest vein in the middle of the drawing. I lean in and get a close look at the exact spot he's drawing. I watch as he shades in a dark crease. Then he moves to the right and tries to add a lighter shading with the pencil by pressing gently. The black charcoal pencil looks way too dark for this section. He grunts in frustration. "I've messed up already."

"You haven't messed anything up," I insist. "Use your fingers to smudge the charcoal, and it'll get lighter."

He rubs the paper too hard because he's frustrated.

"Gently. Take a deep breath and calm down."

His chest rises and falls.

"Let me show you." I use the charcoal pencil to add some soft lines. Then I smudge them gently with my fingertip. "See. Relax and do it gently. Don't attack the drawing. It isn't your enemy."

"That's not as easy for me. You've got perfect tiny fingers." He takes my hand in his and looks at my fingers. "They're ideal for precision. My fingers are too big and clumsy for this." He holds his hand up to mine so I can see how small mine is by comparison.

"Stop making excuses and try it." I reposition our hands. I grab his pointer finger and hold it so it is barely touching the paper. Then I move it to the side, forcing him to smudge the charcoal. "There. See? You did it."

He takes a closer look. "That looks pretty good."

"Yeah. See? You can do it. Now try again." I insist.

He draws another mark and then smudges it to lighten it.

"Good. That's it. Use the kneaded eraser if you want it lighter than that."

I watch as he uses the eraser to achieve the effect he wants.

"See, I knew you could do it." I slide my chair away from the table. "Even with your freakishly big man hands."

He laughs. "They match my freakishly big p—"

"Shut up." I turn my chair around and face my easel. "You've got the hang of it. I'm gonna work on my painting. I'll be right here if you have a question or need help."

"What if I make a mistake and you're not watching?"

"You'll be fine. It's charcoal. It's a forgiving medium."

We sit quietly working for a while. I finish painting the grass on my neighbor's lawn.

Dad pokes his head into my room, "How's it going? Do you kids need anything?" He sounds relieved to see us both seated doing artwork.

I roll my eyes. It's such an obvious attempt to check on us. I've never had a boy in my room before.

"Thanks, but I'm fine, sir," Jason says.

"Okay, I'll be right downstairs. Let me know if you change your mind." Dad leaves.

We work in silence until Jason announces, "I think I'm finished."

I stand and turn around to see Jason's progress. "Wow. That looks great. Stand up and look at it from farther away."

He stands and backs up. "Oh, yeah. I guess that's pretty good."

"It's great. You recreated all the texture on the leaf. Excellent work. I told you that you could do it. Even with those big man hands."

He holds up his charcoal-covered fingers. "I used my pinky a lot. It's my smallest smudge stick."

I smile. "That's good. Your pinky is probably the same size as my pointer finger. So, you should be able to smudge charcoal the same way I do." I wave my pointer finger in his face. "No more excuses."

He reaches up and takes my hand in his. "No way." He compares our fingers. My pointer finger is narrower and shorter than his pinky. "Your tiny fingers give you a major advantage, so you'll always be a better artist than me."

I gaze up into his eyes and blush again.

"At least that will be the excuse I tell myself to feel better about never being as skilled as you."

"Hey," Tonya says.

I look over and see my sister standing in the bathroom doorway. I yank my hand out of Jason's and step back. How the hell did I not hear her come home? I didn't hear her car come in the driveway or her footsteps coming up the stairs. I didn't even hear her come through our bathroom. Did she sneak up on us on purpose?

"Hi," Jason says. "When did you get home?"

"Just now," she steps inside my room. She's in her waitress uniform. Her shoulder brushes the stack of drawings I had on my dresser. They fall on the floor in a heap.

"Thanks," I tell her.

My sister ignores the mess she made. "What are you two doing?"

"We finished our first art class," Jason points to his drawing.

Tonya looks at Jason's work. "A close-up of a leaf," she says dismissively. "So, are we still going to the party tonight?"

"Oh, yeah, right. I forgot. We can still go if you want," he says with no enthusiasm.

"Of course, I still want to," Tonya says. "I'm gonna go get ready." She heads back to the bathroom but turns around in the doorway. "Oh, and don't even bother inviting Kira to join us tonight. You'd have better luck getting a turtle out of her shell." She closes the door to the bathroom and turns the shower on.

I lean over and pick up the mess she made. Jason helps me gather all the drawings. He picks up the last one. It was lying face down on the ground. He turns it over. It's a drawing of his face.

My blood runs cold.

"What's this?" he asks, surprised.

I've never blushed this hard in my life. "Your portrait."

He stares at it for a moment. "Most portraits show the person's neck and shoulders. Why is it so close up? And why is it in color when the rest of your drawings are black and white?"

I cringe. I can't look at him. I keep my eyes glued to the drawing he's holding. "Because your eyes are really green."

"When did you draw this?"

"The night we met," I blurt out. Why didn't I say I can't remember? Or lie and say it was last week?

Realization crosses his face. He knows I've had a huge crush on him since we met.

"It's not a big deal." My hands shake as I flip through the stack of drawings I'm holding. "I like to capture people's most striking features." I hold up a drawing of Liz. "Like Liz's dark hair. You see how the light reflects off her shiny hair?" I don't wait for an answer. I hold up another drawing. "Or my sister's smile. I only used color and drew your face so close up because your eyes are really green."

He doesn't say anything. I can tell by the look on his face that he knows I'm lying.

I need to get the hell out of this room. I set the stack of paper in my hands back down on my dresser. "I should spray your drawing so it doesn't smudge." I walk back to my drafting table and pick up his drawing. "I'll press it between some cardboard so you can take it home. Do you wanna take your portrait home too?" I try to sound casual, like the drawing doesn't mean anything to me. "I mean, I've already scanned it, so you can keep it if you want."

He doesn't answer. He looks deep in thought.

"Do you wanna take your portrait home?" I repeat.

"Yeah. Thanks. My aunt will love it."

"Okay. Give me a few minutes to get this all ready to go." I pick up my fixative spray and head out the door. I head outside to the backyard, place his drawing on the ground, and spray it until the charcoal is set.

When I get back to my room, I'm grateful Jason isn't here anymore. His voice comes from Tonya's room. I press the two drawings between two sheets of cardboard and tape them together for him to take home. Then I head to the living room to avoid Jason and Tonya.

Jason comes downstairs. I hand him the drawings and say goodnight.

I pass my sister on the way upstairs to my room. Of course, Tonya is dressed in a tight, skimpy dress and heels.

"Summer's over. You're gonna be freezing without a jacket," I tell my sister.

"A jacket doesn't go with this outfit," she says. "I guess Jason will have to keep me warm tonight."

I roll my eyes and go to my room.

Chapter Eight

Saturday, September 9, 2023

I'm alone in the living room watching TV. At five to eleven, a car pulls into our driveway. I knew Jason would get her home on time.

"Don't you dare tell them," I overhear Tonya say on the other side of the front door. "I don't wanna get an annoying lecture about how I fucked shit up."

"I already promised I wouldn't. Can you please get your keys out already?" Jason sounds frustrated.

"You just can't wait to get inside and see Little Miss Perfect again," my sister snaps.

I frown and cross my arms.

Something hard hits the ground. I assume those are Tonya's keys.

"Come on. It's cold out here," Jason complains.

I get up and open the front door for them. Tonya's makeup is smudged. Her eyes look red. She has Jason's jacket draped over her shoulders.

"Oh, look," Tonya slurs. "It's Little Miss Perfect,"

"How much did she have to drink?" I ask.

"Way too much." Jason picks the keys up off the ground and helps her through the door. "She had a bad night."

"Oh, I wonder why," Tonya says.

"We can talk about it later after you've sobered up," Jason says. He looks at me, "Where are your parents?"

"They went to bed. A buyer wants to see a house early tomorrow," I explain.

"Help me get her in bed before they wake up to this drama." He drapes my sister's arm around his shoulder.

"Thaaat's right," Tonya slurs. "I'm aaalways the drama queen and Kira is the perfect one."

I take Tonya's other arm and we lead her up the stairs.

"Miss Goody Two-Shoes never does aaanything wrong. She's soooo sweet and wholesome," Tonya yells once we're halfway up the stairs.

"Shut up before you wake up Mom and Dad," I snap at her. "Do you want them to see you like this again?"

"Okay, I'll whisper about how virginal you are instead," she says loud enough for Jason to hear. "She's only kissed one boy, one time."

I want to die of embarrassment. I'm so glad Jason can't see my red face right now.

"Tonya, you're making a total ass of yourself," Jason tells her. "Get in bed and sleep it off." He opens the door to her room and switches on the light.

We get her into her bedroom. I shove her hard. Her butt hits her mattress. "Get your own water and aspirin this time."

Tonya looks too dizzy to respond.

"What's going on in here?" Mom asks.

Jason and I turn to see her standing in the doorway.

"Tonya's drunk again," Jason says.

Dad comes stumbling in after Mom. He looks grumpy from being woken up. "What do you mean *again*? How many times has she been drunk around you?" Dad sounds betrayed. My parents felt safe knowing Jason was driving Tonya home. That's why they went to bed early.

"I've never seen her this drunk before," Jason explains. "But she's been tipsy every time we've gone out."

"Could you all stop talking about me like I'm not here," Tonya complains.

Everyone ignores her.

"I've tried to get her to hang out without drinking, but she never listens to me," Jason explains. "I'm sorry, but your daughter has a drinking problem."

"I do not," Tonya yells. "Just because I like to party with friends—" She stands up suddenly. She turns green. Then she rushes into the bathroom and vomits in the toilet.

Mom rushes in after her.

"I'm sorry I brought her home like this," Jason says to Dad. "I told her to stop drinking, but she didn't listen."

"I think it's about time I talk to Cheryl's parents about what goes on at their house," Dad says.

Jason and I exchange glances. He takes a deep breath. "There is no Cheryl, sir."

"What do you mean?" Dad asks.

"Cheryl is a made-up person," Jason explains.

"What the hell? Why would Tonya make up a friend?" Dad is fuming.

"Some of the kids make up friends, so if they get caught drinking or doing drugs, they can blame it on an imaginary person," Jason explains. "While the parents try to figure out who to call to complain—"

"The kids have time to work out their lies," Dad yells. "Move the drugs and alcohol so no one gets caught." His face is turning bright red. I've never seen him this mad before. "So where the hell does she really go to drink?"

Jason sighs and looks at me. He knows he's about to commit social suicide. "The parties are always at Eric Lawndale's house. I don't know where they get the beer, but they always have a keg."

"Well, then, Eric Lawndale's father is about to get an earful from me," Dad shouts.

"If you can get a hold of him," I say. "Eric's parents travel a lot. That's why all the kids go over there to party."

"Did you know about all of this?" Dad asks me, surprised.

"I knew some of it," I mumble.

"And you didn't tell me what was going on?" Dad yells.

Tonya vomits into the toilet again.

"I didn't know how bad her drinking had gotten," I say.

"And how bad did it have to get before you spoke up?" Dad asks. "When she slipped into a coma from alcohol poisoning or drove into a Mac truck?"

"Don't yell at me. I'm not the one drunk and puking my guts out."

I go back downstairs and flop down on the couch. I'm done dealing with Tonya when she's drunk. Let my parents do it for once.

Tonya embarrassed the hell out of me. She did it to be mean and vindictive. That's how Mom and Aunt Ginny treat each other. Tonya and I promised we would never be that mean to each other.

Jason comes downstairs looking as pale as a ghost.

"Thank you for telling the truth," I say. "You're braver than me."

"Remember when you told me you didn't wanna go to parties because you didn't wanna put Tonya or Mike in the position of being your babysitter?" He moves closer to the door.

"Yeah."

"Well, you're not the one who needs a babysitter." He opens the door to leave. "Goodnight, Kira."

"Goodnight."

I wait until Tonya's in bed, then I head up the stairs to my parents' room. I'm dreading this conversation. My heart is pounding. My mouth is dry. My legs hurt as I make my way up to the top floor of the house to my parents' bedroom.

"It's genetic," my mother says. "Gary was an alcoholic. Tonya inherited this from him."

"Now we have even one more reason to despise that man." Dad is hunched over his laptop. "She's not going to end up like him."

"How could this have happened?" Mom says. "I did everything I could to make sure she didn't turn out like him."

Dad doesn't answer. He's too busy looking at his laptop. "Good. They are open on Sunday. They are open twenty-four hours. Tonya's going tomorrow."

"To an AA meeting?" Mom asks.

Dad looks up at Mom. "To a rehabilitation center in Danvers. I'm emailing them right now."

"Do you really think she needs to be checked into one of those places?" She gets up and stands over Dad to look at his laptop, too. "Do you think it's that bad?"

I knock.

They both look up at me.

"Tonya usually waits and sobers up enough to drive the three miles home from Eric's house," I tell them. "She uses breath mints to hide the alcohol on her breath when she gets home from parties. She drove drunk on the first day of school. She had vodka in her thermos."

Mom gasps and covers her mouth.

"By the time we got to school, she was tipsy. I'm amazed we didn't have an accident. She made me feel unsafe."

It is so quiet you could hear a pin drop. Until Dad says, "Tonya is checking into rehab tomorrow, if I have to drag her there kicking and screaming."

I'm relieved. My father always knows what to do.

Mom starts to cry. She sinks down on her bed and hangs her head low. A sob escapes her lips. I've never seen my mother cry like this. Mom doesn't get sad like this; she gets angry. She should be yelling about how angry she is at my sister, not sobbing on her bed like a little girl.

"I'm sorry I didn't tell you sooner. I was scared. Ratting out Eric Lawndale is social suicide." I turn and head one floor down to my room. The sound of my mother crying feels like a knife in my chest. I remind myself that Dad knows what he is doing. He can fix this.

Chapter Nine

Sunday, September 10, 2023

I wake up to the sound of my dad's voice in the hallway. "So, we can check her in today. That's wonderful. Thank you so much. We'll see you in an hour or two."

"I'll pack her suitcase," Mom says. "You should try to find her keys. She's not driving off today in her car."

"Agreed. It's a good thing we registered and insured the car under my name," Dad says.

A suitcase is wheeled down the hall into my sister's room.

Dad knocks on my door.

I sit up, put on my glasses, and switch on my light.

Dad has my sister's purse in his hands. "There are like nine million compartments in this thing." He sits on my bed. "Come on, help me go through this. A father going through his daughter's purse is an invasion of privacy. A sister doing it is a normal daily occurrence. Help me feel normal, please."

"Okay." I start pulling out the contents. "What do you need?"

"Her car insurance and her cell phone for starters," Dad says.

I find her wallet first and go through all the cards. I hand her insurance card to Dad.

"I'm sorry I yelled at you," he says. "That was messed up. I was angry at the whole world last night. Not you."

It's a huge relief. "Okay. Thanks."

Dad leans in and hugs me.

"You were right. I should've told you."

"Yes, you should have, but as your mother told me, teenage girls and the social pressures they deal with are a totally foreign ecosystem to me. It's like I'm watching that meerkat show on Animal Planet."

I giggle.

"What's happening with your sister isn't your fault," Dad says. "It's not my fault or your mother's fault. It's not even Tonya's biological father's fault. It's Tonya's fault. Now come on. Let's finish this so we can try and get her some help."

I find her dead cell phone next. Dad takes it from me and plugs it into my charger. "She can't take it with her to rehab. Maybe there's something I can find in her text messages to show the police. They need to figure out where the kids are getting the beer."

I'm shocked. "Are you really going to the police?"

"Yes. This isn't just about your sister. The Lawndales have put hundreds of students in danger. Those elitist scumbags have been getting away with too much for too long."

I know Dad is right, but I'm terrified of the shit Jason and I are going to have to put up with in school. When everyone finds out Jason is the one who ratted and my father is the one who went to the cops, we're dead.

Tonya is still asleep at noon.

"Get up," Dad orders.

No response.

"Tonya, get up," Mom says.

I walk through our bathroom to her room and stand in the doorway.

"Go away," My sister mumbles. "I don't feel well."

"Because you got plastered last night. You're not sick. You're hungover. It's afternoon. Get up." Mom yanks the covers off my sister.

"God! What the hell is your problem?" Tonya sits up and glares at our parents.

I've never seen my sister look this bad before in my life. She has vomit on her shirt. Mascara and eye makeup are smudged down her face. Her hair looks like a rat's nest. She smells like alcohol and upchuck. I barely recognize her.

Mom looks furious. "My problem is that last night you were so drunk you couldn't even walk up the stairs. You were so drunk you couldn't stop vomiting. My problem is that you've been lying to us about where you go on the weekends for over a year. My problem is that you drove drunk with your sister in the car."

Tonya looks at me. "You little snitch."

"Don't yell at your sister for telling the truth," Dad says. "We've all had it with you, Tonya. You're days of sneaking alcohol, your parties at the Lawndale house. It's over. You have two choices: you can check yourself into rehab today or move out of this house. You cannot live here with us and keep drinking."

"Fine. Then I'm out of here." Tonya stands. "I can't stand any of you. I've been dying to move out!" She gets up and goes over to her closet to start pulling out clothes.

"If you choose to leave, you won't be taking your car," Dad tells her. "It's registered and insured under my name. I have the keys. You lost the right to it when you drank with your sister in the car."

"What the hell, Dad?" Tonya slams her dresser drawer shut.

"And you won't be taking your cell phone. The phone plan is also under my name. So, if you move out, I hope you can afford to get your own phone, transportation, and housing."

Tonya's voice is wild with rage. "I hate you!"

"Well, I still love you, but you cannot live under my roof and drink," Dad says. "You have thirty minutes to take a shower and get dressed. You can either walk out the door and live on your own, or you can get in our car and check into a rehab facility for thirty days. It's your choice."

"I can't go to rehab for thirty days. What about my job?"

"They'll have to make do without you," Mom says.

"What about school?" Tonya asks. "Do you really want me to miss a month of school?"

"Don't give me that," Dad snaps. "You've made it abundantly clear that you don't care about your grades. You have been coasting by with all D's." Dad looks at me. "Kira, go to your room and lock the door."

I walk through our bathroom, close my door, and lock my sister out of my bedroom.

"Twenty-five minutes, Tonya," Dad orders.

Tonya slams her bedroom door so hard that the whole house shakes.

My sister walks down the stairs like a zombie. She doesn't look at me as she exits our house and gets into the back of Dad's car. He puts her suitcase in the trunk.

"We're heading to the police station to report Eric Lawndale's parents after we get Tonya checked into the rehab center," Dad says to Mom.

I sigh. School is going to be a nightmare on Monday.

"It'll be alright," Mom whispers to me and gives me a quick hug. "We'll be home as soon as we can." She gets in the car.

I go back inside my house and have a good cry. Then I pick up the phone and call Mike and Aunt Ginny. They need to know what's going on.

Then I text Jason. He has a right to know what's going on with his girlfriend. I let him know where they are taking her and how long she'll be gone.

He writes back.

J: Good. I hope she gets the help she needs.

Chapter Ten

Monday, September 11, 2023

I wish I was invisible. I've been getting dirty looks and bitchy comments from people all day. "Narc," a few students murmur as they walk by me in the hall. The word was written on my locker in bright pink lipstick. Liz and I used up all the tissues in my purse, wiping it off.

At lunch, I sit at a table in the back corner of the lunchroom with Liz. She tries to cheer me up by asking, "Do you want my ice cream sandwich?"

"No, thanks. I'm not hungry." I push my lunch tray back.

"I'm sure your sister will be fine," Liz assures me. "Your parents checked her into a great facility. I looked the place up online."

"I don't think rehab is gonna help. Tonya wants to keep drinking. I read online that forcing someone into rehab rarely works. The addict has to be willing to go. My sister can't even stand feeling confined by high school. She's in a treatment center where they allow almost no contact with the outside world. I think my sister is gonna rebel like crazy."

"I hope not," Liz says. "Maybe she'll—"

My lunch tray flies past my head and hits the wall behind me. Mac and cheese lands on my shoulder and in my hair. I look up to see Eric Lawndale looming over our table with a furious expression. "Thanks for ratting us out, you little bitch!" He looks angry enough to snap me in two.

My whole body freezes. I can't remember how to talk.

"I know you narced to your parents when your whore of a sister stumbled home drunk! The cops are on my dad's ass!" He pounds his hand on our table. "My dad is making my life a living hell! So your life is about to become a living hell too!"

"Oh, grow up," Liz snaps at him. "You sound like a five-year-old, Eric. Daddy's mad at me, so I'm mad at you," she says in a baby voice.

A group of students at a neighboring table giggle at her impression.

"Shut up, you fat, ugly bitch!" he yells at Liz.

Nobody talks to my best friend like that. I stand up, snatch Liz's melting ice cream sandwich off the table, and chuck it at him. It hits his chest and leaves a drippy white mess on his black t-shirt.

"You fucking little bitch!" Eric yells

I've made a huge mistake. Liz steps in front of me. I grab her hand and cower behind her. I look around, hoping to see a teacher, a lunch lady, or a janitor. Any adult. I saw three lunch ladies serving food today. They're middle-aged and petite. Way too small to discipline Eric.

"You're so fucking dead!" Eric shoves the table between us to the side. Students nearby scatter.

Liz and I back further into the corner. I close my eyes and prepare to be pounded.

It sounds like a body is slammed into a wall.

My eyes snap open. My jaw drops.

"I knew you were a piece of shit, Lawndale," Jason says. He has Eric pinned up against the wall in a chokehold. "Attacking girls. That's an all-time low, even for you. What the fuck is wrong with you?" Jason sounds furious. I've never heard his voice so deep and raspy.

Eric fumbles trying to remove Jason's forearm from his neck.

Jason slams his hip into Eric's stomach and pushes harder on his neck. "Let me guess," Jason taunts. "Mommy and Daddy don't love you enough to stay at home. They travel all the time to get away from you, so you bully people smaller than you to release your rage. You're pathetic, Lawndale."

Students around us gasp and murmur.

"Sorry, I ain't into this, faggot." Eric shoves hard against Jason's chest.

Jason steps back.

Eric is about to throw a punch until he sees Seth and Mike step up behind Jason. "Here come your queer friends," Eric says in a raspy voice and points to Seth. "Everyone knows he's in the closet. Take him up against the wall."

Mike is about to pound Eric. Seth holds him back.

"Shut up, you piece of shit!" Mike rages. "Why the fuck would you attack my cousin?"

"The little rat needs to be taught a lesson," Eric says in a raspy voice. "My dad could go to jail and be fined two thousand bucks because of that little bitch!"

"Kira didn't rat you out to her parents," Jason says through gritted teeth. "I did."

Eric looks shocked.

"Holy shit," Liz murmurs.

"Kira didn't have anything to do with it," Jason insists. "You wanna pound someone for fucking up your life, I'm right here." He shifts his feet and raises his hands, waiting for Eric to throw the first punch.

My jaw hits the floor. Are they really about to fight? Jason and Eric are about the same height, but Eric's arms and chest are much skinnier.

Eric won't fight here. It's three against one. "You're all so fucking dead. Especially you," he warns Jason. "Your whore girlfriend isn't worth shit. She's screwed everyone in school."

I wish I had something else to throw. "Not you! My sister never wanted *you!* She said you're too stupid to date!"

"And have a small dick," Seth yells, loud enough for everyone around to hear.

Liz laughs. "At least that's what your ex-girlfriend told Tonya," she adds to the lie.

"Yeah," Seth agrees. "Tonya said, that your ex said, that your dick was as small as her pinky finger." He holds up his hand and waves his pinky around for all to see.

Girls around us all giggle and gasp.

We don't even know who Eric's ex-girlfriends are. That doesn't matter. Enough people heard. The rumor will spread.

Eric's face turns bright red. He glares at me and Liz. "This isn't over. You fuckers are dead." He storms off through the closest door. I guess the blow to his manhood was too embarrassing.

I think I held my breath for the whole ordeal, because my lungs burn from my first deep intake of air.

"Are you okay?" Jason asks while brushing mac and cheese out of my hair.

"I'm fine now," I say, trying to catch my breath.

"You should've let me punch him," Mike complains to Seth.

"And let you get suspended for a month?" Seth asks. "No way. I don't wanna face that psycho alone."

"Let's move to another table," Jason says. He picks up my backpack, takes my hand, and leads me to his table on the other side of the cafeteria. I sit between Jason and Liz.

The vice principal enters the room with one of the lunch ladies trailing behind him. Students scatter away from the corner where the argument happened. The vice principal looks around. The only signs of a fight are a lunch tray and food scattered across the floor. "What happened here?" he yells.

Nobody says a word.

We all breathe a sigh of relief.

Jason brushes some more mac and cheese off my shoulder. "Attacking girls. What a psycho."

"He's a psycho with a lot of friends," Mike reminds us. "They're all gonna be out for blood. From now on, you and Liz eat lunch with us."

"Okay," I agree.

"And nobody should walk the hallways alone," Mike says. "We should figure out our class schedules so we can stay in groups."

Mike walks Liz and me out of the school. "I have to get to work." Mike has an after-school job at a supermarket. "My shift starts in half an hour. Let me text Jason or Seth to drive you home."

"I'll take the bus. I'll be fine." I point to my bus, ten feet away. "None of Eric's friends ride on my bus. They are all rich upperclassmen with cars. Go. I'll be fine."

"What about you?" Mike asks Liz.

"My mom's picking me up," Liz says. "She's parked over there." She points to the lot where parents are allowed to wait.

"Okay. Both of you text me when you get home. I have to go or I'm gonna be late." Mike walks away.

The second we're alone, Liz rummages through her backpack. "I forgot my French book in my locker. I need it for tonight's homework. I have to go back for it."

"I'll go with you," I tell her.

"You can't, you'll miss your bus." Liz's phone buzzes with a text from her mom telling her to hurry up. "Shit. I need that book. You get on the bus. I'll be fine." She runs off.

I sigh and walk to my bus. I wish my sister was here. Then I could get home in fifteen minutes. Going home by bus takes about forty. I might as well get used to this. After Tonya graduates, I'll have to take the bus. If she graduates. Who the hell knows what the hell is going to happen after—

Someone shoves me from behind. My glasses go flying off my face. I can't use my hands to break my fall because it's so sudden. I land flat on my face.

"That's what you get, little rat," spits some girl.

I can't see anything. All the people, the cars, the grass, and the trees are shapeless blobs of different colors. I've never been this blind in public before. I feel around for my glasses, but they are nowhere to be found.

I need my phone to call someone for help. My backpack landed next to me. I reach for my phone in the side pocket of my bag. Before I can get it, my backpack is tossed away.

"Snitches get stitches, bitch," the same girl says. She slaps my face, hard. My ears ring.

"I need my glasses. I need my glasses." I start feeling around for them.

"I need my glasses," a group of bitchy girls mocks me. They whimper and laugh at my misery.

I didn't mean to say it aloud. My hand fumbles along the ground looking for my frames. My palms are killing me from the fall.

There is an awful crunching sound as my glasses are crushed under someone's shoe. "Oops," Eric's nasty voice taunts me. I crawl toward the crunching sound. Hoping one lens is intact enough to still see through.

I find my glasses. My fingertip touches the frame.

A foot stomps down and crushes my hand. I scream out in pain as I try to pull my hand back, but it won't budge. There's too much weight on it.

"I guess you won't be drawing with this hand for a while," Eric says. He twists his heel, crushing my hand like it's a used cigarette.

I scream again, loud enough to get an adult's attention, I hope. I try again to get my hand out from under him, but it's no use.

Students around me yell at Eric. "Get off of her." "What the hell is wrong with you, Lawndale?" "Leave her alone."

He ignores everyone yelling at him. Instead, he says to me, "I told you, you're fucking dead."

Is he really going to kill me? Is he going to step on my neck next? He seems crazy enough to do it. I can't die. Tonya will drink herself into an early grave. Mike will murder Eric and go to jail for the rest of his life.

Through the crowd, a familiar voice yells my name. It's Seth. *Thank God.* A punch is thrown. Eric falls back, freeing my hand.

I pull my crushed hand closer to me and cry out in pain. I roll on my side and use my good hand to sit up. I look around and try to get a sense of my surroundings, but it's no use. Without my glasses, I can't even tell where the school is.

"You're dead, motherfucker!" Seth screams. I'm so glad he is close by, but I'm still terrified. I don't know who the girls were who pushed me down, or where they are now. If I stand up, will they hit me again and knock me back down? Seth can't keep them all away by himself.

"Mike, Liz?" I call out weakly for my friends. I want to scream their names, but my voice is too sore to carry far in this crowd.

"Kira," Jason calls my name.

I turn my head in the direction of his voice. "Jason," I try to call out, but my voice is too raspy.

"Jesus Christ," he says when he's close enough to see me. He rushes towards me and crouches down next to me.

I reach for him and cling on tightly with my good arm. The relief that washes over me is overwhelming. His woody herbal scent, his warm hands, everything about him is comforting. He tightens his arms around me. His heart is pounding almost as hard as mine.

"You're okay. You're gonna be fine," he lies. I can tell from his voice that he's worried about the damage to my hand. "Come on. Get up." He helps me to my feet. "You're okay," he whispers again and again. I don't know if he's trying to convince me or himself.

"That's right, run!" Seth shouts.

I hear the frantic shuffle of Eric's footsteps as he flees the scene.

"Run your punk ass bitch back to Daddy!" Seth shouts. "My dad's a cop! You're going to jail, you piece of shit!"

"Seth," Jason shouts. "Some help, please."

"Jesus Christ." Liz runs over to us. "What the hell happened? I left her alone for two minutes."

"I need my glasses," I whisper.

"Find her stuff," Jason says.

Seth retrieves my backpack and glasses. Liz runs to her car to get her mother to help me.

"They're pulverized," Seth says, finding what is left of my frames.

"I can't see anything," I whimper.

"You don't need to," Jason says. "We've got you." He helps me walk towards the car.

"I need my phone. I need to call my parents," I say.

Seth finds my phone inside my backpack. I'm lucky Eric and his friends didn't dump everything out of it and break my phone, too.

"Ay, Dios mío!" Liz's mother, Mrs. Vasquez, cries. She rushes up and looks at my injuries. "Your hand. Ay, Dios mío. You kids all get in my car. I'm taking her to the hospital."

The minivan's door slides open. Jason helps me get in and put my seat belt on.

Mrs. Vasquez starts the engine and pulls out. "What the hell is wrong with these kids? I can't believe how bad schools have gotten. When I was a kid, schools were never this dangerous. Sending your kids to school today is like sending them into a war zone."

"It was two minutes," Liz says from the front seat. "I was gone for two freaking minutes. How the hell did that happen?"

"I'm so glad Mike wasn't there," Seth says. "He would've murdered Eric."

"Keep your hand elevated," Jason says. He puts his arm around my shoulder and wraps his hand around my wrist, keeping my injured hand by my shoulder. "That will help with the swelling."

"Stupid fucking French book." Liz kicks the car in frustration. "I'm sorry, Kira." She sounds close to tears.

"I swear, Liz. I think I'm gonna take you out of public school," Mrs. Vasquez says. "All your parents should take you out, too."

"We need to file a police report," Seth says. "My dad says that parents should always file a report when their kids are assaulted in school."

"Somebody call Kira's parents," Mrs. Vasquez says.

Liz is crying too hard to talk, so Seth pulls out his phone.

Chapter Eleven

Monday, September 11, 2023

Mom's panicked voice comes through the speakerphone, telling Mrs. Vasquez to take me directly to my pediatrician instead of the emergency room. I hear Dad in the background on his own phone. He's calling my doctor's office in a panic. Mom tells us they are already in the car and they will meet us in a few minutes.

A sense of relief passes over me. My parents are on their way. I take a deep breath and lean back. My body goes limp, and my head drops onto Jason's chest. His heart is pounding. I close my eyes. All I want to do is go to sleep. I want to wake up when my hand is bandaged after the doctors have given me painkillers.

"Hey, don't close your eyes," Jason tells me. "You need to stay awake. It's dangerous to let your blood pressure drop after a trauma."

My eyes are so heavy. I don't think I'm going to be able to stay awake.

"Can you turn on the radio, please?" Jason asks Liz. "Something upbeat that Kira likes. Help me keep her awake. Trust me, I know what I'm talking about. My aunt's a nurse."

Liz scampers to pull out her phone and cue up a song. She plays "Cruel Summer."

"Turn it up, please," Jason says.

Liz raises the volume.

Seth starts singing along to all the lyrics. He knows them by heart. Jason looks at him, surprised.

"What? So, I'm a Swiftie," Seth says to Jason. "Don't judge. Taylor is hot, and her music is awesome."

I manage a small smile.

My attention is diverted away from Seth when Jason takes my free hand in his. He's warm and comforting. My eyes are so heavy. I just need to close them for a minute.

Jason's warm breath is on the back of my ear. "Kira, if you want to fall asleep in my arms, you have to get into my bed."

My eyes snap open. I turn and look at him like he's crazy.

"Oh, good. You're awake." There's no guilt or shame on his face; in fact, he looks rather cocky.

I can't believe he said that. I should tell him that was a cheap trick, but my throat is too sore to talk. I look down at my lap and see my hand in his. He gently runs his fingertips along my palm. My heart skips a beat.

"I should've kissed you in the Vatichino room." His breath tickles the back of my ear.

My whole body shivers. He did not just say that. Am I fading in and out of a dream?

"I should've kissed you the day we met."

Heat rushes to my face. I hope the others don't see how much I'm blushing. How can I be hot and shiver at the same time? If I had more experience with guys, Jason wouldn't get to me like this. He must think I'm so lame. He must think—

"Kira." He kisses my forehead.

My breath catches.

He speaks so softly I can barely hear him, "I love the way," his fingertips slide over my palm again, "you tremble when I touch you."

My whole body shakes. I can't breathe.

The car turns sharply into the parking lot.

"Kira's parents are here already," Liz says. "That's their minivan."

My parents aren't going to see me cuddling with my sister's boyfriend. I pull myself free from Jason's arms. He lets go of my wrist, and my hand starts throbbing again when the endorphin rush ends.

Mrs. Vasquez pulls into a space and turns off the engine.

Seth offers to help me out of the car. "I can't see," I remind him. My voice is so sore that I sound like a frog.

"I know." He takes me by my good hand. "I've got you."

I ease out of the minivan onto the pavement. The entire world is a blur around me. Seth helps me stand and take a few steps in the direction of the doctor's office.

My parents rush towards me. Mom takes one look at my hand and cries out, "Oh, my god." She wraps an arm around me.

Dad puts my old spare pair of glasses in my good hand. I put them on. I'm so grateful I can see again. "Let's get you inside," Dad says. They walk me into the doctor's office.

Behind me, Seth asks Jason, "Dude, what the hell was that? What the hell are you doing?"

The door to the doctor's office closes behind me. I can't hear Jason's answer.

My doctor takes one look at my hand and gives us a referral for an orthopedic surgery center in Salem. He tells a nurse to call them immediately to make sure I get seen tonight.

My dad goes out to the waiting room to update everyone as my doctor bandages the cuts on my knees and chin. Dad tells everyone they can all go home. There's no sense in everyone coming to the surgery center with us. I'm relieved that my friends are all gone by the time we leave. I have no idea what I'm supposed to say to Jason now.

The doctors at the surgery center put my hand in a thick cast that runs from my knuckles to the middle of my lower arm. My swollen fingertips poke out of the top of the cast.

I take two painkillers. I turn off my light, lie down, and close my eyes.

My phone buzzes, so I pick it up, and I see a text from Jason.

J: I can't sleep. Worried about u. I hope ur feeling better. Don't b scared. Lawndale will never touch u again. Don't think about the attack. Think about what happened in the car instead.

My eyes are huge.

The three dots on the text screen are jumping and stopping. His message finally comes through.

J: That was so intense. I meant everything I said. I can't sleep because I miss u.

My eyes are bugging out of my head.

The dots are jumping and stopping again. I should put my phone down. I should turn off my phone and go to sleep.

J: Tell me to come over.

Is he insane?

J: Sneak me into your room so I can hold you all night.

My jaw drops. How am I supposed to respond?

J: I know u read all my messages. They r all marked as seen.

Fuck. I drop my phone. *Why didn't I silence it earlier? Why did I keep reading?*

My phone buzzes again.

J: Say something.

My heart is pounding. It's not easy to type with a shaking left hand.

K: No way. My dad will kill u. U r Tonya's boyfriend so stop.

J: I promise u I'm NOT her boyfriend. I'll explain what happened when I see u again.

What the hell? Did they break up? Is that why my sister came home so drunk from that party?

One last text comes through.

J: You should be in my arms right now. Sweet dreams, Kira.

Chapter Twelve

Tuesday, September 12, 2023

The rehab center looks like a cross between a hospital, a therapist's office, and a spa. The common area is filled with plush white chairs and soft footstools. It's as though they wanted a million places for impromptu therapy sessions to happen.

Dad sits in one of the chairs. "I'm sorry you have to do this today. I know you'd rather be in bed right now, but it is really important that your sister sees your injuries before they start to heal. How are you feeling?"

I can't answer him, so I point to my throat and then give him a thumbs down.

"Why don't you go get a cool bottle of water from the vending machine?" Dad suggests and hands me some cash. "That should help for now. We'll get you some throat lozenges as soon as we get out of here."

I nod my head and take the money. I walk back to the vending machines we passed in the lobby. The cool water makes my throat feel a little better.

I make my way back to Dad and notice that my sister has already joined him. I step closer and come around Tonya's chair. I get close enough to notice that my sister looks like a stranger. She has dark rings under her eyes, no makeup on, her hair is pulled back into a ponytail, and she's dressed in sweats. I've never seen her out of the house looking this unpolished.

"If only I'd paid more attention to you, maybe this wouldn't have happened." Dad sounds so guilty.

"How could you pay more attention to me?" Tonya spits out. "Kira needed to be watched every second. If you and Mom stopped hovering over her for one second, she might have walked in front of a car, or fallen down an uncovered manhole."

My jaw drops. Is this the real reason why Tonya insisted I get LASIK surgery as soon as possible?

My sister finally looks up and notices me. She looks almost as shocked at my appearance as I was at hers. She jumps out of her chair and rushes to my side. "What the hell happened?"

"Eric Lawndale wanted revenge," Dad explains.

"Jesus. I knew he was a jerk sometimes, but I never thought he'd attack a girl." Tonya looks at my sling. "What happened to your hand?"

"Eric crushed it under his boot. Kira's pediatrician couldn't treat her hand. We had to take her to an orthopedic surgery center in Salem," Dad lays on the guilt. "They x-rayed your sister's hand. One bone in her palm is broken. Two others are sprained. They said Kira also has soft tissue damage to the muscles, ligaments, and tendons. Hopefully, this doesn't affect your sister's ability to draw."

Tonya's eyes are huge and glassy. She looks pale white. "Shit, Kira, I'm so sorry." She tries to hug me.

I pull away. I hurt everywhere. I don't want a hug from anyone right now. Especially not from someone who resents me. I flop down in one of the big, comfy chairs and look away from her.

"What's wrong? Why aren't you talking?" Tonya asks.

"She's been ordered by her doctor to rest her voice for a few days," Dad explains. "She screamed so loud it hurt her throat."

My sister sits and cups her head in her hands. She looks like her head is about to explode from pressure. "What the hell are you doing here? You should be at the police station pressing charges against Eric." Her hands start shaking. She rests them in her lap, trying to hide it.

"We already did that," Dad says. "He's eighteen and can be charged as an adult. According to Seth's dad, Eric is facing many charges. Destruction of private property for breaking Kira's glasses. Aggravated assault. Assault and battery of a disabled person. Two students took videos of the whole horrid event, so the cops should have enough evidence to arrest him. Eric's cousin Tori is the one who pushed Kira down," Dad explains. "Tori's friend Monica is the one who hit Kira in the face," Dad explains. "Those girls are minors, so they can't be tried as adults, but they can be charged and sent to a juvenile detention center."

Tonya looks as white as a sheet. Her hands shake again. She balls them into fists to try to hide it.

"Are these people your friends?" Dad asks.

"Not really," Tonya says. "I mean, I party with them, but I wouldn't say we were friends."

"So, you'd go anywhere and hang out with anyone as long as they had alcohol? Is that what you're saying?" Dad asks. "Great standards for friends. Is that why you chose to be a waitress? So you could work in a restaurant with a bar? How much alcohol did you manage to take from the restaurant when no one was looking?"

Tonya's jaw drops. "I only did that a few times."

"Your boss called me when you didn't show up for work because I'm your emergency contact," Dad says.

"And what the hell did you tell him?"

"The truth."

Tonya pounds her fists on the chair. "Why the hell would you do that? Why didn't you tell him I'd be away for a while because I'm sick?"

"Because I don't think a restaurant with a bar is the best job for you to have," Dad says. "I'm sure the restaurant has figured out where their missing inventory went. I wouldn't be expecting your job back once you get out of here."

"Oh, my God! You're ruining my life," she yells.

"I'm not ruining your life, but you certainly will if you don't stop drinking. Tell me again how you're not like the other people in here who need help."

"I'm not like the people in here. I can control myself."

"Look at your sister," Dad yells. "This is what *your* drinking friends did to her."

Tonya refuses to look at me again. "They aren't my friends. They never would've been able to do that to Kira if I was there." She glares at Dad. "You're the one who put me in here, so Kira's injuries are your fault."

I pinch the bridge of my nose in frustration. I take my phone out and write my sister a message. I've been scared out of my mind that Tonya isn't going to take rehab seriously. She's doing exactly what I was afraid of. She's rebelling instead of working with the place to get better.

I hand Dad my phone so he can read my message. "Or maybe my injuries are my own fault. I was the one born legally blind. I'm the reason you had to drink to get Mom and Dad's attention."

"I'm glad you finally figured it out," Tonya snaps at me.

"Tonya," Dad shouts, horrified.

"It's true. Kira takes *everyone's* attention." She crosses her arms. "You said Eric broke Kira's glasses." She keeps her eyes on me as she questions Dad. "How'd Kira get away from the bullies?"

"Liz said the girls who pushed Kira down ran away once they saw Eric step on Kira's hand. Seth decked Eric, and that freed Kira's hand."

"She can't see shit without her glasses. How'd she get to the doctor?"

"Liz's mom," Dad says.

"Who helped her to the car?" Tonya's looking for clues.

"Liz, Seth, and Jason."

Tonya's eyes narrow. "Of course, *Jason* was there. He's always around you. Even on *my birthday*, he was alone in *your room* with *you*. Did he rescue you from the bullies?"

I want to curl up into a ball so nobody can see my red face.

"We're getting totally off topic," Dad says. "Tonya, this isn't about—"

"I bet he was soooo heroic," Tonya mocks. "Did he hold you all the way to the doctor's office?"

My face blushes.

"I bet you fell even more in love with *my boyfriend*!" Her words echo off the marble floors.

"Kira, go wait in the car." Dad holds up my phone.

I stand, grab it out of his hand, and rush towards the exit.

"What was on your mind last night as you were falling asleep? Having your ass beaten, or the way my boyfriend's arms felt around you?" Tonya yells after me.

"Tonya, that's enough." Dad snaps.

Tears start rolling down my face. I run out of the treatment center and back to my parents' car.

Jason said they broke up. Why is she still calling him her boyfriend?

My mother is sitting in the front seat, working. The rehab center only allows two visitors at a time, so Mom agreed to stay in the car. She ends her phone call with her client and turns around to look at me. "What's wrong?"

I look at her and point to my throat. I can't answer.

Mom hands me some tissues.

I blow my nose, wipe my eyes, and send Jason a text.

K: My sister is still calling u her boyfriend. What the hell is going on?

Dad comes out of the treatment center a few minutes later. He looks pale as a sheet. He gets in the car and turns to look at me. "Angry mood swings are a common part of the recovery process. Her body is going through a detox. She was sweating and shaking a lot worse when I was here yesterday. She seems physically better today, but mentally, she's a mess. She didn't mean anything she said to you."

I motion the letters "OK" with my hand. I'm grateful Dad doesn't tell Mom what Tonya said.

"After you left, she told me I wasn't really her father. She said she wants her real dad to come get her."

Mom gasps and takes Dad's hand. "She didn't mean that."

Dad looks as hurt as I am.

Chapter Thirteen

Tuesday, September 12, 2023

Doctor Mikelson, the eye doctor I've been seeing for as long as I can remember, retired this year, so I have to see one of his associates. I'm used to a grumpy old man checking my eyes. A young eye doctor, who looks like he graduated from optometry school last week, walks into the exam room.

"Hi, I'm Doctor Russel." He goes through the standard pleasantries with my parents. Then Dad tells him about my blurred vision, double vision, glare, and headaches.

The doctor shines a light into my eye. He holds it there for a long time. Then he moves to my other eye. "And all your eye problems are worse in the morning?"

I nod.

"Do you ever get double vision or glare during the day?"

I nod my head again.

He moves the light a little closer to my eye. He looks for a few more seconds. I can tell from the shocked look on his face that he sees something abnormal.

"I'm going to give Kira the standard visual acuity and peripheral visual field tests to fit her for new lenses." His voice is tight. He scurries closer to the door. "But first, I need to have a quick word with one of my colleagues." He opens the door. "I'll be back in a moment." He shuts the door before we can ask a single question.

"What in the world is that about?" Mom asks Dad. "What did he see?"

"Relax," Dad says. "He's really young. He probably needs guidance from older doctors a lot."

Dad uses the time to check his work messages. Mom can't sit still. She shuffles in her seat so much that I think the cushion is going to get worn out.

I look at my phone. Jason hasn't responded to my text yet, but there are a ton of new text messages from everyone else.

I open Liz's message first.

L: OMG! That looked so hot. What did he whisper to u? He was whispering a bunch of sweet-nothings into your ear, during a TAYLOR song!!!!!!! OMG! I'm worried I'm NEVER going to get a moment like that. PLEASE write me back!!!! I've decided to call this the Car Cuddling Incident. CCI. Have u spoken to him since the CCI? What did he say? Is it weird now? How can it not be? PLEASE write me back!!!! Also how r u feeling?

I lower my phone and sigh. She saw everything. She was in the front seat. Seth was right next to us. How much did he see and hear? How much did he tell Mike? I want to vomit.

I take a deep breath and open Seth's message next.

S: My dad is planning to stop by ur house tonight with an update on the Lawndale case. I'd like to say more but Dad won't tell me anything.

Mike's message makes me concerned.

M: The girls who attacked u aren't in school today. Rumor has it they both got suspended. I want to murder Eric. If the police don't arrest the fucker, I'm gonna kill him.

He really shouldn't write that in a text message. If anything happens to Eric, the police might access Mike's phone records.

Mom stands up and complains, "He said he'd be back in a moment. It's been fifteen minutes. Maybe I should go out and see what's going on."

"Relax," Dad says. "The doctor he needs to talk to is probably with another patient right now."

"Doug, I swear to god, you tell me to relax one more time, you'll be sleeping on the couch tonight!"

I start a group message and include Liz, Mike, Seth, and Jason.

K: Hi. Thanks for all ur concerns. My hand is in a cast. At the eye doctor getting new glasses. Been ordered by my doctors not 2 talk because my vocal cords need to heal. Its really hard to text with my left hand. That is why I haven't gotten back to any of u. Talk to u all in a few days when my voice returns.

It takes me what feels like forever to compose this. Hitting send feels like an accomplishment.

L: That's it? Tell me about the CCI!

Jesus Christ, Liz. Not in the group chat.

S: What the hell does CCI stand for?

M: Cascade Cartridge Inc. They make bullets. Liz, r u planning on shooting Eric

L: No

M: If any1 is going 2 blow that fuckers head off, it's going 2 be me

K: Mike, stop b4 the cops arrest u

J: Cardiovascular Credentialing International.

Oh god. Jason's reading this, too.

J: Is something wrong with Kira's heart?

K: No. My heart is fine.

S: Are you sure it's not still beating rapidly from Jason kissing u in the back of the car? Seth adds a ton of heart and kissing emojis.

M: WTF. What the hell did I miss? Which 1 of my cousins do u like, Jason?

I type frantically. **K: On the forehead. Calm the fuck down. U r all making my hand hurt. Leaving this conversation.**

"That's it." Mom's frustration has reached a boiling point. "It's been almost half an hour. I'm going out there to see what the hell is going on."

The door finally opens. "Sorry to keep you folks waiting," Doctor Russel says as he enters the room. An older doctor follows behind him. "This is Doctor McKinley, one of our ophthalmologists."

"Hello," Doctor McKinley says. "I was finishing up with another patient. So, Kira, let me get a look at those eyes." The older doctor shines a light in my eyes. "You were right to consult me," he tells the younger doctor. "Epithelial edema. We need to do a slit lamp examination to be sure."

"Excuse me," my mom interrupts. "Can you please tell us what's going on?"

"It appears your daughter's eyes have a corneal thickening," Doctor McKinley explains. "It's caused by fluid buildup in the cornea, the clear layer on the front of the eye. This is what caused her blurry vision, light sensitivity, and headaches."

Mom's arms are crossed in front of her. "Why didn't Doctor Mikelson catch this problem last year?"

"I'm not sure. It's possible the fluid buildup wasn't visible then." Doctor McKinley turns to the younger doctor. "We need to do a slit exam today. Perform all the standard exams to fit her glasses and then dilate her pupils for the slit exam."

The older doctor steps out.

"What will this mean for her vision?" Mom asks, annoyed.

"We won't be sure until we get the test results back," Doctor Russel says calmly.

Mom looks like she's about to explode with frustration. Dad takes her arm and whispers in her ear to calm down.

I get all the standard tests. I have to whisper all the letters I can see. My voice sounds so hoarse that the doctor can barely hear me. Just as I feared, my eyes are worse, and I'm going to need a stronger prescription.

I complain via text and hold up my phone. ***K: My glasses are going to get even thicker***.

"They will be thinner," Doctor Russel says. "I'm requesting the opticians give you high-index lenses this time."

My jaw drops.

K: Y didn't I get those before?

"We usually don't recommend them for children. They are more brittle and less scratch-resistant than normal lenses. They need to be handled with more care than regular lenses. If you had been my patient when you were thirteen, I'd have suggested the thinner lenses to you then," Doctor Russel says.

"Why didn't Doctor Mikelson tell us about them?" Mom asks, frustrated.

"Doctor Mikelson was," he pauses to find the right words, "traditional and fixed in his ways."

"You mean ancient and out of touch," Dad says.

Doctor Russel smiles and stifles his laughter.

"He was an idiot," Mom snaps. "How could he treat my daughter for sixteen years and never notice fluid in her eyes?"

"Ma'am, I'm sorry, but I honestly don't know," Doctor Russel says. "Let's get Kira's test results back, and then we'll have more answers for you." He administers eye drops to dilate my pupils. Then dye is dropped into my eyes to check for scratches and damage to my cornea.

I'm taken into another room with a device that looks like a huge sideways microscope. I hold my head against a chinrest and a forehead support. Doctor McKinley shines a bright light into and around my eyes. My neck is getting stiff, and my eyes are watering. When Doctor McKinley finally tells me I can sit back, my chin, forehead, and neck are sore.

Several minutes later, Doctor McKinley comes back into the room to give us the test results. "The slit exam shows that your daughter's eyes have fluid buildup in the corneas. It's causing her corneas to swell and thicken."

Mom draws in a sharp breath.

"The disease is called Fuchs' dystrophy. It's uncommon—"

"Why the hell didn't you figure this out sooner?" Mom looks angry enough to slap him. "We've been bringing our daughter here since she was a baby. You're just figuring this out now?"

The doctor tries to remain calm. "It's rare to see this condition in someone Kira's age. Typically, the disease starts in the thirties and forties, but many people with Fuchs' dystrophy don't develop symptoms until they reach their fifties or sixties. That is why Kira's last eye doctor didn't check for signs of this disease. I can only find one record in the National Library of Medicine of a teenager having Fuchs' dystrophy in 2012. Nobody could've predicted this until the fluid in her eyes was visible with a basic ophthalmoscope," he says with an undertone of *Please don't sue us for malpractice.*

"What kind of treatment is available?" Dad asks.

"Some at-home treatments might help relieve the symptoms. Avoid stress and crying. Get a dehumidifier because humidity makes Fuchs' act up. Saline eyedrops and ointments to help reduce the amount of fluid in her corneas. Dark glasses should be worn in the morning to help with the glare."

"Salene drops? Dark glasses? Can you offer any treatment that we can't pick up at the drugstore?" Mom fumes.

Dad takes her by the hand. "Cindy, calm down. You're making it worse." He turns back to the doctor and asks the dreaded question, "Could Kira lose her vision?"

My heart races. I'm terrified of that happening.

Dad squeezes Mom's hand like he's trying to prevent her from jumping up and biting the doctor's throat if the answer is yes.

"That is highly unlikely," the doctor says, holding up his hands like someone has pulled a gun on him.

Mom and I both take deep breaths

"What's the worst-case scenario?" Dad asks.

"If the fluid in Kira's eyes progresses, she may need a cornea transplant," the doctor explains calmly.

"Oh, my god," Mom murmurs.

"It's actually a fairly simple operation," the doctor assures Mom. "We remove all or part of a damaged cornea and replace it with healthy donor tissue."

I wrinkle my nose. The idea of some dead person's eyes in my head grosses me out.

"Most corneal transplants have a high success rate," the doctor assures us. "But this isn't something we need to discuss today. Ideally, I'd like to wait until Kira is twenty-five before she has that surgery. However, I'm concerned about how rapidly the fluid buildup has progressed. I want to see Kira every six weeks to monitor her eyes," he says with a hint of annoyance. I think the idea of having to see my mother that many times a year is stressing him out. He turns to me, "Kira, have you ever tried wearing contacts?"

I use my phone to answer. *K: I got headaches and I had to take them out.*

"Because your eye's surface isn't smooth and even. Therapeutic contact lenses for people with Fuchs' are available. I'd like to try a few different types of lenses today. They might help ease the discomfort you've been experiencing if fitted correctly."

I smile and use my phone to write many happy emojis.

Nobody wants to cook, so Dad orders pizza for dinner. We don't have much of an appetite after the day we had. At least pizza is easy to eat with one hand.

I'm halfway through my slice when our doorbell rings. My dad gets up to answer the door. "Hello, Sergeant Karlson," Dad says and lets Seth's dad into our living room.

The cop is almost six five, and he has enough muscle mass to be cast as the hero in an action movie. His black police uniform makes him look extra intimidating. He walks like a Terminator. He is nothing like his son. Seth always walks with a spring in his step. He gets none of his lighthearted nature from his father.

"Good evening, Mr. Conway," Sergeant Karlson says in a deep voice. In all the years we've been friends with Seth, his father still isn't on a first-name basis with my parents. "I have news regarding your daughter's attacker."

Mom and I get up and join the men in the living room.

Sergeant Karlson doesn't even acknowledge me or my mother. He acts as if my dad is the only other person in the room with him. "Eric Lawndale has been taken into custody. The video evidence provided from several students' social media platforms gave us probable cause."

I breathe a sigh of relief. I can't stand the idea of returning to school if Eric is there.

"What about the girls who attacked Kira?" Mom asks.

"Monica Humphrey and Victoria Lawndale are both minors. They will both likely be charged with misdemeanors in Juvenile Delinquency Court," Sergeant Karlson explains, still looking at my father. "They will both receive a summons to appear in court. They will likely not be arrested before their trials. Juvenile Delinquency Court usually does not issue warrants for arrests unless there's reason to believe the minor won't appear upon a summons."

"So those two girls could remain in school until their court appearance?" Mom asks, horrified.

"It's up to the school board to determine if they will receive a suspension or an expulsion," Sergeant Karlson explains.

"Which is why we have a meeting with a lawyer first thing in the morning," Dad reminds Mom. "Then we're going straight to the school to talk to the principal," he assures Mom while making calming gestures with his hands.

"I'm not leaving his office until I know those girls are no longer a threat to Kira or any other student," Mom insists. "I wonder how many other students were terrorized by that gang of wealthy brats."

"You did the right thing by pressing charges, Mrs. Conway," Sergeant Karlson says, and then turns back to my dad. "Educators and school administrators commonly ignore bullying. Parents should always press charges. It's the only way the school board is forced to handle the problem." He opens our front door and steps outside. "That's all. Goodnight, Mr. Conway." He shuts the front door before my dad has a chance to say goodnight back.

"Is he incapable of having a conversation with a female?" Mom asks loud enough for Sergeant Karlson to hear from outside. "No wonder he hasn't had a date since Seth's mom left. It's no wonder Seth spends all his spare time with Mike and Ginny."

Dad leads Mom away from the front door. "Would you lower your voice? We need him on our side, Cindy."

Jason finally responds to my texts. Why does he always wait until I'm getting into bed to message me?

J: The night of the party ur sister got drunk to avoid the breakup conversation I was trying to have with her. I'm going to straighten things out with her on Saturday. The rehab center won't let me see her until then. Family members only during the week. I'll call u after I talk to her.

Also, I told Miss Coleman she better give u an extension on all ur art projects until ur hand heals up. She agreed. She also said you could use different mediums, like pottery or

118

photography. I think u should try sculpting clay with ur left hand or taking photos. Let me know if you need to borrow any equipment. Goodnight, Kira.

I drop my head on the back of my pillow. Tonya has every right to hate me. I love her boyfriend. I can't help it. He's so fucking lovable.

Chapter Fourteen

Saturday, September 16, 2023

My doctor insisted I take time off to rest my hand. I've spent the week on the couch with my crushed extremity elevated on a stack of pillows, doing my assignments on my laptop. Typing with my left hand takes forever, but it is a lot less frustrating than trying to write with a pen.

My phone rings. It's Jason. He visited my sister today. I take a deep breath and answer it. "Hello," I say, voice still raspy.

"Hi, Kira. Can you talk? Is your throat healed enough?"

"It's still a little sore, but I can talk for a little while," I tell him. "What happened with Tonya?"

He sighs. "She took it really hard. I'm sorry about that. I thought maybe she'd be more reasonable because she already knew it was over between us. I told her that the last night we went out."

"Then why was she still calling you, her boyfriend?"

"She got drunk at the party, so we couldn't have an honest conversation about why we were breaking up. That's why she came home trashed. She was trying to avoid the breakup. Then she asked me not to tell anyone. She wanted to tell your parents herself. That's why nobody knew we'd broken up. I didn't get a chance—"

My phone buzzes. It's my mom trying to get hold of me. "Sorry. Hold on," I tell Jason, and mute her call. "I still don't understand. Tonya was insisting you were still together."

"I think she was hoping I'd change my mind and stay with her if she sobered up. Today I told her that we were wrong for each other. That we wanted different things and—"

Mom calls again. I mute again.

"I told her that we weren't gonna be a couple even if she sobered up. She took it kind of hard. I feel really bad about it, but I had to get it over with."

Dad is calling now.

"Jason. I'm sorry. My parents keep calling. Something's wrong. I'll call you back as soon as I can."

"Okay."

I switch calls. "What's wrong?"

"Your sister checked herself out of rehab," Dad says.

A chill runs up my spine. "What? How?"

"She's an adult. They can't legally keep her here."

"When did she leave? Where the hell did she go?"

"That is what your mother and I are trying to figure out. She left at about five. The receptionist said that someone in a red sedan picked her up. They said it pulled out of here so fast it looked like they were trying to make a prison break. Which one of your sisters' friends has a red sedan?"

"Kimber," I answer in a tight voice.

"Great," Dad grumbles. "You stay home in case Tonya shows up. Your mother and I are headed to Kimber's house."

We hang up, and I call Mike. He's having a fun night with his friends. I hate giving him the bad news.

"No way. Why would she check out of rehab?" Mike asks, horrified.

"Because Jason broke up with her,"

Mike makes a plan to look for Tonya.

"Don't go to Eric's house," I tell him.

"I won't. Besides, Kimber knows Eric got arrested. Tonya and her wouldn't go there to party tonight. We'll check out the mall and restaurants Tonya loves."

I text Liz next. There's nothing she can do. I just want her to know what is going on.

Our doorbell rings. I rush to open it. *Please be Tonya.* I don't know if my parents gave her house keys back when she agreed to go to rehab. She might need me to let her in.

I yank the door open.

Aunt Ginny is standing on our porch. "I thought you could use some company, and some backup if Tonya comes home."

I hug her. I'm so happy to see an adult.

We sit on the couch talking, discussing all the places Tonya could be. Hoping to come up with a clue. We can't think of anything.

Nine forty. Liz calls me and asks if there's anything she can do.

Ten fifteen. Jason sent several texts asking if everything's all right. I can't talk to him right now.

"I have the worst feeling about this," I admit.

"So, do I. As soon as I got Mike's call that Tonya left rehab, it felt like a black veil dropped over my face. All the color seemed to go out of the world." Aunt Ginny takes my hand. "Maybe I'm wrong. I've been wrong before."

"I hope we're both wrong and this turns out to be nothing."

Ten to Eleven. Aunt Ginny heats up some leftover Chinese take-out in our fridge. I only eat a few bites. I have no appetite. Then she insists we both stay hydrated, so we drink some water.

Eleven twenty. We both jump when we hear Aunt Ginny's phone ring. It's Mike. "We've driven around for hours looking," he says. "I have no idea where she is."

More texts from Jason. He knows what's going on because Mike called him. He asks if there's anything he can do? I don't answer.

"If only we had some way to track her," Aunt Ginny says.

I think back to the day my parents checked Tonya into rehab. They took her car keys and her phone. They took her car insurance card, but they didn't take—

"Her debit card," I say, and rush up the stairs to my sister's room. I grab her laptop and take it back to the living room with me. I open it and turn it on. I know her password. QueenBee1. I open her internet browser and go to her bank's website.

"You're a good detective," Aunt Ginny says.

"Let's see if I can actually get into her account." The browser remembers the username and password, and I can access her account information immediately. Three hundred dollars was withdrawn from an ATM in Salem at 7:20 PM.

A car pulls into our driveway. Ginny rushes to see whose car it is. It's my parents coming home. They had no luck at Kimber's house. Nobody was home. Mom had Tonya's phone in her purse. They sat in the car calling every number in her phone, trying to figure out where Tonya is. Nobody who picked up knew anything.

Twelve thirty. Mike and Seth show up. They can't look anymore. There's nowhere else to look. Mike and I sit down with Tonya's phone. We try to figure out if there's anyone she would go to. Some of these numbers are random guys she talked to once and then never saw again.

One twenty. Mike offers to stay up all night and wait by the phone so we can all go to bed. We're grateful, but everyone's too worried to sleep.

One forty. A car pulls into our driveway. Red and blue police lights get everyone's attention. We all rush to the front door. *Please, God, let this be the police bringing my sister home.*

Dad opens our front door before our doorbell rings.

"Mr. Conway?" the officer asks.

"Yes."

"May we please come in, sir?"

Dad steps to the side and lets two police officers enter our living room. One is very young. He looks like a rookie in his early twenties. The other is middle-aged.

"Are you the parents of Tonya Elizabeth Conway?" the older officer asks.

"Yes," Mom answers. "Please tell us what's going on."

"We're here to deliver bad news," the older cop says. "Your daughter, Tonya, was killed in a car crash this evening."

No.

Mike's arm goes around my shoulder. Seth takes my uninjured hand in his.

"No. That's impossible," Mom insists.

"Was my daughter in Kimberly Davis's red sedan?" Dad asks.

"Yes, sir," the cop answers.

My father's whole body tightens up. His face turns red, and he puts his hand over his mouth like he's trying not to vomit.

It can't be.

"No, no. That's not true," Mom says. "Kimber has a lot of friends. It wasn't Tonya in her car."

"I'm sorry, ma'am. We identified her from the ID in your daughter's wallet," the older cop says.

The younger officer does not speak at all. He watches us all silently, like he is waiting to see who will fall apart.

"No," Mom insists. "My husband took her license and car insurance out of her wallet the day we checked her into rehab. My daughter doesn't even have her license with her."

"Cindy," Dad says. "I only took out her insurance card." He tries to put his arms around Mom.

"No. I remember. You took out her license, too,' Mom says. "I put everything we took out of her wallet into mine for safekeeping." Mom goes to her purse and pulls out her wallet. She starts rummaging through everything, looking for Tonya's license.

Dad turns back to the officers. "Please tell me what happened."

The older cop says, "The accident occurred on Newburyport Turnpike heading south at approximately eleven-thirty this evening. Your daughter was a passenger in Kimberly Davis's car. Ms. Davis was intoxicated with a blood alcohol level of .25 percent. She was driving over eighty miles per hour. Your daughter wasn't wearing her seat belt when the impact occurred. The airbag deployed, but it wasn't enough to prevent your daughter from hitting the windshield. She died instantly from a traumatic head injury."

"No. Airbags are there to prevent that from happening," Mike insists. "That's the reason airbags are put into cars."

"Young man, I am sorry. But Ms. Davis was traveling at over eighty miles an hour. The impact from the crash was so great that the airbag couldn't keep Ms. Conway in her seat."

"Was Tonya scared? Did she suffer?" Aunt Ginny's voice is so tight it sounds like a whisper.

"No, ma'am. Ms. Conway's death was instantaneous."

That's not true. My parents will know what to do. I look at my mom. She doesn't look capable of handling anything right now. She has emptied the entire contents of her purse and wallet onto the coffee table, looking for Tonya's license.

"Are you one hundred percent sure it was my daughter?" Dad asks.

"Yes, sir. We identified your daughter's body from her driver's license. Ms. Davis also helped us identify the body."

The body. My sister isn't a body. She's a person.

"Was anybody else killed?" Aunt Ginny asks.

"No, Ma'am. Everyone else had a seat belt on. The airbag caused some injuries to Ms. Davis's nose and cheeks. She also sustained knee and hip injuries and has cuts from broken glass. There was only one person in the other car. He was lucky. The engine absorbed the impact on the driver's side of the car. If Ms. Davis had crashed into the driver's door, the other driver might have been killed, too. Both he and Ms. Davis were taken to Lahey Medical Center in Peabody."

"Where's my daughter now?" Dad asks.

"Her body has been taken to the morgue. You can have it moved to a funeral home or place of worship for the funeral. I'm terribly sorry for your loss, sir."

"No, no. I'm sorry, but you're wrong," my mom stammers. She gives up looking for the license. She stands up and walks over to the cop with huge, desperate eyes. "It has to be somebody else's daughter. You see, I always make sure my girls wear their seat belts. I've always made sure my girls put their belts on. Tonya always puts her seat belt on."

Dad takes Mom by the shoulders and turns her to look at him. "Cindy."

"Doug. Our girls always wear their seat belts." Mom is facing Dad. Her hands grip his arms and shake him a little. She's desperate for him to tell her what she wants to hear. "You know I'm right. You've never seen Tonya forget to put her seat belt on."

"Cindy."

Tears start streaming down my cheeks. Mike's breathing is shallow and uneven. I know he is crying too.

"Kira," Mom breaks free from Dad and heads towards me. She puts her hands on my face. "Haven't I always made sure you put on your seat belt?"

I can't answer her. My voice won't work. I nod.

"Since the day you and your sister outgrew your car seats. I always made sure you both had your seat belts on. Mike, you too. Don't you remember when you were little? I always made sure you kids had your seat belts on."

"Yes, Aunt Cindy," Mike whispers. "I remember."

"Tonya wouldn't ride in a car with her seat belt off," Mom insists. "It wasn't Tonya. It wasn't my daughter! I'm a good mother!"

Aunt Ginny rushes towards my mother and takes her by the shoulders. "I know you are. We all know." She pulls my mother into her arms.

A dreadful sob escapes my mother's lips. It's a sound I never knew she could make. The sound vibrates through my entire body.

My parents can't fix this. I lower my head onto Mike's shoulder and start sobbing.

Dad rushes towards Mom just in time. Mom's legs buckle, and she almost sinks to the floor. The younger officer, who has been watching like a hawk, steps forward and assists Dad in getting Mom seated on the couch.

It's disturbing to hear your parent cry as hard as a newborn infant. If it wasn't for Mike and Seth holding me up, I might crumble to the ground, too.

"Kira." My father motions for me to come toward him.

I take three steps and fall into his arms, crying. He clings to me for dear life and lets me sob on his shoulder. Then he sits me down on the couch next to my mother. Mom wraps her arms around me and holds me the way a small, crying child would hold onto a doll.

"Kira. You're my good girl. You're such a good girl," Mom whispers it repeatedly.

Mike helps Dad take Mom upstairs to bed. I call Liz. I've never called her at three o'clock in the morning before. Mike sits next to me on the couch. Liz answers with a groggy, "What's wrong?"

127

"Tonya's dead," I say. The words make me cry again. Mike puts his arms around me. Seth takes the phone out of my hand and gives Liz all the details.

"I can't tell Jason," I tell Mike.

"Okay. I'll do it," Mike says.

"Please don't blame him for this," I say.

"The only person I blame is Kimber," Mike spits out her name. "That dumb bitch is the one who should've died. I hope she goes to jail for murder and rots behind bars for the rest of her life."

I look at him, shocked. "Mike."

"Kira," Dad calls me from upstairs. "Why don't you sleep in our room tonight? Your mother will sleep better if she knows you're in the room."

"Okay. Coming." I stand up.

Seth hands me my phone. "Liz is coming over first thing tomorrow."

"Please don't go home tonight," I tell Mike and Seth. I don't want anyone I love to leave here. I want them all where I can see them and hear them.

"We're not going anywhere," Aunt Ginny says as she heads back down the stairs. "I'll sleep in your room, and the boys can crash down here."

I hug her and head up the stairs.

I crawl into bed with my mom. Her eyes are huge and glassy. She looks like she's waiting for me to come to her before she feels safe closing her eyes. "I was gonna do everything differently than my parents. I was gonna do everything right and keep you girls safe," she says.

"Mom, please go to sleep."

"I should have watched her more closely. How long had she been drinking, do you think?"

"I don't know. She was excellent at hiding it."

"I thought keeping you and Tonya away from my father would be enough to keep you safe. I was gonna do things differently. I was gonna make sure you had a safe and happy place to grow up. I'm sorry my temper is so bad."

"Mom, I promise you, Tonya did not drink because of your temper. She drank when she was frustrated over school. She drank when guys disappointed her. I don't think it was because of you. You need to sleep. We all need sleep."

"I'm a terrible mother, aren't I?" Her eyes fill with tears.

I hug her tightly. "Mom, that's ridiculous. Please stop."

She cries herself to sleep.

Dad comes in and turns off the light.

I fall asleep between my parents for the first time since I was five.

Chapter Fifteen

Sunday, September 17, 2023

I wake up in my parents' bed. I was hoping yesterday was a nightmare. That I'd wake up in my own bed today and everything would feel normal. I have a pounding headache from crying. My eyes and head feel like they're about to explode.

Mom's next to me, sleeping soundly. Dad's already up. He put my sunglasses, eyedrops, and painkillers on his nightstand. I reach for them, down two pills, put the drops in my eyes, and lie back with my sunglasses on.

Alma jumps up on my parents' bed. She looks at me with big green eyes and meows. She knows something is wrong. Last night, during the commotion, she was probably hiding under my bed. She was probably waiting for me to get in bed and comfort her. Instead, it was Aunt Ginny who slept in my room. This poor little cat is scared and confused.

I motion for her to curl up with me. She lies down next to me, and I pet her. Usually, she's quiet once I start petting her, but not today. Her meows are long and dramatic. She needs to cry. Just like the rest of us. My eyes start watering again.

Dad comes into the room to tell me that Liz is here. I get out of bed and pull the covers back over Mom. Alma follows me everywhere I go. I walk downstairs to our living room and see Liz talking to Seth and Mike. Our eyes meet. She bursts into tears, and we hug.

The whole day feels like a checklist of awful tasks that need to be completed so we can survive. Mrs. Vasquez hands my dad a few casserole dishes of food she prepared. She tells us to call her if there's anything else we need. Then she tells us she will be back later to pick up Liz. I ask Liz to wait for me to shower and brush my teeth.

"You should eat something," Dad tells me.

"I'm not hungry," I tell him.

"Believe me, neither am I, but I forced myself to eat some cereal. Your body needs nourishment. Please have a bite of something."

I pour a bowl of cereal and take it to the living room so I can hang out with Liz. The food has no taste. After five bites, I leave it on the coffee table uneaten. I'll clean it up as soon as I find the strength to get off the couch.

Our doorbell rings. Dad is in his office. Mom is still asleep. I get up and open it.

Melony is standing in my doorway. Her eyes and nose look red. "I'm sorry."

I step back and motion for her to come in. She steps inside, and I close the door.

"I'm sorry I was such a bitch." She looks at Liz. "I'm sorry I was insensitive about your weight." She looks at me. "I'm sorry, I was jealous. Your sister was so beautiful and I...I was so jealous of her...and you, because you look like her. I'm sorry."

I step closer and pull Melony into a hug.

"I wished her away," Melony cries into my shoulder. "I wished she'd go away because she was too pretty. I didn't mean it!" She clings to me. "I didn't mean it! I want her to come back! I've been up all night telling God I'm sorry. Praying for Him to bring her back!"

Liz comes up and hugs both of us.

"I didn't mean it," Melony keeps saying.

"Of course you didn't," Liz says. "Tonya looked like a Barbie doll. We were all jealous of her."

We sit on the couch together. Melony grabs a tissue, blows her nose, and composes herself. Then she hands me the key ring Seth gave me on my birthday. "I shouldn't have taken this. It's yours."

We sit on the couch in silence for a few minutes.

"Kira?" Mom calls me.

I get up. "I'm downstairs, Mom."

I guess she doesn't hear me. "Kira?" She yells again.

I shout up our stairs. "I'm right here, Mom."

She comes down the steps, rushes towards me, and wraps me in a hug. "Oh, good. You're okay." She pulls back and looks at me with big, scared eyes. "I didn't see you when I woke up."

"I was just in the living room, Mom."

"Where's your dad? Where are Ginny and the boys?"

Dad comes out of his office. "Everyone's fine, Cindy. Ginny and the boys went home for a shower."

"We have showers here." My mom sounds like a little girl.

"They all wanted a change of clothes."

"Oh, yeah. I guess that makes sense," Mom says.

"They will be back soon to help us plan the funeral," Dad says.

The word 'funeral' makes Mom's face wrinkle up. She starts crying again. "I wanted to plan Tonya's wedding."

Dad takes Mom in his arms. "Cindy, please. You've got to pull yourself together. Let's get you in the shower. You'll feel better once you take a shower and eat something." He walks her back towards their bedroom.

I walk back downstairs and flop down on the couch next to my friends. "My mom is losing her mind."

Liz takes my hand. "She's still in shock. It'll wear off soon."

Thirty minutes later, my mother comes downstairs like a cleaned-up zombie. Her eyes look straight ahead, but she doesn't seem to see anything around her. She walks past me and my friends into the kitchen. She eats some fruit and cereal. Five minutes later, she runs into the bathroom and vomits.

"I'm going back to bed," she announces and walks back up the stairs.

My father has the opposite reaction to his grief. He tries to stay so busy that he doesn't have to stop and think. He researches funeral homes. He cleans up everyone's breakfast bowls. Then he pulls out all the old photo albums and starts looking for photos of Tonya to put together a collage. He walks from his office to the shelf where we keep the photo albums so many times, I think he might wear a groove in the hardwood floor.

Our doorbell rings. My dad is the closest to the door, so he gets it. "Hi, Jason," Dad says through gritted teeth.

Liz and I exchange glances. Her eyes are huge.

What is my father going to do? Blame Jason for Tonya's death? Yell at him? Ask him why the hell he couldn't wait until she was out of rehab to break up with her?

"Hi, sir," Jason says. "I am *so* sorry. If I hadn't broken up with Tonya yesterday, she's still—"

"Son, stop. My daughter was an alcoholic. She refused to admit she had a problem. I wish my wife and I had figured out how bad Tonya's problem was last year. If I had put her in rehab as a minor, she'd not have been allowed to check herself out." Dad takes a deep breath. "That's on me and Tonya's mother. Not you. Tonya is to blame, and so is Kimber. Not you. Do you understand me?"

"Yes, sir," Jason sounds like he's fighting back tears.

My dad and Jason exchange a quick hug.

"You have, like, the best dad ever," Liz says to me.

I'm a little freaked out by how logical my dad is being about all of this. He's a pillar of strength for everyone. I'm worried he's going to crack under the pressure of holding everyone else up.

"Can I see Kira?" Jason asks.

"Sure. Come on in," Dad says.

My whole body tenses up.

"Have you seen him since the Car Cuddling Incident?" Liz whispers.

I shake my head no. This is going to be so awkward.

Jason walks inside and exchanges polite hellos with my friends. I'm having a hard time looking at him.

Dad takes the last photo album into his office. "I'll be in here if anybody needs me." He closes the door behind him.

"Let's go in the kitchen and heat up some of my mom's food," Liz suggests to Melony. It's such an obvious excuse to leave Jason and me alone to talk.

I'm glad I didn't pull my hair back today. I look down, and my hair covers my face like a curtain. It's comforting to have something to hide behind.

"Are you okay?"

I shake my head.

"Sorry. That's a stupid question. Of course, you're not okay." Jason sits down next to me on the sofa. It's a large L-shaped couch. There's plenty of room, but he sits two feet away from me. "Is there anything I can do? Anything that you need?"

"I don't think so." I keep my eyes forward.

"Okay. If you think of something, tell me."

"Alright." I hate this awkward tension between us. Our conversations were always so natural.

"Mimi had to work today. I asked her to stop by and talk to your mom later. She's a nurse. She's helped a lot of grieving families. I thought maybe she could, I don't know, help your mom too."

"Thanks."

We sit in silence for a moment.

"Please don't hate me," he whispers.

I look at him for the first time. He looks exhausted and drained.

"Mike said you told him not to blame me for what happened." His voice sounds groggy. "I made him assure me a million times that you don't hate my guts before I came over here."

"I could *never* hate you, Jason."

He slides closer and tries to hug me.

I tense up.

He backs up a little. "But you can't look at me, and I'm not allowed to touch you."

My head hurts. I take my glasses off and place them on the coffee table. I lean back against the couch. "Because I'm guilty as hell. Because the last time I was with you, in the car, it was, um—"

"Intense," he whispers.

I pinch the bridge of my nose. "Inappropriate," I correct. "If I had an ex-boyfriend, I don't think I'd want him curled up in the back seat of a car with my sister. I don't think I'd want him kissing my sister's forehead and whispering *mushy* things in her ear." I turn my head away from him. "The last thing my sister said to me was—" I take a deep breath. "She accused me of—"

I stop myself. I can't use Tonya's words. I can't say *falling in love with*. I'll die of embarrassment. Instead, I say, "—

wanting, her boyfriend. I walked away crying as she screamed at me about you."

He inches towards me again. "Kira, you didn't do anything wrong. She was an addict with an obsessive personality. You heard the things she was saying in rehab. She didn't have a problem. She wasn't like the other addicts in there. I was still her boyfriend. None of it was true."

"I still don't think what we did was okay. People shouldn't cuddle with their sister's ex-boyfriends."

"Kira, when Eric stepped on your hand, I heard you scream so loud it scared the shit out of me. When we were in the car, all I could think was, what if Eric had killed you?" Jason strokes my hair and pushes it behind my ear. "What if he stepped on your neck instead of your hand? What if he'd broken your neck or suffocated you?" He sounds terrified at the thought. "So, I'm sorry if I was too forward and got *mushy*, if that's what you wanna call it."

"I'm not the person everyone lost," I whisper. I sit up and let my hair cover my face again. "Did you ever love my sister?"

"No." He didn't pause for even a second. It's such a quick and easy answer for him. "My entire relationship with Tonya was dysfunctional. I never should've slept with her the first night we hung out."

"So why did you?"

"Because I'm seventeen and stupid. I was drunk, and she was hot. She was kind of insistent about it. It was like she was trying to claim me as hers or mark her territory before anyone else got a chance with me. After that, she was kind of obsessed with me. But, Kira, I swear I did *not* use and discard your sister," he insists. "I wouldn't do that to anyone. Believe me, I tried really hard to connect with her after we had sex. I couldn't talk to her about anything important. No matter how hard I tried, my conversations with her were meaningless. Especially compared to my conversations with you."

"Well, no wonder she took the breakup so hard. If someone I'd slept with felt so indifferent about me, I'd be devastated too."

He sighs. He knows I'm right.

"When you visited her in rehab, the day she died. What did my sister say about me?"

"She asked me to stay away from you until she got over me."

"And you came over here anyway?" I ask softly. "You think you don't need to respect her wishes because she died." My eyes water again.

"I just didn't think about it like that. I don't think she needs to get over me anymore."

"Because people don't exist anymore when they die?" It's a fear that's been nagging at me. Where the hell did my sister go? How can a whole person disappear?

"What? No. Kira, I believe people still exist after death. I've sensed my mom around me my entire life."

"Jason, I'm sorry, but I really don't think you should be here right now." I look away from him. "I know everything my dad said to you was right. I know that, but I feel like—" my voice cracks "—I feel like we killed her." Tears are pouring down my cheeks.

"Kira, no. You didn't do that to her." He pulls me into his arms. I shouldn't let him, but I don't have the strength to pull away. He places his hand on the back of my head and whispers, "You'd never do that to her. She knew how much you loved her."

His arms feel wonderful. I want to sink into his embrace, but I can't. "I'm sorry." I pull away. "You should leave. I think my sister is right. You should stay away from me for a while."

He turns my face so he can look me in the eyes. "Kira—"

"It hurts too much to be around you."

He looks devastated. His green eyes look almost grey.

I'm in the elbow of the couch. There's no more room to slide away, so I stand up. "I'm sorry." I pick up my glasses. "I'm sorry." I hate how much I hurt him, but I can't get over the guilt. "I'm sorry, Jason." I turn and head upstairs to my room and close my door. I need to cry alone.

Chapter Sixteen

Saturday, September 23, 2023

My family has never been religious, so a funeral parlor seemed like a better place for Tonya's funeral than a church.

I sit in the front row and wait for guests to arrive. I stare at a closed casket. On the left side, there's a huge photo of my sister smiling and looking beautiful. On the right side is the photo collage of Tonya's life that Dad put together.

Seth is the first one to arrive. He looks so different. His blonde hair is styled back with product, and he's dressed in a suit.

"Do you think she's really in there?" I point to my sister's casket.

"I'm sure her body is in there. I think her soul is in a much better place than that box." He takes my hand. "Why is it a closed casket?"

"The damage to Tonya's face was severe. The mortician could've put her face back together for a small fortune, but Mom and Dad have missed so much work since I was attacked. The funeral costs a lot of money. They spent a lot of money on a casket, so they decided not to pay for cosmetic surgery for a corpse."

"Oh. Yeah. I guess that makes sense." Seth shifts in his seat.

"They put her in the dress and heels she wore during her birthday," I say. "It seems crazy for me to think of her all dressed up in a nice outfit with her face smashed in."

"Kira, I'm sure your sister looks beautiful in heaven."
I smile and look at him. "Do you really think so?"
He turns his head sharply and stares at me. "I'm gay."
"What?"
"I'm gay."
Is my brain malfunctioning? My jaw hits the floor. There's no way. "Stop messing with me."

"I'm not messing with you, Kira. I'm gay. And I'm in love with Mike."

"But you're obsessed with boobs."

"I pretended to be to hide the truth. I don't find boobs appealing."

"You have a crush on Taylor Swift."

"I know she looks like a goddess, but I'm not attracted to women. Not even her," Seth says. "But I love her music. It's helped me pine for Mike for years."

My eyes are so huge that I must look like an owl.

"Sorry to blurt it out. I've been dying to say it out loud to someone. Plus, it seemed like a great way to stop your mental diarrhea."

"My what?"

"Mental diarrhea. We all have it. Your aunt is feeling guilty for missing Tonya's last birthday and for not spending enough time with her. Mike's been torturing himself, insisting Tonya would be alive if we'd found her that night. I keep doing it too. Imagine saving her, over and over again. It's not helping."

"Mel is guilty for being jealous of Tonya's looks. She thinks God took Tonya away because she wished for it."

"Yeah. That's mental diarrhea. We all have it." Seth puts his arm around me. "Your sister will always be young and beautiful in heaven and in our memories. It doesn't matter what her body looks like inside that box." He kisses my forehead.

I drop my head onto his shoulder. "I like the real you, way more than the obnoxious boob-obsessed horndog you pretended to be."

"I was desperate to hide that I'm gay from my ex-military father."

"What's RoboCop gonna say when he finds out?"

Seth looks back at his father, seated in the back row. "He is gonna lose his shit. My dad doesn't do emotion. That's why he's in the back by himself."

"Sergeant Karlson." Mom rushes over to him.

"What's my mom doing?" I ask Seth.

He turns around to look. "She's showing my dad a photograph."

I sigh. "That's a photo of my grandfather. We haven't seen him in years. My mom's worried the evil bastard is gonna show up here today. She's probably asking your dad to keep an eye out for him and remove him once he starts making a scene."

"If that fucker shows up, I'll help throw his ass out," Seth assures me. "Mike has so much repressed rage because of that asshole. I'm worried Tonya's death is gonna cause Mike to snap."

I look at him, surprised. "Wow, you really are in love with Mike."

"Yep."

"Does Mike know that?"

Seth cringes. "Yes and no. We had a moment. It was wonderful. Then it was awful. We haven't talked about it. Now I don't know what to say to him. I have no idea where I'm gonna go after I tell my dad the truth."

"Well, why don't you wait until things smooth over with Mike before you tell your dad?"

"Because I've been keeping this secret since I was twelve years old. It's been exhausting." He looks at Tonya's casket. "Life is too fucking short to live a lie. I have to tell my dad. Best case scenario, Dad loses his temper and can't look at me for a while. Worst case scenario, he kicks me out of his house."

"If that happens, you come right to my house."

"But your parents are going through enough right now. I don't want to—"

"Seth, you come right to my house. Do you understand me?"

"Yes."

"Good."

"I love you." He kisses my forehead.

"I love you, too."

"You know my dad is back there watching us," Seth says. "I nagged him to lock Lawndale up and throw away the key. My dad thought maybe I was furious because that psycho hurt my girl. He's hoping I'm in love with you."

I giggle. "You might be the only person on the planet who could make me laugh today, Seth."

Aunt Ginny drifts toward the front of the room and hugs me. She looks so different. She dyed her hair back to its natural brown color. She's dressed in a pantsuit. I've never seen her in anything but jeans or hippy-witch clothes before. "You look nice," I tell her.

"Thanks. I needed a makeover."

"You look like…an adult."

She smiles and kisses me on the cheek. Then she goes up to the front podium and goes over her notes. She is the official funeral celebrant. My aunt's life has always been a mess, but she has many opinions about the afterlife. She seemed like the right person for the job.

Attendees begin to arrive. Students from Tonya's class fill empty seats. Some of her teachers. A few of our neighbors. They all come to pay their respects.

Liz and Melony show up with their parents. My friends both hug me. "Jason and his aunt are here," Liz whispers to me. "They are sitting in the back. I thought you should know."

Seth whispers something into Melony's ear.

She smiles. "Really?"

He whispers again.

"Oh. Thank you for letting me know. I feel so much better."

Mike walks up to me, looking disheveled. His brown hair looks like it hasn't been washed in days. He looks exhausted and malnourished. His blue eyes are sunken in. He's in black jeans and a black t-shirt. His hug has all the warmth of a marble statue.

"Mike, are you eating and sleeping enough?"

He shrugs. "Not really."

Seth steps up to us. Mike walks away without so much as a hello. Seth and I exchange shocked glances.

"You see. Shit's weird between us," Seth says.

I sigh, and we sit back down.

Dad sits in the chair next to me, and Mom sits next to him. Mom turns around one more time and scans the room.

"Cindy, your father isn't going to show up here today," Dad assures her.

"We can't know that for sure. It would be just like him to show up here and scream at me for never letting him get to know my daughters." Mom sounds like a scared little girl.

"You have a police officer in the back row watching all the entrances," Dad assures her. "I asked some of my old work colleagues to watch out for your dad, too. If he shows up, he's getting bounced before he can say one word to you."

Mike sits down next to my mother, but says nothing to her. He keeps his eyes straight ahead and crosses his arms.

Aunt Ginny leans towards the microphone. "Thank you, everyone, for being here today. It means a lot to our family that so many people showed up to pay their respects."

Mom, Dad, and I link hands and prepare to get through this.

My aunt takes a deep breath. "Tonya was beautiful. She was outgoing and popular. She was the kind of person others looked at and thought, 'That girl has it all.' Maybe that is why it took so long for all of us to figure out she had a problem. I've spent the last few days asking myself why I didn't see it. How could my niece hide her alcoholism so well? Was it because Tonya used breath mints? Because she snuck sips of alcohol when nobody was looking. Because she was so good at hiding how much she needed alcohol to get through the day."

Mom sighs. Dad puts his arm around her.

"Tonya was always a free spirit," Ginny says. "When she was a little girl, she loved to ride her bike too fast, swing too high on the swing set, swim too far out in the ocean. Her parents and I were always reminding her to slow down, to calm down, to be more careful. As a teen, all she wanted to do was graduate from high school and move to a big city. There was never any appreciation for being the age she was. All she talked about was how great everything was going to be later when she was older. Later, when she graduated. Later, when she was an adult." Ginny sighs. "Her desire to be free caused her to be trapped in an addictive cycle that led to her death."

A lot of people are crying. Somebody blows their nose.

"Death changes all of us. It has certainly changed me," Ginny says. "I've always been someone who desperately tried to hold onto my youth. My bathroom is filled with serums, creams, and electric facial devices that all promise to give me my twenty-year-old face back. My son is afraid of all the stuff in the cabinet. I had to assure him that my electronic muscle stimulator is only for my face."

The crowd laughs.

"Recently, I've felt like aging might not be such a bad thing. Maybe it's a privilege that only some of us get. Maybe instead of hating any signs of aging on my body, I should be grateful I've gotten to live this long." She takes a deep breath. "I'd give anything to bring Tonya back. If I could. I'd sacrifice forty years of my life and become a wrinkled eighty-year-old right now, if it meant I could have my niece back with us. If God would let me, I'd switch places with her. We are not supposed to outlive the younger generations of our family. Losing an eighteen-year-old, it's against nature." Her voice cracks.

More sobbing sounds come from people behind me. A bunch of teenage girls are taking it really hard.

Ginny composes herself. "My family isn't religious. We decided to have a non-religious funeral. I've always been Cindy's flaky, weird, Wiccan sister who runs the Witchcraft shop in Salem. I seemed like the only family member qualified for this funeral." She pauses. "We all want to believe in a higher power watching over us. For a long time, I've believed in many powers: the gods and goddesses embodying natural forces. At least I used to. It's a comforting idea, but maybe it's not as necessary as we think. If the gods could let someone so young fall into such darkness, what good are they?"

Gasps and murmurs come from the crowd.

"As I look around this room at all of you, I see more love and support than I've ever felt from the uncaring universe." Ginny sighs. "Maybe this is all we have. And maybe it's enough. So now I am gonna open this up to all of you. If any of you have any stories of out-of-body experiences, dreams, or messages from your loved ones, please come up here and share them."

Dead silence. Nobody says a word. I hear people squirming in their seats.

"Anyone?" my aunt asks.

People in the crowd exchange glances.

I wish I had enough courage to get up and say something. I'll burst into tears before I get one word out.

I look at Mike, sitting three chairs away. He is in no mood to get up and speak about anything other than how he hates the whole world.

"Anyone have anything to say about any spiritual experiences?" My aunt looks embarrassed. She's realizing that this may have been a huge mistake.

Jason stands up and heads towards the front.

"Oh, thank god," Ginny says.

People giggle.

My aunt looks up towards the heavens. "That's just a saying. I'm still pissed at you."

More laughter.

Aunt Ginny hugs Jason and then steps back and lets him have the microphone.

"Hi, everyone," Jason says. "Ginny asked for a story about the afterlife, so here's mine. My mother died giving birth to me."

Some gasps come from the crowd.

"Just in case you're not already sad and depressed enough. I thought I'd share that."

Some giggles.

"She asked for it," he points to Ginny.

More laughter.

"My Aunt Mimi raised me," Jason explains, "When I was about five years old, I started having dreams about a woman with strawberry-blonde hair and green eyes."

Jason is too far away for me to see clearly, but I can tell he's looking at me. I can feel his eyes focus on me from across the room.

"In the dreams, she'd always appear in my room and sit on my bed," Jason explains. "We'd have long conversations. She always wanted to know about my life. Who my friends were? How school was going?

"She had an accent. I had never met someone with an accent before, so I didn't know what it was. One morning at breakfast, I told my aunt about the woman who visited me in my sleep. At first, my aunt thought I had an imaginary friend. Then I said, my friend told me to give you a message: 'You're going to be a great nurse.' Mimi had been thinking about going to nursing school. She hadn't told anyone. When I said that, my aunt's face turned white."

Murmurs come from the crowd.

"It was like I had read Mimi's secret thoughts. Then my aunt asked me what my friend looked like. I said she had green eyes, strawberry-blonde hair, and she talks differently than we do.

"My aunt looked shocked. She got up from the breakfast table and got out her old photo album. I had never seen a photo of my mother before. I was only five, and Mimi didn't know how to tell me about my mother's death. She opened the photo album and said, 'This was your mother, Niamh. She grew up in Ireland. She spoke with an Irish brogue.

"Skeptics always question my story," Jason says. "Maybe I already saw a photo of my mother, but didn't remember seeing it. Maybe I heard Mimi say something in passing about nursing school. Maybe I saw an Irish actress on TV who resembled my mother, and my five-year-old brain turned the actress into an imaginary friend. Maybe there's some reasonable explanation for how this happened."

I can feel Jason looking at me. He's so intensely focused on me that I have to turn and drop my head on my father's shoulder.

"I know that the woman in my dreams was my mother," Jason insists. "Her hands. The freckles across her nose. The exact color of her hair. They were identical to the woman in the picture." Jason pauses to take a deep breath. "My mother still visits me sometimes. I haven't had any dreams about her lately, but I've been talking to her a lot the past few days. Asking her to help Tonya cross over or adjust to the afterlife. I feel better knowing there's someone there for Tonya on the other side."

My mom starts crying again. She's relieved to hear that.

"So, the point of this story is, I fully believe that nobody ever really dies. They just go somewhere else, or everywhere else. Tonya couldn't wait to graduate and leave this town. I think now she can go anywhere she wants. Thank you."

He steps down from the podium.

After the service, my family stands at the entrance of the funeral parlor. All the attendees line up to walk past us and tell us how sorry they are. I nod, smile, and say thank you like a robot.

Mimi and Jason approach us. Mimi hugs my parents and then hugs me. It's actually warm and comforting. It feels like being hugged by an aunt I've known my whole life.

My mother bursts into tears before she hugs Jason. It's loud in the room. A lot of people are talking and shuffling around. I can't hear exactly what my mother says to Jason. I'm assuming she's thanking him for what he said and telling him she doesn't blame him for what happened to Tonya.

Jason lets go of her and steps in front of me. Our eyes meet. He looks like he is dying to wrap his arms around me and pull me close.

I drop my eyes and stare at the lapels on his jacket. "Thank you for what you said."

He leans in and strokes the back of my hair. "I understand if you need space right now, but I'm here for you." He kisses my cheek and then moves his lips to my ear. "Because I love you."

My heart explodes in my chest. My legs shake.

He walks away from me before I get a chance to respond.

I have to take a seat before I fall down.

It's the end of the night. Aunt Ginny and Mike are the last guests to leave our home. My dad walks them to the door and says goodnight. He closes the door behind them. His hand locks the door. His arm drops to his side. For the first time in days, he's still.

I sit on the living room couch, looking at him.

Mike and Ginny make it to the car. Their engine starts. Their car pulls out of our driveway. My father should turn the porch lights off. He should go upstairs to sleep, but he doesn't. He just stands there.

I get up and move towards him, "Dad?"

His eyes meet mine. He looks exhausted.

"Are you okay?"

"I don't have anything else to do. There's nothing else – I can do for her." He looks broken.

I walk up to him and wrap my arms around him tightly. I've never heard my dad cry like this.

Our pillar of strength finally crumbles.

Chapter Seventeen

Sunday, September 24, 2023

Our fridge is filled with food dropped off by well-wishers. We eat reheated meatloaf in silence. The empty chair at the table hurts us. It doesn't help that it is pouring rain outside. Everything seems dark and grey.

My phone buzzes on the coffee table in the living room. I ignore it. I need to ask an important question. "Dad?"

He looks up from his meatloaf.

"Did you mean what you said to Jason the other day? About how you don't blame him for what happened to Tonya?"

Dad looks at me, surprised.

"You don't think it was his fault she died? Do you?"

My phone buzzes again.

"No, I don't blame him, Kira. Don't get me wrong, when I first opened the door and saw Jason standing there, part of me wanted to pound him into oblivion." Dad's fist hits the table.

I jump and look at my father, surprised. It's not like him to be so reactive.

"Then I saw the expression on his face," Dad explains. "He looked so guilty. He looked terrified to come here and face us. In that moment, I knew, if I blamed Jason for causing your sister's death, I'd ruin his life. There has been enough tragedy lately. So I stopped myself from yelling and said something rational."

"But did you really mean it when you said it wasn't Jason's fault?" I ask. "Deep down, do you resent him?"

"No, Kira. I don't resent him."

I smile at him and look at my mom. She seems oblivious to our conversation. She pokes her meatloaf with her fork. Then she forces herself to eat it.

"Mom? Do you agree with Dad?"

She looks at me. "About what?"

149

"About what he just said," I say.

"Sorry, I wasn't listening. What were you talking about?"

"If Tonya's death was Jason's fault," Dad snaps at Mom.

"Oh." Mom lowers her eyes to her food. "I don't think so. I blame myself mostly." She pokes at her food again.

"What about Kimber?" I ask.

My mother sighs and looks away.

I look back at my dad. "Mike keeps saying the most awful things about her. He says he hates her guts. He says they should lock her up and throw away the key. He says she should rot in jail forever."

"That bitterness isn't going to hurt anybody but Mike," Dad says.

"So, you guys don't hate Kimber?"

"No, Kira. I don't hate her. I just hate what she did. That girl's life could be ruined. She is being charged with manslaughter. That's a mandatory minimum sentence of five years. The judge could sentence her up to twenty years," Dad explains.

I'm horrified. "Twenty years? I don't want Kimber to go to jail for twenty years. It's not like that will bring Tonya back."

"Me neither," Dad says. "If you want, we can write letters to the judge asking the court to be lenient. Maybe when Kimber gets out of jail in five years, she can still do something valuable with her life." He sighs. "But that's how I feel now. In five minutes, I might feel rageful again and want Kimber to pay for killing your sister." He squeezes my hand. "I'm trying really hard not to let this get the best of me."

"Me too." I look at my mother. She's in her own world.

Our doorbell rings. Dad turns towards the door. He almost gets up, but then he stops himself and looks at Mom. "Get the door, Cindy."

"Would you get it? I can't deal with anyone right now." She pokes her food again.

The bell rings again.

"Get the door." My father's voice is tight with frustration.

Mom keeps her eyes down. "I asked you to get it..."

"I've done enough!" Dad yells.

I look at him, shocked. My father never loses his temper like this. I look at my mother. Her eyes are as wide as mine.

"I picked out the funeral home," Dad says through gritted teeth. "I had Tonya's body moved to the funeral parlor. Ginny and I planned the whole service. I picked out the casket. Ginny and Kira picked out a dress to bury Tonya in. I picked out the flowers. I put the whole event together. All while you've shuffled around this house like the undead. Listen to our daughter when she's asking us important questions," Dad motions to me.

The bell rings.

"And get up and get the fucking door!"

Mom slams her fork down, gets up, and walks towards the door.

The bell rings frantically, like a desperate person is poking the button.

My mother yanks the door open. "Seth," she says, surprised. "What's wrong?"

Dad and I exchange surprised glances and then get up to join Mom at the door.

Seth is standing in our doorway with a suitcase at his side. He's soaked to the bone from the rain. His blonde hair is plastered to his head. His eyes are red and glassy. "My dad kicked me out."

"What? Why?" Mom asks, concerned. "Why in the world would he do that?"

"Because I told him I'm gay," Seth murmurs and starts crying.

"Get in here." Mom takes his hand and leads him inside our house.

"I'm so sorry," Seth says. "I can't go to Mike's. Things are weird with him. He's so angry, I don't even recognize him. I don't have anywhere else to go."

My mom pulls him into a tight hug. "Don't worry about that," Mom says. "You can stay here as long as you want. We have a furnished basement. It's yours for as long as you need it." She takes his suitcase and wheels it towards the basement stairs. "Come on. Let's get you cleaned up and in some dry clothes. Are you hungry?"

"Yes," Seth answers.

"I'll get you some meatloaf as soon as you change into some dry clothes." She takes his suitcase down the stairs. Seth follows her.

Dad and I exchange surprised glances. We sit back down at the table.

A moment later, Mom comes up from the basement and then rushes to get Seth clean towels. "Kicked his own son out for being gay," Mom says under her breath. "That is the stupidest thing I've ever heard."

Once she's sure Seth has everything he needs, she goes to the kitchen to get him a plate. "Homosexuality has existed for as long as humanity has existed," Mom says, placing Seth's food down.

"Yeah," I agree. "RoboCop should look at some ancient Etruscan pottery."

"How could anybody be such a homophobe in 2023?" Mom asks. "The next time I see that man, I'm gonna give him a piece of my mind."

Seth comes upstairs in dry clothes and takes a seat. "Thank you." He starts eating.

Mom cuts her food and takes a big bite. "You can stay here as long as you need to, right, Doug?"

"Of course," Dad says.

"The couch in the basement is a pull-out bed," Mom says. "I'll make up your bed after dinner. This makes me so mad. I should call your father tonight and yell at him."

"I don't think that would do any good," Seth says. "Once he gets an idea in his head, it's impossible to change his mind."

"We'll just see about that." Mom gulps down her juice like she hasn't had any liquid in days. "I have a lot of experience dealing with difficult fathers." She pours herself another glass. Then she eats a big forkful of mashed potatoes. She takes a deep breath and looks at me. "Kira, I don't blame Jason."

I look at her, confused. "Okay."

"Teenagers break up every day. Most teenagers don't go on deadly drinking binges with drunk drivers after a breakup. As for Kimber, she made a horrible mistake. She didn't hurt your sister on purpose. I'm going to work hard to forgive her."

Mom takes another huge bite of food, chews, and swallows it. She hasn't eaten a full meal in days. It's good to see her appetite return.

"The only person I can't forgive is my father. He hurts children on purpose." Mom slams her fist on the table. "I spent Tonya's funeral terrified that prick was going to show up and make the worst day of our lives even worse." She throws her silverware down on the table. "It's not Kimber's fault Mike is so angry." She looks at Seth, "And Mike isn't angry because of anything that happened between the two of you."

"Okay, thanks," Seth says awkwardly.

"My nephew is rageful because my idiot of a sister exposed him to our abusive asshole of a father!" Mom grabs her plate and throws it against the wall.

Alma sprints off the living room couch and runs upstairs.

The blue wall is smeared with brown gravy and white mashed potatoes. We are all dead silent.

"This is *so much better* than being at my dad's house," Seth says.

I look at him, shocked.

"Seriously," Seth says with a mouth full of mashed potatoes, "this is a way healthier environment than living with RoboCop."

I giggle.

"Can I throw something too?" Seth asks. "Not my plate, though. I'm hungry." He shovels more meatloaf into his mouth.

Mom and Dad laugh for the first time in forever.

Chapter Eighteen

Monday, October 2, 2023

I put a head strap on the arms of my glasses. Then I lay the top of my hair over the strap and use a round clip to make a low ponytail. These frames won't fall off my face, no matter how hard someone pushes me.

Seth drives me to school. It is so weird being back. I walk by the front of the school where my hand was crushed, and a chill goes through me.

Seth sees that I'm a little freaked out. "Nobody's gonna mess with you. Word has gotten out that my dad's a cop, and your dad has a lawyer who scared the hell out of the principal. Everybody knows Lawndale is in jail. His bitch cousin and her friend got expelled. You'll be fine."

Nobody talks to me as I walk through the hallway. I hope all the students are too preoccupied with their own lives to worry about the girl assaulted in front of the school a few weeks ago, or the girl whose sister died. I want to be invisible.

A couple of senior girls stop me in the hallway between classes to tell me how sorry they are about Tonya. I thank them politely, but then find I have nothing else to say to them, so I excuse myself and head to my next class.

Halfway through the morning, it starts to feel good to return to normal. I go to each class, listen, take notes, and answer if the teacher calls on me. It feels good to focus on day-to-day tasks instead of pressing charges against criminals and planning funerals.

I sit with Liz and Mike at lunch. Seth and Jason stay at another table on the other side of the cafeteria. "Don't you think you should talk to Seth?" I ask Mike.

"Don't you think you should talk to Jason?" he snaps.

"We've already talked. He's giving me space," I say.

"Have you said anything to him since he told you he loves you?" Liz asks.

"He never said that to me," Mike yells at Liz. "Why don't you mind your own business?"

Liz looks at him, shocked. "I was talking about Jason and Kira."

Mike looks away, embarrassed. "Oh, sorry."

"Alright. That's it," I yell at my cousin. "We aren't putting up with this chronic bad mood of yours anymore. You don't get to yell at Liz like that."

"Sorry, Liz," Mike says.

"You're taking me somewhere after school," I insist.

"Where?" Mike asks

"Meet me by the flagpole after school. I'll tell you where we're going then."

"Why can't you tell me now?"

"Because I'm not giving you time to think of an excuse to get out of this."

"Fine," Mike says through gritted teeth. "I really am sorry, Liz."

"It's okay. Greif makes us all edgy," Liz says.

Mike's brain finally processes the information he heard. "Jason told you that he loves you?"

I blush. "I'm not telling you anything until you tell me exactly what happened with you and Seth."

"Fine. Then we won't talk about it." He goes back to eating his sandwich in silence.

Art class is next. Miss Coleman welcomes me back with a smile. "I'm so sorry about your sister. I remember your drawing of her. She was so pretty." That is the most personal I've ever seen her get with a student.

She tells me that I've missed two painting assignments. One with impressionist techniques. The other is an abstract painting. She tells me I have until the end of the fall semester in December to complete them. I can either wait until the cast comes off to paint them or come up with alternatives I can do right now.

"Like what?" I ask.

"That's up to you. Your boyfriend came to me demanding I be flexible. He suggests you try sculpting clay with your left hand or photography."

"He's not my boyfriend." I correct her.

She looks at me doubtfully. "You might wanna tell him that. In all my years of teaching, I've never seen a student so concerned about another student's grades."

I blush. "He's not my—it doesn't matter."

"Kira, I want *you* to come to me with some alternative medium ideas, and I'll approve them. If you wanna do sculpture or photography, tell me. The point is, I want *you* to pick them, not your—whatever he is, unboyfriend."

"Okay."

"You'll still need to keep up with current assignments, too. The good news is that for the rest of the semester, we're studying and recreating Jackson Pollock and Louise Nevelson. You should be able to create splatter painting and installation sculpture with your left hand."

I meet Mike at the flagpole at the front of the school. He looks so tired, I almost feel bad asking him to do this. "Where are we going?" he asks as soon as he sees me approaching him.

"You'll see when we get there."

We walk in silence to his car. I get in the passenger side, use my phone to locate the address, and then slide it into his phone holder. "Take me there, please."

He looks at me like I'm insane, but starts the car and follows the GPS. He turns up the radio. We don't speak for most of the drive.

"Why the hell are we going to Salem Hospital?" Mike says as we get close.

"I wanna see the other person involved in the car crash."

"Why?"

"You'll see why when we get there."

He sighs and whispers under his breath. "This is so stupid."

We find a space in the front and walk inside the main entrance. "Can I help you?" the receptionist asks.

"We're here to visit a patient," I explain.

"What's the name?"

"Kimberly Davis," I say quietly.

"What the hell, Kira?" Mike snaps at me. "You said you wanted to visit the other person involved in the car crash."

"Kimber was the other person."

"No. Kimber is the criminal. The other person is the poor bastard in the car she hit. I can't believe you tricked me into bringing you here. I thought Kimber was in a hospital in Peabody."

"My parents found out she was moved here."

"I never would have come if you told me the truth. Screw this, we're leaving." He walks to the door.

I refuse to follow him.

He turns to look at me. "Come on."

"No."

"Damn it, Kira. I can't leave you here. Let's go."

"No." I grab him by the shirt. "You've been in a scary, rageful mood ever since Tonya died. You couldn't even grieve with us at the funeral. You just sat there like a machine. We're going to see Kimber because it'll help."

"Help? If I see that fucking bitch, I'm gonna strangle her. How will that help anyone?"

"You're not gonna *see* her. You're gonna stand outside her room as I talk to her."

"No way."

"Mike. This isn't just about you. My sister is dead. I need you to do this for me. You haven't done anything for anyone since the night Tonya died. Stop being such a selfish ass and help me do this."

"Fine. But if I end up killing her and going to jail, this is on you."

I walk back to the receptionist. "Kimberly Davis's room, please."

She stares at us with a shocked expression. "She's in police custody. Family members are only allowed to visit her. Are you family?"

"No. I'm a friend."

"I'm sorry. I can't give you her room number."

"Please. It's really important."

"I'm sorry, young lady, but no."

"Is Dimitra Drakos here tonight?" I ask. "We're friends with her, son—I mean nephew. Who is practically her son."

"I'm sorry, young lady. I can't give out a hospital employee's information. If you really know her son, I suggest you call him about getting in contact with her."

I sigh.

"Well, thanks for your time," Mike says. "We'll be going now."

I look at Mike. "Please call Jason and ask him if his aunt is working tonight."

"You call him. I didn't wanna do any of this."

"I can't call him."

"Why?"

"Because things are weird between us. If I call him, he's gonna think it's because I don't need any more space. I don't wanna give him any false hope. Please call him."

Mike looks like his head is ready to explode. He pulls out his phone and dials Jason.

It rings four times, and then Jason picks up. "Hey. What's up?"

Mike holds the phone between us so I can hear too. "My cousin has it in her head that she needs to see Kimber for closure, or some weird-ass shit like that. The hospital won't let us in to see the convict. Is your aunt working tonight? If so, is there any way she can get us in?"

"My aunt's home right now," Jason says.

My heart sinks. There's no way we can get inside to see Kimber without her help.

"Hold on. She's in the other room," Jason says. He explains the situation to his aunt. Mimi takes the phone and asks to speak to me. "Hi, Kira. What are you doing, sweetheart?"

I walk a few steps away from Mike so he can't hear me. "I wanna tell her I don't hate her," I whisper. "I want her to know that." Tears form in my eyes again. "Mike is so angry—all the time. He keeps talking about horrible things he wishes would happen to her. I don't even recognize my cousin anymore. I think if he sees her, he'll stop hating her. She's not a monster. She's my sister's friend."

"I'll be there in twenty minutes," Mimi says. "I'll get you in to see her."

I'm so relieved. "Thank you."

She hangs up.

I compose myself and hand the phone back to my cousin. We sit in the lobby and wait.

Half an hour later, Mimi arrives. She comes in carrying a tray of cookies with a plastic lid.

My heart races when I notice Jason with her. "What's he doing here?"

"He heard you crying. Did you honestly think he wouldn't show up?" Mike asks.

I keep my eyes on Mimi. "Thank you."

She pulls me into a hug. "Are you sure you wanna do this?"

"Absolutely. I have to."

"Okay," Mimi takes my hand and leads us past the receptionist.

"You're not going to get in trouble, are you?" I ask her.

"I doubt it. I can get you to her door, but we'll have to get around the officer assigned to guard her."

"A cop is guarding her door?" I ask, surprised.

"She's a prisoner in police custody awaiting trial. She's a flight risk," Mimi explains. "Don't worry. I have a plan. Officer Simmons loves cookies." She takes us to the hallway by the nurse's station. "Wait here. I have to change. I'll look more official in my uniform." She disappears into a changing room.

"This is ridiculous," Mike complains. "Don't you think?" he asks Jason.

"It seems kind of brave to me," Jason says.

"Oh, you're all nuts." Mike takes a few steps away from us and pulls out his phone. Leaving me alone with Jason.

"I really do think what you're doing is brave," Jason says.

"Thank you." I lean back against the wall because there are no chairs to sit in.

"Most people would never be this forgiving, you know." He stands next to me.

I look towards my cousin. "I think Tonya would want me to do this. For Kimber and for Mike."

"Probably," Jason agrees.

I can almost sense Tonya here with us right now. I have a weird feeling I'm being guided to do this. Is my sister's spirit here with us? Looking out for Mike? Glaring at me for wanting to cling to Jason right now?

"You still can't look at me?" He sounds so hurt.

I sigh. "Jason. It's not because I blame you." I force myself to turn and look him in the eye. He looks drained and exhausted like the rest of us. "I don't blame you. Nobody does."

He looks so relieved, he almost smiles.

All I want to do is wrap my arms around him so we can comfort each other. I resist the urge. I look away and back up.

"I'm trying to give you space," Jason says.

"Thank you."

He moves closer. "But it's impossible for me to hear you crying on the phone and not want to come help."

I sigh. "I'm sorry." I close my eyes and drop my head back against the wall. "I really didn't mean to pull you into all this drama today. That's the last thing I wanted."

"Kira, I don't mind the drama." His need to hold me is overwhelming. He moves in close enough to whisper in my ear. "I told you I'd always be here for you. I meant what I said to you at the funeral."

My heart races. *Please don't say it again.*

"I—"

"Please don't. I can't deal with—" I have to move away from him to compose myself. "I can't deal with any more emotions right now."

"Okay. Sorry."

Mimi finally comes out dressed in nurse's scrubs. She takes the lid off the platter and tells all the nurses to take a cookie. A bunch of people come over to grab one.

Mimi leads us to Kimber's room. There's a cop outside the door. "Hold on," Mimi tells us to hang back. She walks up to the cop. "Officer Simmons. How are you tonight?"

He smiles. "Fine, ma'am. Thank you."

"Didn't you mention that you love chocolate chip cookies? There's a tray of them at the nurse's station."

"Really?"

"I have to go in and take Ms. Davis's vitals again. Why don't you go get yourself a cookie while I examine her? They're soft-baked and disappearing fast."

"Thank you, ma'am. I'll be back in five." He walks away.

She motions for us to come.

"Your aunt is a genius," I whisper to Jason. I turn to Mike, "Please just stand in the doorway and listen."

I open the door and I step inside.

It feels empty and lifeless in here. Kimber lies motionless in her bed. Is she asleep? I step closer and get a better look. Her face, eyes, and nose are still swollen from the airbag. Her arm and leg are bandaged. There's a cuff around her ankle, keeping her chained to the bed.

She turns her head and sees me. Her breath becomes rapid and shallow. Her eyes become huge and terrified. She snaps her eyes shut and turns her head away.

I take one step closer.

Her whole body turns away from me. The cuff and chain on her ankle slide along the bed. She wishes she could get up and run away from me.

"Kimber, please. We don't have much time." My voice comes out as a whisper. "Can you *please* tell me what happened to my sister?"

Kimber sighs. "Tonya called me and said she was checking out of rehab." Her voice is so groggy, I barely recognize it. "She said she didn't belong there, and she couldn't take another second of it. She asked me to pick her up. She wanted beer so badly that she practically begged me to bring some. I used my fake ID to buy a six-pack." Kimber turns her body slightly towards me, but keeps her face turned away. "I picked her up in my car. She was so happy and excited to be free. Tonya popped open a beer and guzzled it down. I've never seen anybody drink so fast. She was starving for it." Kimber insists, perhaps to remind me that Tonya is also at fault.

"I'm sure she was," I agree.

"Tonya said she was gonna move to New York the next day, and she asked me to come with her. I agreed because I was sick of my mom and dad nagging me. We were so stupid," Kimber mumbles. "The whole plan was so stupid. We planned to sneak into our houses the next day when our families were out to get our stuff, but that night, we were gonna party like the world was ending. We finished the six-pack and stopped at a convenience store for some flavored vodka and more beer. We drove up and down the 95, going nowhere. We were just happy to be back together, getting drunk.

"A sad song came on the radio. Tonya got really upset over the breakup and started crying. Her last words were, 'Why doesn't he love me?'"

I gasp. I glance towards the door. Did Jason hear that?

Kimber says, "I answered, 'Because he's an idiot. Forget him and get another beer.' I changed the station so she wouldn't cry. There was more beer in the backseat. Tonya took her seat belt off to reach into the back and get more. She cracked open another can and drank it down." Kimber's voice starts shaking. "I don't know how I ended up on Route One. I thought I was still on the 95. Freeways don't have traffic lights," Kimber's voice cracks.

"I know," I agree.

"We were singing along and laughing. And then...I don't even know how to describe it. My car hit another car so hard. My airbag went off. I felt my nose and ribs break. Everything stopped but the fucking radio. It kept playing the upbeat song we had been singing. I cried out for Tonya. I asked if she was alright. She didn't answer me. I turned off the radio. I don't know how I reached it, but I managed to poke the button. I pushed the airbag away from my face and called to her again. That's when I turned and saw her."

Kimber starts sobbing. "Her body was pitched forward. She was lying in an awkward position. I could only see the side of her face. It was covered in blood. I screamed her name over and over again. I screamed, 'Tonya, say something to me!' She didn't answer. I wouldn't let myself believe she was dead until the police and ambulance came."

Tears are streaming down my cheeks. I can't think of a single thing to say.

"You should kill me," Kimber whispers.

I gasp.

"Do you have a pen on you? Hand it to me and I'll drive it into my throat." She holds her hand up. "I don't want you to go to jail. Your family has been through enough. I'll do it myself."

I take a deep breath and try to figure out what to say. I can't find my voice yet.

"I should've died in that car accident. God is a sick, twisted bastard for keeping me alive. I've been praying for him to bring Tonya back and take me instead. He doesn't answer."

I cover my mouth.

"Please hand me something sharp. Anything." She holds her hand up again. "Do it. I shouldn't be alive."

I take her hand in mine and sit on her bed.

She clings to my hand for dear life, but she turns her head further away from me.

"Kimber. You made a horrible mistake. You're going to jail for it. You don't deserve to die for it," I whisper.

Her shoulders convulse in a sudden sob as tears tumble down her cheeks. "Why don't you hate me? You should hate me."

I turn her head and make her look at me. "Because you didn't hurt anybody on purpose." I lean in and hug her. "You were my sister's best friend."

She pulls me into a hug and we cry together.

"Tonya died on September sixteenth," I say. "You have a few choices. You can let yourself die from guilt. Or you can serve your time, get out of jail, stay sober, and help other people stay sober. I'll come visit you every year on September sixteenth. In jail, at your gravesite, or the home you live in after prison."

She holds on tighter. "You promise? You'll really visit me?"

"I promise. Please don't make me visit your grave, Kimber. God kept you alive for a reason."

"Thank you, Kira."

I hug her one more time, and I stand up to leave. I have to compose myself before I can step out into the hallway.

Mimi is crying. Jason has his arm wrapped around his aunt's shoulder.

I look at my cousin. Mike's face is red with repressed emotions. He looks like he is ready to explode.

Mimi leads us all to the nearest stairwell. Mike and I go in alone.

I turn him to face me. "Do you still want to kill Kimber?"

He doesn't answer. He breaks down in tears. I hug him, and he holds on to me so tightly that my ribs hurt. His whole body shakes as he sobs in my arms. "I couldn't save Tonya. I couldn't save her." He says it over and over again between sobs. "I knew she was drinking too much, and I did—fucking nothing! Why didn't I fucking do something?"

"Mike, the same questions are in all of our minds. None of us imagined it would get this bad. You can't save someone who doesn't want to be saved." I squeeze him tightly until he calms down.

"I'm never gonna let anything bad happen to you," he says.

"I know. I'm never gonna let anything bad happen to you either. Why do you think I brought you here today? I wasn't gonna let that grumpy, angry lunatic replace my cousin."

He smiles and takes a deep breath.

I pull a tissue out of my purse and hand it to him. "Let's go home."

Mike nods.

I take his keys and leave him standing in the stairwell for a second. I open the door and hug Mimi. "Thank you."

"Your parents are going to be so proud of you," she says.

I smile at her and turn to Jason. "I don't think Mike should drive right now. Can you give us a ride to my house in his car and have Mimi pick you up after?"

"Yeah, of course," Jason says. "Anything you need."

"Thanks." I hand him Mike's keys.

"You kids go ahead," Mimi says. "I'm gonna change into my clothes before I get talked into working on my day off."

Mike, Jason, and I take the stairs down to the lowest level and then walk out to Mike's car. We drive to my house in silence.

We walk into my living room. Seth is sitting on the couch. He sees the three of us walk in looking like death. "What happened to you guys?" He stands up. "You all look like hell."

Mike takes three huge steps in Seth's direction. He grabs Seth and pulls him into a hug.

"Okay, what's going—"

Mike kisses him right on the lips.

My eyes are huge. Then a huge smile spreads across my face. Jason and I exchange shocked glances.

"Let's go downstairs and talk," Mike suggests.

Seth smiles. "Okay."

They disappear into the basement.

"Wow," Jason says, smiling. "They look surprisingly good together."

"I know, right?" I look at him and smile. "It's like they've always been a couple, but didn't know it yet."

Jason looks at me knowingly, like he is thinking the same thing about the two of us.

"Thank you. For being there for us and for driving us home. I'm exhausted." I yawn. "I think that was the most exhausting experience of my life. I need to go lie down and take a nap." I head towards the stairs and stop on the bottom step. "Your aunt will be here in a few minutes to pick you up, right?"

"Yeah. She texted. She's on her way." He steps closer. "Are you really exhausted? Or is it too hard to be around me?"

I look at him, standing by our front door. A bad memory makes me frown.

"Kira?"

166

"I remember you standing in that exact spot kissing my sister goodnight," I whisper.

He inhales a sharp breath.

I remember my heart breaking when I saw that kiss. I remember crying myself to sleep that night after I found out they'd slept together.

"My whole relationship with her was a mistake. I wish I'd never touched her," he says under his breath.

I hate that I'm hurting him by keeping my distance. "It won't always be this way. I just need some time."

He smiles. "Good." It's the first time in weeks I've seen a genuine smile. He opens my front door. "Have a good night, Kira.

Chapter Nineteen

Monday, October 9, 2023

I walk into my art class and find my teacher sitting at her desk.

"Miss Coleman. I'm dropping out of art for the rest of the semester."

She looks shocked. "Kira. That would be a huge mistake. You're one of my most talented students. I'd hate to see you—"

"My mind is made up. I still have no idea what alternative medium ideas to use for my makeup assignments. My sister died. I have no desire to create anything right now." I tell her. "It takes me twice as long to do all my regular schoolwork and homework. I can't work as fast as the other students with one good hand and bad vision. After school, I have to catch up on my schoolwork and then start my homework. I'm exhausted. I need a break."

"Kira. Please don't drop out. One of the reasons I chose sculpture and paint splatter is because it would be possible for you to do those assignments with your injured hand."

I'm shocked that she would care enough about me to rearrange her curriculum. "I'm sorry, Miss. Coleman. You didn't have to do that."

"I wanted to. What if I try to find a different way to accommodate you? How about I give you credit for being my teaching assistant?"

"I think you've already done enough to accommodate me. I can't ask you to do more. Besides, I really need this period in study hall to catch up on all my required classes. I'm so far behind, I'm drowning. I already went to the office and dropped this class. I just came here to tell you in person."

She looks a little hurt. "Okay, Kira. I hope to see you back next semester."

"I'm not sure yet. I'll let you know." I walk out of the classroom feeling like I put down one-hundred-pound weights.

I get off the bus and walk towards my house. My aunt's car is in the driveway. Aunt Ginny and my mom had plans. I walk into my living room and see my mother lying on our couch, crying her eyes out. Her head is in Aunt Ginny's lap. I guess the girly shopping day wasn't that fun.

"What happened?" I ask, concerned.

"We were at the mall," Aunt Ginny says. "We saw a mother with her two daughters. They were about your age and your sister's age."

Mom cries harder.

It is so weird to see my mother and aunt getting along. I remember them being at each other's throats my whole life. I feel awful for my mom, but it is good to see her getting along so well with her sister.

Then I realize, I will never have a moment like this with Tonya again. I used to cry with my head on Tonya's lap. When I fell off the swing set and got hurt. When I was upset that my first kiss was such a disappointment. When anything bad happened, I'd lie down on my sister's bed and she'd hold me.

Jealousy is a horrible emotion. It builds inside of me until I can't stand to look at my mother and aunt anymore.

I go to my room and close the door. I cross our bathroom to Tonya's bedroom door. I haven't been in here since she left for rehab.

I crack the door and switch on the light. Her room is dark and cold. There's no life or energy in here. It feels like a void.

Tonya's phone is on her nightstand. The bed is made. The waitress uniform my sister wore on her last day at work is still on top of her hamper, along with the last dress my sister wore on her last date with Jason. The heels she had on are still by her bed where she left them.

I don't know why Mom made the bed, but didn't clean up anything else.

"Where the hell did you go? How does a whole person just vanish?"

I sit on her bed and close my eyes, hoping that I'll sense something. I don't feel anything. I grab her pillow and hug it.

"Are you still here? Do you even still exist?" I smell her pillow. It has lost all of Tonya's scent. It feels like God took every part of her away from me. I can't see her or hear her. I can't smell her. Then I remember *her perfume.*

I jump off the bed and grab her perfume off the bathroom sink. The bottle is almost empty, so I'll use it sparingly. I spray a little on her bed and pillow. I sit back down on her bed, close my eyes, and inhale her scent.

I like your new glasses; I imagine her saying.

"Really?" I whisper.

Yeah. They're so much thinner than your last pair. People can see your eyes now. You look really pretty.

"I went to see Kimber."

I know. I think you may have saved her life. I'm really proud of you.

"Tonya. I miss you so bad it hurts. How am I supposed to get through high school without you?"

I'll still be with you, I'm just…

"Dead."

That is so inappropriate. The PC term is "corporally challenged."

I laugh through my tears. That is exactly the type of joke my sister would make.

It feels like I'm really talking to her. "You're not here to help me deal with things. Jason keeps telling me he's in love with me. He's so *intense*. He freaks me out."

No response.

"I'm sorry I fell for your boyfriend. I feel awful about it."

Silence.

"Tonya?"

Nothing

I smell her pillow again and inhale the scent of jasmine. "Tonya?"

Still nothing. I guess she's not ready to talk about this.

I get home from school today and hear Mimi's voice when I walk through the door.

"I never let Jason call me mom. I loved his mother. I wanted him to know who she was." Mimi explains. "But that boy is my son. If anything happened to him, I don't think I'd be able to go on. I can't imagine how painful this must be for you. How are you holding up?"

"I'm still breathing," my mother says.

I slip through the front door as quietly as I can. I'm glad my mother has someone she can talk to. I don't want to interrupt their conversation. I manage to go unnoticed as I close and lock the door behind me.

"I tried to go back to work last week," Mom says. "Everything was fine until I thought about dinner. I thought I'd make pasta and meat sauce. Then I thought, Tonya doesn't like meat sauce. I have moments like that where I forget she died for just a moment. Coming back to reality is always a shock to my system. I had to go home. I feel horrible because Doug is drowning in work without my help. I know I need to go back to the office, but I don't want potential clients to see me sobbing behind my desk." She sighs. "Doug thinks I should see a grief therapist."

"How do you feel about that?" Mimi asks.

"I don't think it'll help," Mom says. "I don't think anything can help."

I open the closet door to hang up my jacket. They finally notice me.

"Hi, sweetheart," Mimi says to me. "How are you holding up?"

"I'm dealing with it as best I can. It actually helps to be back at school. It's good to do normal things again."

"Well, thank God you're more mature than me," Mom jokes and motions for me to sit on the couch with them. I sit next to her, and she pulls me into a hug. "You're such a good girl. Mimi told me what you did for Kimber. I'm proud of you." She kisses me on the cheek and hugs me tightly.

"Mom, I'm not five anymore." I pull away.

"You're still my baby." She pulls me back and holds me like I'm an infant. She's been doing this a lot since Tonya died.

"You said I'm more mature than you," I remind her.

"I don't care. You're still my baby."

Mimi laughs at us.

I roll my eyes. "Okay, Mom. Whatever. I'm a baby with a ton of homework. I'm going upstairs." I stand up. "It was good to see you, Mimi."

"Kira, wait. Before you go, I need to talk to you," Mimi says. "I need your help."

"With what?"

"Jason and I love your living room. I came over to ask your mom's advice on how to make ours look half this good. Your mom says you're the one who helped her put this room together."

"It's true," Mom says. "Kira inherited her art skills from Doug's mother." She looks at me. "I wish you could've known your dad's parents."

"What happened to them?" Mimi asks.

"Doug's mother died of cancer," Mom explains.

Mimi's eyes widen, and she shakes like a chill went through her.

"Doug's father couldn't take the grief. He aged twenty years overnight. He only lasted one year without her," Mom explains.

"I'm sorry. That's awful," Mimi says quickly. She looks uncomfortable and changes the subject. "Anyway, if you can help me with my living room, I'd greatly appreciate it." She shows me a picture of her living room. "See how plain it looks?"

The walls are beige. Her couch is grey. The black coffee table looks like it is made of plywood. There's no rug or pillows. The hardwood floors look cold and uninviting. The black coffee table stands out as the most noticeable feature in the room.

"It's awful, isn't it?" Mimi asks. "I have no artistic abilities. I have a mathematical and scientific brain."

"It could definitely use some work," I agree.

"What do you suggest? I have a budget of two thousand dollars."

"An area rug, curtains on the windows and throw pillows would help to spruce up the room and make it look cozier."

"Okay, but I hate picking all that stuff out. I always pick individual pieces that I like. Then I put them together and they clash."

"Hold on. I have an idea." I pull my laptop out of my backpack and sit down on the couch. "Email me that photo."

Twenty minutes later, I've downloaded an interior design software. I've uploaded her picture and recreated a similar empty room. "

I make the walls a light blue, similar to the color of our walls. I find a blue oriental rug similar to the one we have. I let her keep her grey couch, but I add two green throw pillows and a blue-green throw. I paint the molding and window sill a light grey to match the dark grey couch. I add a wooden coffee table with a glass top. I use the app to add some knick-knacks and some impressionist and Renaissance-style art to the walls. When I'm done, it looks like a cross between dark Victorian and boho chic.

"I love it," Mimi says. "That's what I want."

"You can order everything online and have it delivered."

She's amazed at how fast I did it. She thought she was going to have to go to many stores to find all this stuff. Older people never understand how to make the most of technology.

"Use the painter's tape to make sure the walls are blue and the moldings are grey."

"I'll have Jason paint the living room," she says. "He's much better at that kind of thing. Maybe you could come over and help him."

I try really hard not to react. I don't want Mimi or my mother to know what is going on. "I don't think I'd be much help," I hold up my cast. "Besides. He is really creative. I'm sure painting a wall will be easy for him."

Seth and Mike come home. "Hi, Aunt Cindy," Mike says. "Is it okay if I have dinner here tonight? My mom is busy closing up her store, and she said we're having TV dinners tonight. Yuck."

"Sure, Mike," Mom agrees. "I'm making a plain marinara tonight. Nothing fancy."

"It's a million times better than a TV dinner," Mike says.

I look at the time. It's already after five. "I have to get my homework started. I'll email you a copy of the picture of the room so you can use it to paint and decorate," I say to Mimi. I close my laptop and pick up my backpack. "See you later."

"There was one more thing I wanted your help with," Mimi says. "Jason's birthday is next Saturday, the twenty-first."

"Oh, yeah. I remember he mentioned his birthday was in October," I say.

"His friends from Connecticut are visiting," Seth says. "It should be fun." He sits down at our dining room table and takes out his schoolbooks.

"Kira, Jason really loved your cupcakes. He said they were the best he's ever had," Mimi says. "It's his eighteenth birthday. My baking skills are as lousy as my decorating skills. I always buy him a cake. But eighteen is kind of a big deal. I'd love for him to have a homemade cake."

"I don't know if I can bake right now." I hold up my cast again.

"I'll come over and help you," Mimi says. "I'll pay you for all the ingredients, too."

"It's not just my hand. I was out of school for a long time. I have a lot of work to catch up on. Besides, I don't wanna give him any sense of false hope that we—" I stop myself before I say too much. "I just don't think it's a good idea."

"You'll at least come to the party, won't you?" Mimi asks. "It's Saturday, the twenty-first."

"Maybe," I lie. There's no way I can go to that party. "I'll see if I can move things around."

"Okay, sweetheart. I hope you come. I think it would mean a lot to him." Mimi says.

I'm not responding to that. "I'll see you later." I head upstairs.

Will you come over and help Jason paint the living room? Will you bake him a birthday cake? Will you come to his party? Is she trying to get us together?

My mom spends the whole meal watching everyone interact
while she nibbles on her pasta. Her plate is only half-eaten
when she stands and says, "I'm exhausted. I'm going to bed.
You guys clean up."

"You slept for thirteen hours last night," Dad reminds her.
"You woke up at noon today."

"And now I'm tired again," Mom snaps at him.
"Goodnight." She charges upstairs to her room.

My father looks frustrated. "I thought Ginny and Mimi
could make her feel better, but she's still in a funk." He stands.
"I have to get her some help. She can't go on like this. Can you
kids clean up?"

"Sure," Seth says.

"Thanks. I gotta research some grief therapists in this area."
Dad disappears into his office.

My parents are so different. I miss the people they used to
be.

"Kira," Mike says, snapping me out of my thoughts.
"Remember when my mom asked people to get up and talk at
Tonya's funeral?"

"Yeah, why?"

"That was such a stupid thing to do. You ask people
beforehand if anybody wants to say anything at a funeral. You
plan it out carefully. You don't just ask for anyone to stand up
and talk on the spot."

The memory makes me feel so uncomfortable. "I know, that
was so cringe."

"Pure cringe," Mike agrees. "My mom looked like she was
about to die of embarrassment."

I giggle.

"I swear, I think I heard crickets chirping outside. That's
how quiet the crowd was," Mike says.

I laugh harder. "That moment gave me the worst
secondhand embarrassment."

"Jason rescued my mom from public humiliation," Mike
says.

"I know," I agree.

"I haven't known Jason for very long, but he's one of my best friends. He didn't judge Seth and me when we got together. Some friends I've known since kindergarten won't talk to me anymore.

I frown. *How can anybody be so close-minded?*

"Jason is there for you every time you need him," Mike reminds me. "At Tonya's birthday party. At her funeral. He saved you from Eric in the cafeteria. He stayed with you after you were attacked and made sure you got to the doctor. When we saw Kimber, he came to the hospital because he knew you were upset."

I sigh. "You're saying I have to bake Jason's birthday cake, aren't you?"

"Ding, ding, ding," Seth says. "We've got a bingo."

I look at Seth, "Okay, but you have to help me sift the flour, butter the pans, and do all the other stuff."

"Okay," Seth says.

"And I'm still not going to the party," I insist.

"Uh-huh. Sure," Mike says.

"Why don't you admit that you want him?" Seth asks.

I blush. "Just because Jason looks like a Greek god, that doesn't mean that everyone wants him. Tastes vary." I walk away from the table. "You guys clean up. My hand hurts. Goodnight, boys."

I go upstairs and text Liz and Melony about going to the Taylor Swift movie. I tell them I have to see it on the twenty-first. It's my only free night.

Chapter Twenty

Saturday, October 21, 2023

Liz is sixteen and a half. She can finally drive without an adult in the car. Her mom is letting her take the minivan tonight. I'm excited for the first time in months.

My hand is still in a cast, but at least the fingers sticking out of the plaster look normal again. Last night, Liz gave me a manicure. The pink polish made me feel better. It inspired me to polish up my whole look. I used tweezers on my neglected brows and gave my hair a much-needed deep conditioning.

I'm not putting my hair in my signature ponytail tonight. I leave it hanging down my back. I can't believe how long it is. Usually, I keep it cut to my shoulders. It grew fast this summer. It hangs down my back in brown waves.

I decide to finally try putting in my new contacts. I don't want to deal with glasses sliding down my nose as I dance with the other Swifties in the movie theater. The last time I wore contacts, I had a headache in ten minutes. I'm skeptical about whether these lenses will be different, but I pop them in my eyes and hope for the best. After ten minutes, they feel fine. I decide to take a chance and leave these contacts in until bedtime.

I make up my face. I have fun playing around with eye makeup. I blend soft purple and brown shades on my eyes. I add liner and mascara, and I can't believe how big my eyes look.

My phone buzzes with a message from Mimi.

M: Hi sweetie. I can't pick up the cake. I have to run to Target to get air mattresses and extra pillows for Jason's friends to sleep on tonight. Can you drop the cake off?

I text Seth and ask him to come get it.

S: I'm already at Jason's. U bring it.

I don't have time for this. Liz is going to be here any minute to pick me up. I'm not even dressed yet. I change into a pink blouse and a white mini skirt. I grab my nude tights out of my drawer.

I text Mike and ask him to pick up the cake. I try to put tights on with one good hand. This is a huge pain. I get it halfway on my left leg when Mike texts me back and tells me he's already at the party, too. I text Seth and Mike and remind them that I am going to the movies with Liz tonight. That she will be here any minute to pick me up.

I yank the stupid tights all the way up my left leg and start on the right leg. Then Liz texts me.

L: Can't order the tickets. The site keeps crashing when I try to order them on my phone. Can u try on ur computer. B there in 10 to pick u up.

I grunt and reach for my laptop. There are a few tickets left for the seven fifteen showing. I pick our seats and click the order button. The website won't load the next page. I keep getting a blank white page with the stupid rotating circle.

I grunt and go back to pulling up my tights. The website crashes, and I have to start all over again. There are fewer seats now.

I choose two seats again. It takes forever for the next page to load, so I keep working on my tights. I pull up on the left side of my leg, then the right side. Left, right, left. I get frozen out of the website again. "Goddamn it!"

I text Mike and Seth that I can't drop the cake off because I don't have time. Seth tells me he will clean up after dinner every night for a week if I bring the cake over tonight.

I try one more time to buy the tickets. The damn site crashes again. "To hell with this." I yank the damn tights off my body and throw them on the floor in a heap. I don't need them anyway. I'm going to be dancing in the movie aisle with Liz. That will make me hot.

I go directly to Taylor's website and try to order there instead. I put on my jewelry as I wait for the page to load. I wear the rose quartz necklace my aunt gave me. She says it's supposed to stimulate the heart chakra. I have no idea what the hell that means. It looks good with my pink top.

I put on socks and my tan boots. I look in the full-length mirror on the back of my closet door. *Whoa. I'm hot. When the hell did this happen?*

I didn't realize my B cups could be noticeable in any top, but this Empire waist blouse makes them look bigger than usual. My face looks really pretty without those damn thick glasses. My legs don't look like sticks anymore. My hips finally got a little wider than my waist. A stranger looks back at me in the mirror.

Maybe I look hot because Tonya isn't here to outshine me. It's going to be nice not being in her shadow anymore.

The thought is horrifying. Why did I think that? I stare at myself in the mirror. "That is bullshit. I'd gladly smash my face into this glass if it meant I could have my sister back."

Liz messages me that she's here. I grab my purse and run out of my room. My parents are having the same old argument in the living room.

"Do you know how much money we'll lose if I have to hire someone to do your job?" Dad asks.

"I'm sorry, I'm not there to be your slave anymore," Mom says, "I'm sorry I spoiled you by spending my entire adult life supporting your dreams instead of going after my own."

"What dreams?" Dad yells. "You never mentioned wanting to do anything else."

I rush down the stairs.

"Where are you going?" Mom asks.

"Out with Liz?"

"Who is driving?" Mom asks.

I cringe. "Liz."

"No way," Mom says.

"She's old enough to drive on her own," I insist. "Liz's mom let her take the car tonight."

"A sixteen-year-old inexperienced driver. No," Mom says.

I look at my dad. "We're only going to the movie theater at the mall."

He sighs. "Text us when you get there and be home by eleven."

I smile.

"Doug," Mom yells. "Are you crazy? I said no."

"Our daughter can't spend her entire life in this house, Cindy. They are just going to the movies. Liz is a smart, responsible girl. Kira will be fine."

I walk past them. I get my purple velvet jacket out of the closet and put it on.

I go to the kitchen, get the cake out of the fridge, and head out the door. I can still hear my parents yelling as I walk down our porch steps. I refuse to let their argument bother me tonight. I'll worry about them later. It's Taylor Swift night.

"Whoa, you look…different," Liz says. "Gorgeous, actually."

"Thanks." I slide into the passenger seat.

"Now I look underdressed." She looks down at her Eras tour sweatshirt and jeans.

"You look great," I tell her.

"What's that?" Liz points to the container.

"Jason's birthday cake. Can we make a quick pit stop at his place?"

"Sure, but it'll have to be fast if we want food before the movie," Liz says. "I'm starving. Did you get the tickets?"

"No. I had the same problems you did. I'll try again on my phone."

She starts the engine. I try again to order tickets from another ticket website. There are four tickets left. I take the two closest to the screen and try to check out. The damn signal drops. "Jesus. Why can't I buy these damn tickets?"

"I think Swifties are all online trying to get tickets for tonight. I knew I should've bought our tickets a few days ago," Liz says. "Keep trying."

My battery dies. "What the hell? I plugged my phone in last night."

Liz points to her charging cable and tells me to plug in my phone. Then she hands me her phone to try to get tickets. I go to another website, but this site is even more glitchy than the last. We decide to buy tickets when we get to the theater.

Liz finds a parking space near the apartment complex.

"They are gonna invite us to join the party," I say on the way inside. "Don't get guilted into staying."

"Kira, I've been dying to see this movie for weeks. Nobody could convince me to miss it tonight."

It feels weird not heading to my aunt's apartment on the third floor. We go to unit B4 instead. I can hear classic rock playing and the sound of people laughing.

Liz knocks. "Why do teenage boys always sound like primates when a group of them get together?"

Someone makes a farting sound. It's so loud it has to be fake. It makes everyone inside crack up.

She knocks again. "I mean, seriously, listen to them. They all sound like a bunch of Neanderthals in there. I swear, I'm not gonna date anyone until college. High school boys are so—"

The door opens. A boy with dark hair opens the door. He has a round, friendly face. He reminds me of a huggable teddy bear.

A huge smile spreads across Liz's face. "Hi."

He looks Liz up and down and smiles back at her. "Hi, I'm Will. Jason's friend from Connecticut."

She responds with a breathy, "Of course you are." Then she bites her lower lip.

I look at my friend, surprised. I've never seen her so instantly taken with anyone.

"I'm Liz. This is Kira." She motions to me. "It's nice to meet you."

Will's eyes don't even glance in my direction. He hasn't looked away from her since he opened the door. "Are you guys here for the party?"

"Actually," I say, "we're only—"

"Yeah, we're here for the party," Liz cuts me off. "I mean, we brought the cake. Nobody would drop off a birthday cake and not stay for a slice."

I look at her and frown.

"Cool. Come on in," Will says. "You're just in time. We're about to order the food." He leaves the door open for us and goes back inside.

"Liz, what the hell?"

"Please, please, please, can we stay? Did you see how cute he is? He's just...wow."

"Liz?"

"We can see the movie next week. Please."

"Fine," I whisper. "But if Jason gets even remotely mushy with me, you have to take me home."

"I will."

"Immediately."

"I promise." She steps inside.

I'm going to regret this. I step inside Mimi and Jason's living room and notice the walls have been painted with the blue paint I picked out. It's a calming color, but it doesn't help relieve my stress. My anxiety spikes. I can't tell how many people are here because everyone's talking and laughing over each other.

I go into the empty kitchen and lean back against the counter. Maybe I should tell Liz I'm sick to my stomach and take an Uber home.

"You look gorgeous." Jason enters the kitchen and steps closer to me. He's in jeans and a green sweater that matches his eyes.

"Thanks, I made you a cake," I blurt out.

He scans my outfit up and down.

I hold the large Tupperware container in front of me. "Mimi asked me to make this for you. It's the same recipe as the cupcakes you liked."

"Awesome. Thank you. She said a special cake was coming, but I had no idea it was yours."

"Can I put this in your fridge?" I ask. "It's decorated, and I don't want the frosting to run."

Jason opens the fridge and moves things around to make room. I place the cake container on the top shelf, close the door, and turn around.

He's a foot away from me. "So, who'd you get all dressed up for?" His green eyes seem to glow.

"Taylor Swift." I pull my jacket closed, and I slide to the side to put some distance between us. "Liz and I were supposed to go see her movie tonight and—"

"And you thought she was going to see your outfit through the movie screen?" He raises his eyebrows. He thinks I'm lying.

"Yes," I lean back against the sink. "And Taylor would love my outfit so much that she'd invite me to meet her in person.

Then we'd bond instantly and she'd be my surrogate aunt and older sister figure for the rest of my life."

He tries really hard to stifle his laughter.

"Don't judge me. A billion other girls my age have the same dream. I'm not alone in my insanity."

"So why are you here instead of with your surrogate aunt?"

"The show was sold out."

"Oh, that's too bad. I'm so sorry to hear that."

"No, you're not," I accuse him.

"You're right. I'm not. I'm really happy to see you."

"I'll stay as long as you don't get mushy."

He smiles. "What the hell does that even mean?"

"You know what it means."

"Something with a soft consistency. You might wanna avoid the sour cream and onion dip tonight. It's probably too *mushy* for you."

I frown at him.

He laughs at my expression.

"Kira." Mimi rushes over and hugs me. "I'm so glad you came." She takes me by the arm and walks me into the living room. Everyone's sitting around their table playing cards. Liz sits next to Will, smiling at him, patiently waiting to be dealt into the next hand.

Mimi introduces me. "Kira, this is Will and his sister Annette, Jason's friends from Connecticut."

Annette looks stunningly beautiful, but also as hard as nails. Her long hair is jet black. Her arms and neck are covered in black tattoos. Her top is low cut, displaying large, pushed-up breasts. She looks at me like she hates me. Then she takes a second look, and her expression softens.

"Hi. It's nice to meet you," I say.

"You too," Will says.

Annette just stares at me.

"I'm Mike's cousin. Seth's my roommate, old friend, and surrogate brother."

"Kira is my interior decorator," Mimi says proudly. "She helped me with this living room." Then Mimi walks me around the whole room proudly displaying every piece I selected and gushing about how great everything turned out.

The portrait I drew of Jason is hanging on the wall. My heart stops. I'm so embarrassed. The night I drew this, I swore I'd never let another person see it. I didn't even want my sister to see it. Now it's hanging on his living room wall. It looks professionally framed with a green mat that matches his eyes.

"You had it framed?" I ask Mimi.

"Of course I did. I needed some artwork for the walls, remember?" She scans my outfit. "Let me hang up your jacket, sweetie."

I take it off and hand it to her. Then I look back at the drawing.

"I told you my aunt would love it," Jason says. He brushes past me as he leans over to pick up a menu off the coffee table. He hands it to me. "Order whatever you want."

I scan the Greek dishes. "This looks expensive."

"I decided to only invite people I really care about," Jason says. "We have way fewer guests than Mimi planned. That means we can afford way better food."

"So, nobody else is coming?"

"No, this is it."

I breathe a sigh of relief and look back at the menu. Some hair falls over my face.

He tucks my hair behind my ear. "I know how much you hate big parties."

I look at him, stunned. "You didn't only invite a few people tonight because of me, did you?"

He doesn't answer.

"I mean, you didn't even think I was coming, right?"

He fidgets. "I just had a feeling you'd show up tonight. Order anything you want off the menu." He goes back to the table and sits.

I tell Mimi what I want, and she calls to place the order. Then she announces she's going to pick up the food because she doesn't trust the restaurant to get the order right unless she's there to check everything's correct.

"Did you find everything you needed at Target?" I ask.

"What? Oh, right. I had enough towels for everyone, so I didn't need to go?"

"You said you needed bedding," I remind her. "You said you needed it so badly, you couldn't pick up the cake."

"Right. Well, it turns out one of Jason's friends decided to stay at a motel tonight, so we didn't need an extra air mattress."

"Convenient," I say, and cross my arms. I know she's lying.

She puts on her jacket, grabs her purse, and rushes out the door to get away from me.

Mike and Seth bring in some extra chairs from Ginny's apartment so everyone has a place to sit.

The only seat available is between Will and Annette.

"Do you two know how to play poker?" Annette asks Liz while motioning to me.

"No," Liz says.

"How about we play UNO?" Will suggests.

"Great idea," Liz says, smiling at Will. "Everyone knows that game."

Annette grunts and starts gathering up the regular playing cards and poker chips. "How about a game of pin the tail on the donkey?"

"Excuse my sister," Will says. "She's twenty-one. She's way too old and cool to be at a party with teenagers. So she's gonna pout like a small child all night over not getting her way. So mature."

"I'm just saying," Annette says. "We could've been in Boston or New York City at an eighteen-to-enter club. I could've gotten you both drinks, but no. You wanna stay home and play UNO."

"Nobody feels like drinking after what happened recently," Jason reminds her.

Annette's hands freeze in place. She stops gathering up chips. "Right, sorry. I forgot."

"Alright. Who's up for UNO?" Seth asks, breaking the tension. He grabs the deck out of the media cabinet, sits back down, and starts dealing the cards. "Where's Melony tonight?" Seth asks me.

"On a date," I explain. "She met a guy from Salem High named Derik. He looks a lot like you, Seth."

He smiles. "Good for her."

Liz stares at Will from across the table. "So, how long have you and Jason been friends?"

"Kindergarten," Will says.

"Wow, kindergarten," Liz says, smiling. "That's a long time."

"Mimi was more lenient than my mom and dad, and she was always at work," Will explains. "We'd watch all the movies and play all the games my parents wouldn't let me get. I was at Jason's place all the time."

"Yeah, they only spent time at our house after they hit puberty. Jason liked to gawk at me," Annette adds proudly.

"You had a huge crush on your friend's older sister," Seth teases. He finishes dealing and turns over the first card. Red nine.

"That happens when you're twelve," Jason says.

"It happened when you were fourteen," Annette teases him.

I stop arranging my cards and glance at Jason. He frowns at her. Everyone gets quiet. Curious about what she meant by that.

"Shut up, Annette," Will says.

Seth breaks the ice again. "Mike, go. It's your turn."

Mike puts down a red two.

"Point is, I loved being friends with this guy." Will points at Jason. "Until we reached puberty."

Liz is gazing at Will so hard she doesn't realize it's her turn.

"Don't start," Jason warns him.

"Why?" Liz asks, confused, and finally puts down a yellow two. "What happened?"

Will jumps up. "I need to change the song to fully explain this." He goes over to the laptop plugged into the speakers.

"Will, don't play it," Jason warns.

Will ignores him and starts playing Van Halen's "Everybody Wants Some."

"It's Jason's theme song," Will teases. He grabs an open gift box off the coffee table and sits back down. "You see, Liz, every time I was interested in a girl, she'd get a huge crush on my best friend. It was so annoying. It happened so many times."

"It did not," Jason insists. He puts down a yellow three.

"Ever since we were twelve years old, every girl I knew would be like," he makes his voice high-pitched. "Will, what's your friend's name again? Jaaaaasoonnn. Yeah, that tall, dark, and handsome guy you're friends with. He's *so* yummy."

We all laugh.

Jason turns red.

"Every girl," Will insists and slams down a blue three.

"It wasn't every girl," Jason insists.

"I bet it was," Seth teases. "That's because Jason looks like–" he looks at me "–how'd you describe him, Kira?"

My eyes widen.

Seth smirks. "Oh, right. You said Jason looks like a Greek god. Isn't that right?"

Jason smirks.

I send Seth a death glare. "I am not in this conversation. I am casually playing Uno." I put down a blue four.

"Remember Jessica?" Will asks Jason. "The girl I worked with at the ice cream parlor when I was fifteen."

"No," Jason says.

"Well, I remember her. I had a crush on her that whole summer. She let me dry hump her once. I was so in, until you showed up one afternoon for some ice cream, and her eyes bugged out of her head." He does the high-pitched girly voice again. "Will, is that your friend? He's so hot he could melt all the ice cream in here. What's his name? Oh, Jaaaaasoonnn."

Everyone at the table cracks up laughing. Annette changes the color of the game with a red four. "The dry humping left my brother with blue balls for the rest of the summer."

"Shut up, Annette. This is the best part of the song. Everybody wants some," Will sings along. "Like Kelly. You remember Kelly?"

Seth puts down a red six.

"No," Jason says.

"Well, I do," Will says. "She showed up the first day of school, sophomore year. I had a crush on her as soon as I saw her. The second day of school, she walked up to me and asked, 'Who is that guy you were eating lunch with yesterday? He's sooooooooo hot. Yum, yum. Everybody wants some," he sings in a high-pitched girly voice.

We all laugh again.

189

"You wanna see the birthday present I got Jason?" Will opens the box and pulls a t-shirt with the words, 'Everybody Wants Some" printed on it.

"I'm never wearing that in public," Jason grumbles.

Mike laughs and puts down a red zero.

"I swear, I never had a chance with any of these girls," Will complains. "At one point, I thought I was gonna die a virgin because of Jaaaaasoon."

"Will, since I've moved away, how many times have you gotten laid?" Jason asks.

It's Will's turn to blush bright red. His lips purse together, and he blinks several times. "That's not the point. That doesn't matter."

Everyone cracks up again.

"I think we all know the answer." Jason holds up a blue card with a zero on it. He throws it down on top of the pile of cards. "There you go, Blue Balls Zero," he says to Will. "That's your new nickname. I'm gonna get you a blue t-shirt with your new nickname on it for Christmas."

I laugh so hard tears form in my eyes, and my stomach hurts.

"I assure you, Will. You didn't miss anything," Jason says. "Most of those girls were snobbish and wanted me because of the old money they thought I had. They all lost interest in me when they found out I was estranged from the entire Dimitriou family."

"If they were that shallow, they didn't deserve either one of you," Liz says.

"I'm confused. I thought your last name was Drakos." I ask Jason.

"It is now," Jason says. "Mimi and I legally changed it before we moved so our ex-family wouldn't be able to track us down. We chose Drakos because I've liked dragons since I was a kid."

"Do your new friends know the story of why you left?" Annette asks him.

"No," Mike answers. "What happened?"

"I don't think we need to get into that," Jason says.

"I think they should know," Annette says, looking right at me. "Can I tell them?"

"Fine," Jason says. "But hurry and finish before Mimi gets back. It's a sensitive subject for her. I don't want her to get upset."

"Three years ago, for Jason's fifteenth birthday, his father gave him a beautiful new Mercedes," Annette says. "You should've seen this car. It was brand new. Totally decked out and way too extravagant for a fifteen-year-old."

"He's not my father. Let's call him Sperm Donor or Damien," Jason reminds Annette.

"Okay, Sperm Donor said Jason needed a car to practice with. The whole thing was a manipulation. Sperm Donor was trying to drive a wedge between Jason and Mimi," Annette says.

"It started out really subtle," Jason explains. "Damien moved back to Connecticut after living in Manhattan for fifteen years. He said the car was too nice to park at my aunt's apartment. He said the car had to be kept at his house. It was a way to keep me coming over to visit. Then he gave me a room at his place and told me I could sleep there whenever I wanted. It was a bit uncomfortable, since his new wife was only twenty-five years old. Making her closer to my age than his."

"Then Damien started making up messed-up lies about Mimi," Annette adds.

"Like what?" I ask.

"Ridiculous crap, like Mimi didn't make enough money as a nurse to give me the lifestyle I deserved," Jason says. "It was the same lies my grandmother had been saying to everyone in town about Mimi for years. That Mimi was the worst nurse in our hospital. Some patients refused to be treated by her because of the lies. It was humiliating for her.

"My ex-family also said that she didn't get married and have kids because she was so selfish, she couldn't make a relationship last. They said the only reason she wanted to raise me was because no man wanted to have kids with her."

"Assholes," Mike says.

"Uh, yeah," Annette agrees.

191

"The difference is, I hadn't been wanting a relationship with my grandmother my whole childhood," Jason says. "I wasn't willing to listen when she said these things. I wanted a father, so I actually listened when he said these lies."

"Then, two years ago, Mimi got ovarian cancer," Annette says.

Liz gasps.

Mike and I exchange shocked glances.

"Fuck," Seth murmurs.

No wonder Mimi looked upset when she found out that cancer caused my grandmother's death.

"Probably due to all the stress these assholes put her under for years," Jason says.

"When she got sick, nobody in her family offered to lift a finger to help her," Annette says. "These people are sick and twisted. Mimi needed chemo and radiation. She couldn't work as a nurse anymore. Her health insurance would only cover payments for half the treatments she needed. Do you think her mother or brother offered any financial assistance?" Annette asks me.

"I doubt it," I say. I look at Jason, "What did you do?"

"I sold the Mercedes and used the money for Mimi's medical treatments. As soon as she was healthy enough, we moved away."

"Tell them the worst part," Annette says.

"I found out that Sperm Donor decided to run for mayor," Jason says. "Having a family to flaunt in front of the camera helps when you're running as a conservative candidate with family values. He didn't want a relationship with me. He only wanted me to pose for his campaign photos."

"Fuck him," Mike says. "I thought my dad was the biggest piece of shit in the world, but yours is worse."

Aunt Ginny never married Mike's father. She waited years for a proposal, that never came. Not even when she got pregnant. Not even after the baby was born.

"If that fucker ever shows up here, I'll help you kick his ass," Mike adds.

We hear Mimi's keys in the door. "Nobody says a word about the cancer," Jason warns. "She's sensitive about it." It's his turn. He puts down a draw-four card.

Will grumbles and takes four cards.

"I just thought you should know what a good person he is," Annette says to me. "Before you decide to throw him away like a piece of trash again." She gets up before I get a chance to respond.

We clear the games, cups, chips, and dip so Mimi can set the table. She asks for my help, and we make the table look cozy with cloth napkins, mats, and her best set of crystal glasses.

It's crowded at the table because there are eight of us at a table meant for six. I end up seated next to Jason.

We all enjoy the appetizers as Mimi plates everyone's food in the kitchen. This is the best hummus I've ever had. I dip more pita bread and enjoy another bite.

"I hope that spread isn't too *mushy* for you," Jason teases.

I frown at him with a mouth full of food.

He laughs at my expression.

My chicken souvlaki skewers over rice are delicious. I haven't had an appetite in almost two months. I forgot how enjoyable food could be.

After dinner, Mimi asks me to please bring out the cake.

"Wait until you taste this," Mike says to everyone. "Kira is the best baker."

"You mean the pickiest one," Seth says. "I helped her bake this cake. You know what she had me do? She had me sift brown sugar. Sift the flour sure, but the brown sugar? I've never heard of that."

"Brown sugar gets clumpy," I say. "Sifting it makes the batter extra fluffy."

I go to the kitchen to get the cake. I get the candles and lighter out of the drawer Mimi said they'd be in. I get the cake out. I try to figure out where I'm going to put eighteen candles without messing up the "Happy 18th Birthday Jason" lettering.

"I can see why he wants you," Annette steps inside and looks me up and down. "You're beautiful."

The way she says it makes me uncomfortable. "Uh, thanks." I look towards the living room, hoping somebody else will walk in here so I don't have to be alone with this girl. Everyone is laughing at one of Seth's funny stories. I'm on my own.

She steps even closer. "I mean, your facial features, wow. Round eyes, a perfect little nose, and lips full enough to be kissable. And your figure. You're so petite, but you have just enough curve. You're like a little doll. You should let him play with you."

My jaw is on the floor.

"Or you could let me join in, too. I'm good with virgins. I took Jason's virginity."

I glare at her and murmur, "Congratulations." I jam a candle into the cake. "And you're here to pick up where the two of you left off?"

"Oh, would it make you jealous if I moved into your territory?" she mocks.

"He's not my boyfriend. Do what you want." The idea of Jason having sex with this girl makes me want to vomit. I take a deep breath before I do something stupid like smack her in the head with my cast.

"Relax," Annette says. "We could never be a couple. Jason is way too monogamous for me. I'm bi and poly. I like to play with a lot of different people." She steps closer to me and looks me up and down again.

"I'd rather get a root canal than have sex with you."

"Oh, you have some spunk. Good. You'll need that to keep up with him. I trained him well. I assure you, he'll know exactly what to do with your perfect little body."

I look at her like she's a pervert. "And I take it from the comment you made earlier, he was only fourteen when you started *training* him. Add pedo to your proud list of prefixes."

She giggles.

I frown at how unbothered she is. I thought that was a good insult.

"Calm down. I was underage, too. I was only seventeen, so don't call the cops."

I almost smear the y at the end of birthday. "Would you go away and let me focus on what I'm doing?"

"Right, the cake of all cakes is being decorated. You're the best cook and baker in the world. You make every room cozy with your artistic skills. You're so domesticated. Even your hair is the color of dark brown sugar."

"What's your point?"

"Jason has spent his entire life living in crappy apartments and eating take-out off of tray tables in front of the TV. He only has one loved one, and he thought he might lose her to cancer. What do you think it is that he wants the most?"

I remember how much Jason loved hanging out with my dad when he came over. I remember how happy he seemed sitting at my dining room table, eating dinner with my family. He's laughing and joking around right now with my cousin.

"A found family," I say.

Annette raises her eyebrows at me. "Yep. You got it. You're surrounded by people who love you. You're sweet, nurturing, and creative. You're everything he could ever want, wrapped up in a beautiful package, and you broke his heart into a million pieces. Do it again and I'll kick your ass."

I'm stunned. I drop the candles on the table and face her. "I didn't break his heart. We didn't break up. We were never a couple. He was my sister's boyfriend before she died."

"So you didn't tell him it hurt too much to be around him. If it hurts too much to be around him, what the hell are you doing here? Be with him, or go away so he can get over you. Keeping him in limbo is fucked up."

That's it. I glare at her. "Have you ever lost a sibling?"

"No."

"When Will and you both fall for the same person and then Will dies in a horrible car accident before you can resolve your issues, then you can give me advice on how to handle this whole situation. Until that happens, fuck off!"

Annette looks taken aback for the first time. "Fair enough." She backs up.

That was enough to get Mimi's attention. She comes into the kitchen. "What's going on in here?"

"Nothing. We were clearing something up." Annette looks at me with big, guilty eyes. "I really am sorry about your sister." She leaves the room.

I gulp down a glass of water to extinguish my rage.

"Are you okay?" Mimi asks.

I take a deep breath. "I'm fine. Don't worry. There will be no more drama tonight." I finish arranging the candles. "Do you wanna light these?"

She helps me get all the candles lit and then tells everyone in the living room to take their seats. I carry the cake out and place it down in front of Jason as everybody else sings "Happy Birthday." I take my seat next to Jason. I'm too pissed off and guilty to sing along.

"Are you okay?" Jason asks.

I force a smile. "I'm fine. Make a wish."

He knows I'm upset about something. He reaches for my hand under the table and squeezes it. I know what he's wishing for as he blows out the candles.

"I'm gonna go to the bar by my motel and find an adult to play with," Annette announces as soon as she's done with her slice.

I feel better as soon as she leaves.

Mimi hugs Jason and wishes him a happy birthday. She says goodnight to all of us and goes to bed.

Seth and Will have been discussing who their favorite stand-up comedians are. Seth turns on Jason's TV and cues up his favorite Bo Burnham special.

There isn't enough room on the couch for six of us, so Will blows up the air mattress he's going to sleep on tonight. He makes his bed and pushes it up against the wall next to the couch. Will and Liz prop throw pillows against the wall and lie back together. They look like they are in their own little world.

The temperature is dropping outside. I'm getting cold. I really wish I had tried harder to get those tights on earlier.

Jason notices how cold I look. He drapes Mimi's throw over me and sits down between me and Seth. It is a tight squeeze with four of us sitting on the couch. Jason's weight makes the cushion dip, and I keep sliding towards him.

My boyfriend! I remember Tonya yelling. I move closer to the arm of the couch. I try to keep my distance, but every time my body relaxes, I end up sliding closer to him.

"Would you stop squirming," Seth complains. "I ate two big slices of cake and now my stomach is queasy."

"Sorry, Seth." I try to sit totally still. Two seconds later, gravity pulls me closer to Jason again.

"It's okay," Jason whispers. He pulls the blanket over himself, so we're sharing it. He slides closer to me and takes my hand under the blanket. "You're allowed to curl up next to me."

Allowed? Would Mike and I even be here tonight if my sister was still alive? She'd still be heartbroken over the guy I'm cuddling with. If I pull my hand away, it will feel like a rejection. I don't want to hurt Jason's feelings, so I let him hold it.

Liz giggles at something Will whispers to her. It must be nice to meet someone and connect immediately. Someone who you don't find intimidating as hell. Someone who isn't out of your league. Someone who isn't ten times more experienced than you.

I sigh and sink deeper into the couch. Jason is radiating warmth. My chills disappear. It's going to be a long, cold winter. If he was mine, I'd be able to cuddle with him whenever I felt cold. Cuddling with him has always felt wonderful. *If he put his arm around me, I'd feel even warmer.* The thought makes my hand tighten in his.

He smiles at me and kisses my forehead.

If my sister was alive, she'd be so pissed at me right now.

This stand-up special is one of Seth's favorites. I've seen it with him before at my house. I'm not as surprised by the jokes as everyone else. I'm too focused on the feeling of Jason pressed up against me. I love the sound of his deep laughter when he cracks up at a joke. How can someone's laughter be sexy?

My eyes are getting heavy. I was up late baking his cake, and I'm tired. I catch myself nodding off and force myself to sit up. A moment later, my eyes slide closed again, and my head drops onto Jason's shoulder.

A joke makes the rest of the group crack up.

I jolt awake and lift my head off Jason's shoulder. "Sorry."

He lets go of my hand. "For what? Falling asleep on my couch? If you're tired," his fingers caress my outer thigh, "feel free to go lie down on my bed."

I jump. I turn and look at him, shocked. "That's not...um."

"Not what?"

"Not a good idea. You'll be bored with me in five seconds."

Jason looks at me like I'm crazy.

Seth pauses the video. "I'm thirsty." He and Mike head to the kitchen.

Jason turns towards me. "You really believe that?"

I blush. "Well, yeah. I mean, you started at *fourteen*?"

He looks shocked. "I'm gonna kill Annette," he whispers under his breath.

"I get the feeling you've had a lot of girls in your bed." I turn beet red and look away. "I'll suck by comparison." I remove the blanket and stand up.

I find my purse and phone. Ten twenty-eight. I walk closer to Liz. "It's time to go."

"I know. Just give me a minute," she says. She and Will both have their phones out and are exchanging contact information.

"I'm gonna get my jacket." I go to the hall closet. I can hear Mimi snoring softly in the master bedroom, so I try to be as quiet as possible.

Jason steps up behind me. "I didn't sleep with any of those girls Will mentioned."

My jaw drops. I turn and look at him.

He fidgets, running a hand through his hair and shifting his feet. "If that's what's bothering you."

"I didn't think you did."

He steps closer. "Kira, I've only had sex with three people."

"Oh." I smile. Tension drains from my shoulders. "I guess, I just assumed it would be way more because you're so, um—"

He raises his eyebrows and waits for me to finish.

"Well, I mean, you know how good-looking you are." My cheeks flush.

He sighs, "Kira, Damien looked a lot like this when he was younger." He points at himself. "He'd fuck anyone he could use and discard."

My eyes widen.

"That young wife I mentioned earlier, she aged quickly after a few years of being abused and cheated on." His hands ball into fists. "He did the same thing to my mom. My ex-father drains the life out of people." He pauses, looks away from me, and runs a nervous hand through his hair again. "I don't want to be like him."

I step closer and try to get him to look at me. "Jason, you're *nothing* like him."

He keeps his eyes on the ground. "Are you sure about that?" His voice comes out in a low whisper. "People around him end up dead."

"I feel like we killed her." That's what I'd said to Jason the day after Tonya died. Guilt gnaws at me. "Don't you dare," I say in a voice way too deep and commanding to be mine. "Don't you dare blame yourself for what happened to my sister." I step closer and wrap my arms around his shoulders.

He wraps his arms around my waist.

"I didn't mean what I said to you," I whisper against his neck. "I don't think we killed her. I've been thinking about this a lot. She started drinking way before she even met you. You didn't drain the life out of her. She did that to herself. You're nothing like your father."

He inhales a sharp breath. "Really? Because I have to see him every time I look in the mirror."

I turn my face into his neck. "Then focus on your green eyes and remind yourself that you are like your mother."

His arms tighten around me. I'm enveloped in his warmth. I inhale his scent. He exhales, feeling relieved to finally have me in his arms. His heart beats against mine. I can feel his need for me radiating off of him. My heart flutters. A warmth flows from his heart chakra and pours into mine. Rose quartz really does work.

His fingers stroke the back of my hair. Then his hands cup my face. My breath catches. He senses how nervous I am, so he kisses my forehead first. His lips on my forehead and cheek are warm, familiar, and comforting. I relax against him and take a deep breath.

His lips on mine make me tremble in his arms and whimper against his mouth. He kisses me slowly but with so much passion that my knees tremble. I hold onto his shoulders to steady myself as I kiss him back. His fingers thread through the back of my hair, and he deepens the kiss. *I don't suck at this.* Relief washes over me. I hold him tighter.

He reaches over and opens his bedroom door. Both his arms wrap around my waist tightly, and he lifts me off my feet. I gasp and tighten my arms around his shoulders. He carries me into his bedroom, turns around, and sets me down on my feet. He pushes the door closed behind me. The room becomes pitch black. He leans towards me, and I'm pressed back against the door.

His lips find mine in the dark. His kiss is more urgent this time. More demanding. My fingers thread through his thick, gorgeous hair. I kiss him back with just as much passion. My whole body starts to shake against him.

"God, Kira," he whispers in my ear. His hips push closer. He's already hard. The thin material of my miniskirt feels like nothing is between us. I gasp and whimper as a surge of energy goes through my entire body from the contact. "Tell me again how bored I'll be with you," he whispers.

I gasp and pull him closer.

He pushes his hips into me harder. "Stay with me tonight."

I can't tell him yes, but I don't want to tell him no either. I lean back against the door.

He cups my cheek. His fingers slide down my neck and caress the bare skin under my collarbone. I relax against the back of the door and close my eyes. His fingers feel wonderful. It's so good to feel something other than overwhelming grief.

His hand cups my breast.

I gasp and pull him closer. I don't need to worry about doing anything wrong or being bad at this. I can just relax and let him teach me.

He moves his hand lower. His fingers slide under my blouse and gently caress the bare skin of my lower stomach.

"Jason?"

"I know," he whispers in my ear. "You're a virgin." His fingers slide down my hip to the hem of my skirt and then

caress my inner thigh. "Every little touch is such a big deal."
One slow finger slides up my inner thigh.

"Jason?" My whole body shakes.

"Kira. Stay with me." He runs his finger against my panty line.

I tremble like a leaf.

"I'll make your first time so good, Kira," he whispers in my ear. He gently caresses my clit over the outside of my panties.

"Jason. God." I cry out. Moisture gathers between my legs. I have to hold on to his shoulders to stay standing.

"So good." His finger moves against me slowly.

I gasp, then whimper.

"Stay with me tonight." He kisses me softly on the lips. He moves his lips to my ear. "Stay with me, Kira. I'm so in love with you."

My heart is going to burst out of my chest.

His fingers move my panties to the side.

Did he do this with my sister? The thought makes me tense up. *Did he do this with her in this room?* "Stop."

He pulls his hand away.

"Sorry. Too soon." He pulls me into a hug. "We don't need to do anything else tonight. We'll take this as slowly as you need to. Please stay with me tonight. I'll just hold you all night long." His arms tighten around me. "I love you. I just wanna know that you're mine."

I can't be his. Why did I let this happen? What the hell was I thinking?

"What's wrong?" he asks, concerned. "Did I scare you that badly?"

I shake my head.

"Then what is it?" He holds me tightly. "Talk to me."

"Jason, my mom is…" I gasp for air, "holding on by a thin thread. I hear her in my sister's room late at night, talking to somebody who isn't there anymore."

His arms tighten around me.

"She is losing her mind. We went shopping. She found a sweater in my sister's size and pulled it off the rack. She forgot Tonya was dead for a split second. She had a meltdown. Ginny had to rush her out to the car." My eyes fill with tears. "The next day, Mom got an email from the school about the upcoming senior prom and graduation ceremony. It made her have another meltdown. She's not eating. She spends fifteen to twenty hours a day in bed."

"Kira, I'm so sorry," he whispers.

"My dad is the opposite. He's working nonstop. He's not eating or sleeping right either because he's working eighteen hours a day. I don't recognize either one of them."

He sighs. He can't think of anything to say to make me feel better.

"Jason, they didn't like any of the other boys Tonya dated. My dad said that my sister hit the jackpot when she found you. I can't tell them you're mine now."

He's frustrated. His breath is rapid and shallow.

"If a sweater and an email are enough to make my mom hysterical, what will that do to her?"

"I don't know," he admits. "What do you wanna do? See each other in secret until they can handle us being together?"

"No. I can't do that." My voice cracks. "Do you remember what Tonya's last words were?" *Why doesn't he love me?*

Jason's body tenses up. He lets go of me.

"Kimber told us when—"

He switches on the wall light. He looks so frustrated. He backs away from me. "You wanna know why I didn't love Tonya?" He takes a deep breath. "She was selfish. She didn't listen to a word I said. I told her a million times I did not wanna move to New York. That I had no interest in being a model or an actor. She still had this story built up in her head of the two of us together in that city pursuing *her* dreams. She was always pushing her own narrative. Always taking advantage of everyone!"

"She didn't take advantage of people!"

He looks at me like I'm naive. "The first night I hung out with her, she took advantage of both of us. She kept encouraging me to drink. I went along with it because everyone else was drinking, and I wanted to fit in. I knew I had to sober up, so I let her take me upstairs to lie down. The second I hit the mattress, she crawled on top of me and started kissing and grinding on me. I knew I should've told her to stop, but she was hot and I was drunk. As soon as it was over, she made some snide comment about you. About how you didn't have enough courage to admit how much you liked me. She said your loss was her gain."

My eyes water again. "She wouldn't say that."

"She said it. She was a selfish, obsessive alcoholic. That's why I didn't love her. Checking out of rehab and getting in Kimber's car was as selfish as sticking a gun in her mouth and pulling the trigger."

My eyes are bugging out of my head. A realization sweeps over me. "You hate her." I can't listen to him talk about my sister for another second. "I have to go." I turn around and reach for the door handle. "I shouldn't have come here tonight."

He leans his weight on the door, keeping it closed. "Wait." His arms wrap around me from behind. He clings to me. "Kira. I don't hate her. I just hate what she did."

"It doesn't matter." I push his arms away. "This is an impossible situation. Your friend Annette is right. I need to stay away from you so you can forget about me. Stop chasing me. I'm too young to be your found family." I open the door. "Now you can hate me and my sister." I open the closet and grab my jacket. I rush away.

Everyone in the living room has a stunned expression.

"Are you okay?" Mike asks.

"I will be as soon as I get the hell out of here." I grab my purse.

Mimi comes out of her room. "What's going on out here?" she asks in a groggy voice.

I look at Mimi, embarrassed. "I'm sorry." I look at my friends. "Goodnight, everyone. Liz, please, we need to go now."

I rush down the stairs.

Chapter Twenty One

Sunday, October 22, 2023

I wake up feeling miserable. I cried myself to sleep last night after I got home from the party. At least the crying made the throbbing between my legs go away for a little while. My mind knows Jason and I are done, but the rest of my body is craving him like a drug.

Why did I go to that party? I should have taken an Uber home after I dropped the cake off. Why did I hug him? Why did I kiss him back? Because he's gorgeous and I love everything about him. At least I did until he said all that awful stuff about Tonya.

I'm chilly. The fall temperature dropped overnight. I pull my covers up to my nose. It doesn't make me feel warmer. If I had stayed with Jason last night, I would have woken up in his arms. I'd be warm, comfortable, and judging by how amazing his fingers felt between my legs, totally satisfied.

The words he whispered in my ear are torturing me. *"I'll make your first time so good, Kira."* The throbbing between my legs intensifies. *"Stay with me, Kira. I'm so in love with you."* My heart flutters again.

I roll over and burrow down lower into my bedding. The water from my parents' shower is running one floor above me. They're awake. There is no way I'm relieving the tension myself right now. Every cell in my body wants Jason. I wish I hadn't stopped him. I wish I'd gotten into his bed.

And then my mother would have lost her mind worrying about me. When I got home last night, she was waiting for me in the living room when I walked in the door at 10:55. She wasn't reading a book or watching a movie. She was just sitting there, looking at the door. She looked so relieved when I got home, I thought she might cry.

There is no way I could have stayed with Jason. If I had texted Mom that I wanted to sleep at Liz's house last night, she would've called Mrs. Vasquez to make sure I was safe and sound. If I had said I was crashing at Mike's, Mom would've called Aunt Ginny. Mom would have made herself sick with worry. Then, when she found out where I really was, in bed with Tonya's ex-boyfriend, her head would have exploded.

My head hurts from crying. I sit up, put in my eye drops, and put on my dark glasses. I pick up my phone and see new messages from Jason. My heart races. My hands shake as I open them.

J: If you want me to stop resenting your sister, stop letting her drive a wedge between us. You aren't the one who is supposed to look out for your mother. It's supposed to be the other way around. She's the parent. Punishing me for loving you instead of Tonya isn't going to bring her back to life.

Monday, October 23, 2023

Another eye exam. More light shines directly into my dilated eyes. It's more uncomfortable this time. I keep closing my eyes to avoid the light. Doctor McKinley keeps reminding me to keep my eyes open.

The doctor returns with the results quickly this time. "The fluid in Kira's eyes has increased rapidly. She has entered stage three of Fuchs' dystrophy. A corneal transplant is inevitable at this point. However, given Kira's young age, I'd still like to avoid the procedure as long as possible. At this point, Kira must avoid crying and stress."

"My sister died. How am I supposed to stop crying?"

Dad takes my hand.

"Have you considered putting Kira on antidepressants?" Doctor McKinley asks.

I love that idea. The idea of a pill that can numb my emotions sounds wonderful.

Dad looks horrified. "No. I don't want my daughter overmedicated."

"Mr. Conway, I understand your concern. I wouldn't be the one to prescribe that medication. You would have to talk to her pediatrician. All I can tell you is that if your daughter doesn't stop crying so much, she could need a corneal transplant in a year to avoid losing her vision. If we can avoid this surgery until she's older, that would be the best solution for her eyes."

I touch my father's arm. "I think it's a great idea. I want to talk to my doctor about it."

Dad gives me a concerned look, but agrees to make an appointment with my pediatrician.

Tuesday, October 24, 2023

I take my first antidepressant pill this afternoon.

Wednesday, October 31, 2023

I can't bring myself to get dressed up this year. Tonya and I would always do my ghost, princess, or pirate makeup. She'd help me put wigs on. Help lace up dresses. Help me look pretty or ghoulish. Whatever I felt like being, she'd help me create the look. She wasn't a selfish bitch. Jason was wrong about her.

I'm not going to the Halloween dance with Liz and Melony. I want to forget it's a holiday. I turn on the TV. I watch *Mean Girls*. No Halloween-themed movies tonight.

Alma jumps up on the couch with me. She curls up on my lap and lies down. I pet her, but she doesn't purr the way she usually does. She stands up and meows at me. I pet her again. She is used to my cute aggression spiking when I pet her. I usually cuddle her close, kiss her head, and pet her like she is the cutest being on earth. My emotions are turned off. Like I flicked a switch and they went out like a light bulb. Maybe they're tucked away in a box and shoved into a storage unit in my brain.

She moves off my lap and goes to find another place to sleep.

I go to bed early because I want this stupid holiday to be over. My brain and body aren't torturing me with memories of Jason tonight. I think the antidepressants are wonderful.

Wednesday, November 15, 2023

My cast finally comes off. My hand still looks swollen, and the skin looks disgusting. It's so dry and flaky. My doctor gives me exercises to do and tells me to use ice packs to help the swelling go down.

Saturday, November 18, 2023

I try holding a pencil in my hand and writing my name. It's difficult, but I manage to do it.

Monday, November 20, 2023

"I talked to my lawyer today," Dad says at dinner. "The video evidence of Kira's assault, and all the witnesses who were available to testify for the prosecution, were enough to get Lawndale to plead guilty."

"Really?" I breathe a sigh of relief.

"Yes. A trial would've been a long, difficult process and most likely led to a guilty verdict. He's going to jail for three years."

"I'll drink to that," Seth says and raises his glass.

We all clink glasses.

"Also, that father of his is facing jail time for serving alcohol to minors," Dad says. "I know the Lawndale house was put on the market today. Probably to help pay the father's legal bills. It's rumored that the rest of the family is moving away."

I look at my mother. She says nothing. She cuts and chews her food like a robot.

"The Lawndales picked another realtor to sell their house. They didn't come to me. I can't imagine why." Dad cuts his steak again. "I'd never sell that property even if I had a chance. It should be bulldozed to the ground, in my opinion."

Wednesday, November 22, 2023

I bake all the desserts for Thanksgiving and a birthday cake for Mike. His birthday is November 24th. I have two special occasions to dread celebrating without my sister. I don't take the time to sift any ingredients. I don't care if everything tastes mediocre.

Thursday, November 23, 2023

Aunt Ginny helps me do all the cooking because Mom is too depressed to get out of bed. When dinner is ready, Mom comes into the living room. She brushed her hair and put her makeup on, but she still looks bedraggled. She takes a few bites of food and goes back upstairs. Dad is angry at her for not eating the meal Ginny and I spent two days preparing. Mike looks depressed that his birthday is so disappointing.

Friday, December 15, 2023

I pick up one of my drawing pencils and start sketching. It feels so good to be drawing again. I ignore the pain in my hand. I sketch out a basic face. The nose is small, and the lips are full and pursed together. I overshadow the eyebrows because my hand moves frantically. The eyes come out hooded and glassy.

It's Tonya's face, the last day I saw her alive. She's glaring at me for stealing her boyfriend.

I crumple the paper and throw it away. I should feel upset or scared, but I don't. I don't feel like drawing. I don't feel anything.

Saturday, December 16, 2023

I go to the perfume store in the North Shore Mall with an empty bottle. It's busy in here. I look around for the same perfume, but I can't find it. A salesgirl finally asks if I need help.

"Yes. Do you still carry the jasmine perfume?"

She looks at the bottle. "Yes, we have it right over here." She walks over to a shelf I missed. "Here you go." She hands it to me.

I go to the checkout. "I'm buying this for my sister."

The cashier doesn't look at me like I'm crazy for buying a Christmas gift for a dead person. Instead, she smiles and says, "I'm sure she'll love it."

I smile back. "Yeah. Jasmine is her favorite fragrance." I enter my debit card and put in my PIN.

"Do you want it gift-wrapped?"

"No, thanks. I wanna wrap it myself."

"You're a good sister." She hands me a small shopping bag with my purchase. "Merry Christmas."

Monday, December 25, 2023

I wake up early and sneak into Tonya's room with her wrapped gift. I sit on her bed and place the gift on her pillow.

Nothing happens. Am I stupid for doing this? "I guess I should open it for you." I unwrap the bottle and spray a little on her pillow. I close my eyes. "Merry Christmas, Tonya."

Merry Christmas, Kira.

"I love you. Remember when I was little and I'd come in here to sleep when I got scared?"

I remember. You'd always fall asleep fast because you felt safe in here. You were so cute when you were little.

"I love you."

I love you, too.

"I don't care what *he* thinks. I know you weren't a selfish person."

Nothing

"I haven't spoken to him in weeks. Nobody talks about my sister like that."

Still nothing.

"Tonya?"

No answer. I guess she's still not ready to talk about this.

"Kira," Seth knocks on my door. "Are you up? Your dad is ready to open gifts."

I jump off my sister's bed and head back to my bedroom.

"Hey. What were you doing in Tonya's room?"

"Giving her a Christmas gift."

He looks concerned.

"Don't worry. I'm not losing my mind. I know she's dead. I just need to feel like she's still here sometimes."

"I understand. I'm sorry if it's weird having me here this morning. I can stay in my room if you wanna open gifts with your parents."

I hug him. "No. Having you here helps. The house doesn't feel so empty."

We head downstairs to our gifts in the living room. "Merry Christmas," Dad says and forces a smile.

"Shouldn't we wait for Mom?" I ask.

"She's gonna sit this one out." Dad hands me my first present.

Saturday, January 27, 2024

I skip Melony's seventeenth birthday party. I tell her I have a cold.

Wednesday, February 28, 2024

Mom refuses to do anything for her birthday. She doesn't want a cake or any gifts. We let the day pass like any other. My mother manages not to have a meltdown today, so I guess it was worth it.

Friday, March 15, 2024

"I can't wait to see Will again," Liz gushes during lunch. "Do you think it'll be weird to see him in person again?"

He's coming this weekend for her birthday.

I nibble on my turkey sandwich.

"I'm sure you guys will have as much to talk about in person as you do over the phone," Melony says.

"I hope so," Liz says. "I've lost fifteen pounds. Do you think he'll notice?"

"You FaceTime with him every day. I'm sure he's already noticed," Melony says

Liz smiles. "So anyway, about my birthday dinner. We'll meet at Amigo's at seven."

"Can I bring Derik?" Melony asks.

"Sure," Liz says. "The more the merrier."

I sit back and let my friends gush about their boyfriends. I'm happy for them both, but I can't share in their excitement.

"Anyway, I need a final head count to call and make the reservation. It's me, Will, my mom, and both of you, Derik. Are Seth and Mike coming?" Liz asks me.

"Probably. I'll ask them again." I text them. Mike responds with a yes.

"Great, that's eight. We're gonna need a large table for eight, or possibly nine," Liz gives me a desperate look.

"Don't tell me Will is bringing his sister," I say, annoyed.

"No. He's not bringing her."

"Good," I say, relieved, and take another bite of my sandwich.

'It's just that Will doesn't feel right about coming all the way here and leaving his best friend at home on a Saturday night. Is it alright if Jason—"

"No."

"Come on. Mike, Seth, and Will are all coming. That's all of Jason's friends. I understand how Will feels. Can't you tolerate Jason for one meal?"

"No."

"Kira. It's been five months. Can't you tolerate being in the same room with the guy by now?"

"Liz. Doctor's orders. I have to stay neutral. I'm on antidepressants. Everything about the guy stresses me out. If you want, I'll stay home Saturday so your boyfriend can bring his best friend."

"That's not what I want," Liz says. "It won't feel right if you're not there. I guess I'll have to explain this whole awful situation to Will and hope he's okay leaving Jason home."

"Thank you," I say and push my lunch tray back. This conversation is ruining my appetite.

"Have the two of you really not spoken in six months?" Melony asks.

"Jason keeps tabs on me. He texts my dad to make sure my eyes are alright. I know Seth and Mike tell Jason things about me, too."

"But you haven't said anything to each other? Not even hello when passing in the hallway?" Melony asks.

"I keep my eyes down and pay attention to where I'm walking. I don't know when I pass him in the hall. If he passes me, he's nice enough to leave me alone. I can't wait until he graduates and I don't have to worry about running into him at school anymore."

"That is so extreme," Melony says. "I can't believe after that kiss he gave you, you're never gonna talk to him again. I'm waiting for someone to kiss me like that," Mel says. "Don't get me wrong, Derik isn't a bad kisser, but I've never had a kiss where my knees shake and a guy has to hold me to keep me from falling."

"Me neither. That is so hot," Liz says.

"Oh, God, guys. Don't start." I cover my face.

"Tell us the story again," Melony says. "Especially the part where he picked you up and carried you into his bedroom."

"Mel. Stop."

"Come on, humor us. That's never gonna happen to me," Liz says. "No guy is ever gonna pick me up and carry me into his bedroom. Not unless he has a forklift."

I stare her down. "What'd I tell you about that shit? Stop being mean to my friend. That is such a shitty thing to say about yourself."

"It really was an awful thing to say about yourself," Melony agrees. "But let's get back to the story. Was his room pitch black when he started kissing you again? That is so hot."

"Yeah, until he switched on the light and called my dead sister the bitch of all bitches. Is that hot too?"

My friends are finally silent.

"Can we please stop talking about him? He's going to know we're talking about him and start looking over here. Or worse, come over and say something."

"Are you kidding me? He spends every lunch glancing over here," Liz says.

"He does not. Shut up."

"Uh, yeah, he does," Melony agrees. "I bet if I look over there right now, I'll catch him looking." She turns around and looks at the table where Seth, Mike, and Jason are sitting. "Yep, he's looking."

Liz looks over there, too. "He totally is." She waves at him. "Liz, cut it out."

"Kira, I'm not gonna ignore him the way you do. I'm dating Jason's best friend. Jason is friends with your cousin and surrogate brother. His aunt is friends with your mom. He's one of us. He's not going anywhere. You need to deal with that."

I stand up and grab my backpack. "Yeah, well, I don't need to deal with that *today*." I carry my lunch tray to the garbage bin, dump the rest of my food out, and exit the cafeteria.

Saturday, March 16, 2024

I have no enthusiasm for Liz's birthday party. I can't deal with Will looking at me all night like I'm the asshole who hurt his friend. There is no way I'm going if Jason might show up. I send a group text to Liz, Mel, Mike, and Seth that my stomach hurts, and to have fun without me tonight. I wish Liz a happy birthday and tell her to stop by tomorrow so I can give her my present.

I veg out in front of the TV all night. I get a text around eleven. I figure it is Liz getting back to me about coming over tomorrow.

It's not from Liz. It's from Jason.

My heart pounds. I close my eyes and take a deep breath. *I don't care.* I lie to myself. I drop my phone and go back to the Lifetime movie I was watching. Lifetime and Hallmark movies are great at entertaining me while making me feel nothing.

What did he say? I look at my phone. *I don't care. I don't care. I don't care.* I go back to the movie, but I can't pay attention to the plot. I have to know what he said. I pick up my phone and open his message.

J: We all know ur not sick! Liz tried to have fun, but she couldn't stop wondering if u lied to her. It ruined her night. Is it easier to hurt ur BFF than be around me?

My blood is boiling. I can't remember the last time I felt this angry. Who the hell does he think he is, overpowering my antidepressants? I want to text him back and tell him that my friendship with Liz is none of his business. That nothing about my life is any of his business. That I'm not his anything. But that would mean we were officially talking again. I throw my phone down on the couch and try to go back to the movie.

Sunday, March 17, 2024

I grab my phone as soon as my eyes open. Liz hasn't gotten back to me about coming over for her birthday gift. She's not responding to any of my texts, so I'll call her as soon as I wake up.

She answers on the first ring. "Were you really sick last night?"

"Yes." My voice is too high-pitched to sound natural.

"You're lying. It's so obvious. You're a terrible liar, Kira."

I sigh. "Okay. I'm sorry." I sit back against my headboard. "I couldn't deal with seeing Jason."

"Don't blame him. You've been lying to get out of every special occasion. You told Melony you were sick on her birthday too."

She's right. I did. "I'm sorry, okay? I hate special occasions. I hate birthdays because Tonya isn't here to celebrate with us."

Liz sighs. "Kira, I feel horrible about Tonya's death. We all do. But you don't get to use it as an excuse to disappoint your friends."

I know she's right. "Okay. I'm sorry. It won't happen again. Can I come by your place today to give you your gift?"

She pauses. "No thanks. I really don't want to see you today. I'm too mad."

My jaw drops. I've never heard Liz this angry.

"I thought we were best friends," she yells

"We are."

"Really? Because I wasn't even invited to your last birthday party."

My heart sinks. She's still angry about that. I don't blame her.

"After last night, I don't know where we stand."

I'm sick to my stomach. "Liz, please don't say that."

She hangs up on me.

My head spins. I can't stand this sick feeling in the pit of my stomach. I reach for my antidepressants and take my daily pill.

Monday, March 18, 2024

I sit down with Melony and Liz at lunch. Both my friends are glaring at me as I take my seat.

"I'm sorry, you guys," I say.

"I can't believe you lied to avoid both our birthday parties," Mel yells. "That is seriously messed up."

I look down at my lunch tray. I'm like a small child being scolded. "I know. It won't happen again."

"It better not," Liz mumbles.

"I didn't do it to be mean," I explain.

"We know," Liz says. "You did it because you're grieving. Tonya has no more birthdays, so you feel weird about celebrating ours."

I look at her, surprised. It's nice to feel so understood.

"You get a free pass because of Tonya's death," Melony adds.

I smile.

"I get it. Birthdays are weird for you because you can't have them with your sister anymore," Liz says. "But they're important for us, especially now. I'm never going to have another sweet sixteen. It's something my best friend should be there for."

My smile drops. "I'm sorry."

We eat our lunch in awkward silence.

After school, I have another eye exam. Doctor McKinley says there are no visible changes to my eyes. I'm doing something right.

Saturday, April 13, 2024

I bake Seth a birthday cake. We have a small party for him at our house. He spends the entire night looking towards the window, hoping his dad is going to show up. Hoping that tonight will be the night they work out all their issues. He's supposed to go out with Mike and Jason afterward, but he's too depressed to do anything. He goes downstairs to his bed as soon as he finishes his cake.

Tuesday, May 7, 2024

Dad's birthday. I bake him a cake. I bought him a new tie. I got him a card that reads, "Best Dad in the World." We go through the motions like we're supposed to. Doing this without Tonya makes me feel like shit.

Wednesday, May 29, 2024

Seth gets dressed for his prom. He looks nice in a tux. He slips out before my mother sees him. He heads to Ginny's for prom pictures with Mike. I'm sure Mimi is taking pictures of Jason tonight, too. Everyone's getting photos of the seniors tonight. Except for my mother. She's upstairs in her room crying.

I muted all of Jason's Instagram posts so I don't have to know who his prom date is. Will he hold her close on the dance floor? Will he screw her tonight in a hotel room in Boston? *I don't give a shit. Not anymore.* I lie to myself.

I should be thinking about my sister tonight. Not the guy who drove a wedge between us before she died. I spray the jasmine perfume and sit on Tonya's bed. I close my eyes and imagine her in a pink prom dress. Her hair is all done up in a French twist. A pink corsage on her wrist.

"You look beautiful," I whisper and shed a tear for the first time in months.

I'm getting into bed when my phone buzzes with a new text. I sigh. Nobody ever texts me this late at night except for Jason.

J: My senior prom sucked. Tried to have fun with my date, but I couldn't. I was with the wrong girl.

I lower my phone and sigh. He's still not over me.

Friday, May 31, 2024

Mike, Seth, and Jason graduate from high school today. My dad goes to the ceremony. Mom and I can't bring ourselves to go. I stay home with Mom.

Wednesday, July 10, 2024

"What do you wanna do for your birthday this year?" Dad asks me at dinner.

I think back to my birthday last year. Tonya helping me get ready in the bathroom. Meeting Jason. Falling into his arms. If we'd never met him, would Tonya still be alive? Would her drinking have gotten out of control? Would she still have gone to rehab? Would our lives be totally different now? There's no way to ever know.

"Nothing," I tell him. The idea of asking my friends to celebrate my birthday after I bailed on theirs makes me feel guilty.

"Come on, seventeen is a big deal."

"Seventeen isn't a big deal. Sweet sixteen is a big deal. Eighteen is a big deal because you're an adult. Seventeen is meaningless."

"No birthday is meaningless. Why don't we go back to the museum? You liked that so much last year."

I look at him like he's insane. "Dad, the last thing I wanna do is repeat what I did last year."

"Fine, we can do something else."

"Why don't we have a small party here?" Seth suggests.

"Oh, my god. I cooked a feast for you on Thanksgiving. I wrapped and opened gifts on Christmas. I baked all of your birthday cakes. Except for Mom, because she's smart enough to realize that celebrating all these stupid fucking days without Tonya feels like shit! When the stupid holidays ended, I felt like I finished fighting a war. All I wanna do is pretend my birthday is a normal fucking day so I don't have to feel like shit all day that my sister's dead."

I get up from the table, go to my room, and slam the door. I open Facebook and remove my birthday from my profile so nobody sends me any messages this year.

Dad comes up to my room and knocks.

I open the door.

He looks furious. "Everyone in this family is going to a grief counselor."

Friday, July 12, 2024

"So, how have you been doing, Kira?" my therapist asks. She sits with a notebook on her lap, ready to write down anything I say.

"I'm doing the best I can."

"Why do you think your father encouraged you to come here?"

"I don't wanna celebrate my birthday without my sister."

"That's understandable. Special days often magnify feelings of loss. How were the holidays for your family?"

"Awful. We did everything to try and feel normal, and I still felt terrible. I wish everyone would forget about all special occasions for the rest of my life."

"Did you ever experience these feelings of dread regarding social situations before your sister died?"

"Yes." I explain about my bad vision. How I always feel like I'm going to bump into something and make a fool of myself. How I only go to social events if I know everyone there and am familiar with the place. "The Lawndale house always seemed terrifying because of all the drinking."

"What about school dances? Do you ever attend those?"

"No."

"Why not? Nobody drinks at those events. Adults always supervise. Aren't they held at the school?"

"Yes."

"Isn't that a familiar place?" the therapist asks.

"Yes"

"Yet you choose not to go. What's scary about a dance?"

"I hate large gatherings. They make me panic."

"What's the worst thing that could happen at a dance?"

"I could trip over something. I could bump into someone and spill punch all over us both. A million bad things could happen because of my bad vision."

"If your eyes were better, would that make your social anxiety go away?"

"I don't know. Maybe. Probably."

"Kira, if you don't mind, I'd like to spend the rest of our time together giving you an assessment to help me properly diagnose you." She opens her laptop and reads me a series of statements.

I feel overwhelmed by my emotions. Strongly agree. I have physical symptoms of anxiety, such as sweaty palms. Strongly agree. When I experience a strong emotion, I usually know why it's hitting me. Agree. I get upset or angry easily. Agree.

When the assessment is over, she closes her computer and says to me, "You mentioned your friend Liz earlier. You mentioned missing her birthday recently. How do you think Liz would feel about never celebrating a special occasion with you again?"

"Terrible."

"Do you think your friendship with her will survive if you never celebrate anything with her again?"

I sigh. "No."

"How would you feel if you and Liz were no longer friends?"

"Way worse."

"Do you think it would be possible to find friends who wanted to let all special occasions pass them by?"

"No."

"If you never celebrate again, what do you think your life will be like?"

"Lonely."

"Then perhaps we should find a way for you to cope with the loss of your sister so you can be there for others again."

"Fine," I sigh.

Saturday, July 13, 2024

I go to a sleepover at Melony's house. We sit around Melony's desk painting our nails. My friends gush about their boyfriends.

"Derik's make-out skills have gotten better," Melony says. "He used to use way too much tongue, but now he uses the correct amount."

I sit silently painting my nails with a base coat.

Liz giggles. "Will has always been a great kisser. He didn't try and French me until the time was right. When the kiss built to the right moment, you know?"

"That's what I'm saying," Melony says. "You don't stick your tongue in someone's mouth as soon as the kiss starts like this." She rams the brush into her pink polish and rotates it round and round while making kissing sounds.

Liz laughs.

I don't find it funny. "Can you pass the purple polish?"

Liz slides the bottle over to me and goes back to her conversation with Melony.

I paint my nails in silence. I wish I'd stayed home.

Monday, July 29, 2024

Mike and Aunt Ginny come over for dinner. We sit around the dining room table eating spaghetti. My mom and dad sit at opposite ends of the table, not talking to each other.

"I mean, who needs to graduate with one hundred thousand dollars of debt?" Mike asks. "That's why we all applied to online colleges. Why pay all that money to sleep in crappy dorms and eat awful cafeteria food?"

"It might take Mike, Jason, and me forever to graduate, but at least we won't have a buttload of debt," Seth says.

"I think it's a great idea," Dad says. "Do you have any idea what you're going to major in?"

"We're both gonna major in marketing." Mike looks at Seth. "You tell them. It was your idea."

"Mike and I wanna open our own comedy club," Seth says. "The Northshore doesn't have one. If you want to see live stand-up, you have to go to Boston."

"That's a great idea," Dad says, smiling. "I'll be there every weekend."

"Jason's taking classes online, too." Mike changes the subject. "He's majoring in creative writing."

I look down at my plate and twirl my spaghetti.

"The great thing about taking online classes is that you can attend from anywhere. Jason has decided to visit his mother's relatives in Ireland. His grandmother gave him the money for the ticket. He's gonna go for an extended period of time. Maybe get a job there."

The acid in my stomach churns. I lower my fork. I can't take another bite of this food. I look up and see Mike staring at me, looking for a reaction.

"He might stay there for a few years. You can do that and still take classes online in the US. His mother's family is really excited to get to know him." Mike raises his eyebrows at me.

"Good for him." I look back down at my food.

"I have some big news," Aunt Ginny announces.

We all look at her. I'm grateful for the change in subject.

"I'm getting married." Ginny holds up her hand, displaying her engagement ring.

Am I hallucinating? What the fuck?

"What?" Mom frowns.

"I'm getting married." Ginny squeals.

Mom and Dad exchange shocked glances.

"I didn't even know you had a boyfriend," I say.

"We've been seeing each other for six months," Ginny explains. "We met at a bereavement support group eight months ago. After two months of flirting, he finally asked me out. And now, *I'm getting married*."

"Ginny, don't you think you're rushing into things?" Mom asks.

"Relax, the wedding won't be until next summer. At that point, we'll have been together for a year and a half."

"Who is he and what's he like?" I ask before my mother can come up with another snarky comment.

"His name is Rick. He's a lawyer. He's brilliant and sweet. He has a seven-year-old daughter named Lily. He lost his wife to cancer two years ago."

"How come we've never met him?" Dad asks.

"This isn't another online romance, is it?" Mom asks. "You've met him in person, right?" Ginny's last two relationships started online with people who lived out of state.

"Yes, Cindy. I met him *in person at a bereavement group eight months ago*," Ginny repeats slowly, like my mother is an idiot. "Mike's met him several times."

"He's a great guy," Mike says. "His daughter Lily is adorable."

"Lily loves Mike," Ginny says. "She's so excited to be getting a brother." Ginny turns to me. "Lily can't wait to meet you, Kira. She's already told her friends all about her cool older cousin."

"Okay," I say flatly. This all seems ridiculous to me.

"The only reason you haven't met him yet is because I wanted to be sure it was serious." She looks at her diamond ring. "It's serious. You can all meet him at our engagement party next Saturday. That's why we came over for dinner tonight. To tell you to cancel any plans. I will see you all on Saturday."

"Where are you all planning to live?" Mom asks. "Your apartment?"

"Do you need a hearing aid? Rick is a successful lawyer. Lawyer." She repeats slowly. "He makes great money. Mike and I will be moving into his house soon. He has a furnished basement for Mike to live in during college."

"I still think it sounds like you're rushing into things way too fast," Mom says.

Ginny sighs. "Can't you be happy for me? I knew you'd find a way to ruin my good mood."

"I'm just saying…" Mom rambles on and on about how Ginny's moving too fast.

"Excuse me, I need more Parmesan cheese," Dad lies. There is a container of it right in front of him. He picks up his plate and goes into the kitchen.

I lean over and whisper to Mike, "Is this really happening?"

"Yes, Jason's really going to Ireland."

I roll my eyes. "Not that. Is this guy your mom's engaged to as great as she says?"

"You always do this," Mom complains to Ginny. "You meet someone and cast them in a role in your life like you're casting a movie."

"Always, always, always! Cindy's favorite word," Ginny complains. "Nobody can change because they are *always* going to be the way Cindy perceives them. You're the most closed-minded person in the world!"

"Yeah, Rick is awesome," Mike says to me. "But I doubt they'll actually get married. Grandpa will ruin this relationship for my mom, like he ruined all her last ones. Everyone in this family is great at fucking up potentially great relationships." He glares at me.

"Shut up," I say.

"You know, when I invited Jason to join us on your birthday, I wasn't planning on introducing him to Tonya," Mike says.

I look at him shocked.

"I knew he was perfect for you the first day we met him," Seth adds. "We all know you're in love with him."

I blush. "I am not."

Mike crosses his arms. "You're so full of shit. You have no self-esteem. Grandpa fucked you up, like he fucked the rest of us up. Get some confidence before Jason moves away, falls in love with an Irish girl, and stays in Ireland forever."

I push my chair back and stand up. "I've lost my appetite."

"Whatever. Stay in therapy." Mike stands up, too. "Sort out your grandpa trauma before you get old and bitter like these two morons!" He yells while glaring at our mothers.

They stop fighting and look at Mike.

"What the hell does that mean?" Aunt Ginny asks, offended.

I go up to my room. I've had enough of all of them.

Friday, August 9, 2024

Dad and I walk back to the therapist's office for my weekly visit. "Hello, Mr. Conway. Please have a seat," my therapist says.

Dad and I both sit in the plush chairs in the room.

"I've made a diagnosis based on my time with Kira and the test I administered. I believe that Kira is suffering from post-traumatic stress disorder. I believe that to be the cause of Kira's social anxiety. A stressful life event, such as being attacked by a bully or losing a sibling, may lead to an increase in trauma-related mental health symptoms."

"The bully attack and her sister's death were the traumatic events," Dad says.

The therapist takes a deep breath. "Sir, Kira has struggled with social anxiety disorder for years. She has panic attacks in social settings. Unfamiliar people are terrifying to your daughter."

"That's not true. Kira has a good group of friends she sticks with, but she isn't awkward around strangers," Dad says.

"Does your daughter attend school dances or other social events?"

"No, but that's because she's introverted."

"Sir, at her sister's eighteenth birthday party, Kira spent most of her time doing tasks like emptying garbage cans and refilling snacks to avoid socializing. Kira didn't socialize until friends she's known for years showed up. New people scare her."

Dad looks at me. "Is this true?"

"Yes," I admit.

Dad leans back in his chair. "I'm so sorry. I had no idea how bad things have been for you." He looks back at the therapist. "Why is Kira like this?"

"Lots of things can cause childhood PTSD. Car accidents or train wrecks, animal bites, natural disasters, such as floods or earthquakes. Did Kira experience anything like that before the age of six?"

"No, nothing like that," Dad insists.

"Given Kira's irrational fear of people being judgmental or hurtful towards her, it's likely her anxiety stems from a hurtful person. Unfamiliar people, even peers her own age, seem to provoke an irrational fear in Kira. Was she exposed to a person who may have been verbally or emotionally abusive?"

"No," Dad insists. Then his eyes widen like he's remembering something awful. "Oh, I guess there were a few awful incidents with my wife's father. He's a horrible, malignant narcissist, but Kira hasn't seen him in years. We became estranged from him when Kira was five."

"So, then it's possible and highly likely that Kira experienced trauma before the age of six," the therapist repeats.

Dad looks at me with the guiltiest expression on his face.

"I can't remember any of it." I hope that will make him feel better.

Dad asks for a copy of the therapist's report to show Mom.

Saturday, August 10, 2024

"Kira, wake up."

I was in a deep slumber. My body refuses to move. All I can do is give an annoyed grumble.

"Kira," Mike whispers again. "Come on. Wake up."

My eyes open. It's still dark outside. Why the hell is he waking me up in the middle of the night? "What's wrong?" I ask, concerned. I assume it must be an emergency.

"Nothing's wrong. I just need you to come somewhere with me."

"In the middle of the night? No. I'm going back to sleep." I roll over and close my eyes. "If you wake me before sunrise again, it better be because someone we love is dead or dying."

"It has to be now. It has to be this early."

"What time is it?"

"Five."

"Are you nuts? Nothing is open this early."

"Exactly. I need you to get up, Kira."

"Why? Where are we going?"

"I dare you to get out of bed and see. Come on."

I look at him like he's insane. "How are you so wide awake?"

"I haven't gone to sleep yet," he explains. He was spending the night in our basement with Seth. My parents and aunt don't care what the boys do together because Mike and Seth can't get each other pregnant. The boys are also both legally adults, so my basement has become their love nest.

"Your boyfriend invited you to spend the night with him, and you stayed up all night long. Are you nuts?"

"Probably, now come on. It's important." He takes my hand and pulls me out of bed. "It will only take about an hour. Then we can both come back and sleep. You don't even have to get dressed. Stay in your jammies."

"Fine," I reach for my glasses. "But if I'm a grump at your mom's engagement party later, it is your fault."

"I have a feeling everyone is going to be a grump at my mom's engagement party."

I leave my pajama pants and top on. I'm too tired to change them. I put on my sneakers and jacket.

We head out the front door and get in his car. Mike turns on the engine.

"Where the hell are we going?" I yawn.

"Oh, I'm sorry. Is it annoying when a family member forces you to go somewhere and doesn't tell you where the hell you're going?" he teases. "I can't imagine how annoying that would be."

I cross my arms and look out the window. I'm too tired to deliver a smart-ass comeback.

Mike drives us to Waterside Cemetery in Marblehead. My stomach knots up. I haven't been here since the funeral. "What the hell are we doing here, Mike?"

"You'll see." He parks his car on the street, turns off the engine, and gets out of the car. He goes to his trunk and takes out a box.

The gates are closed because they don't open until 7:30 in the morning. Mike helps me get over the small stone fence surrounding the cemetery. It's a quarter to six. The sun is starting to rise. It looks like it is going to be a rainy day.

We walk to Tonya's grave in silence. I hesitate when we get close. I don't want to see her burial site again.

Mike turns around and looks at me. He sees my sad expression. He tucks the small box under his left arm and takes my hand in his. I'm like a small child clinging to someone's hand for comfort.

We stand over Tonya's grave. My parents and I picked out a tombstone with engraved flowers surrounding her name. Tonya

227

Elizabeth Conway. Beloved Daughter and Sister. August 18, 2005, to September 16, 2023.

Mike puts the box on the ground and opens it. He picks up a water balloon in his right hand. He looks at the tombstone. "I am so fucking pissed at you, Tonya!"

I look at my cousin like he is crazy.

"Jason's right," Mike says. "Checking out of rehab and getting in that car with Kimber was as selfish as putting a gun in your mouth and pulling the trigger. Your drinking turned you into a self-absorbed bitch!" He throws the water balloon at the grave. It bursts into a million pieces and splatters all over her name.

"Jesus Christ, Mike! Is this really necessary?" I'm horrified.

"Oh, I think it is." Mike picks up another balloon and looks back at the grave. "I think my mom is stupid enough to invite Grandpa to the engagement party. I hate the bastard. Who the fuck am I supposed to talk to about this now? Kira doesn't remember him. Thanks for leaving me all alone to deal with this shit without you!" He throws a second balloon.

I think I'm going to be sick to my stomach. "Mike, what the hell are you doing?"

He turns towards me and takes me by the shoulders. "Getting you fucking mad! It's about damn time. You brought me to Kimber because I was furious and needed to release it. You're the opposite. You're numb. Get fucking mad, Kira!"

"I'm not mad at Tonya. I'm just sad she died." My eyes water.

"Bullshit!" He picks up another balloon and looks at the grave. "We are all pissed off at you, Tonya. Your mother is a zombie. Your dad is a workaholic. My mom lost all her faith. And why? Because you loved alcohol more than all of us. Have another fucking drink, Tonya!" He throws another balloon.

I notice the smell. It's the same smell that came out of Tonya's thermos. These are filled with more than water.

Mike turns me towards her grave. "Tell her how pissed off you are."

I can't say anything. I'm crying too hard.

"She fucking left you, Kira! Tell her how fucked up that is!"

I take a deep breath. "I'm mad at her for messing up all our special occasions," I whisper.

"Don't tell me. Tell her." Mike motions towards the grave.

I look at the tombstone. "I'm mad at you for messing up all our special occasions." It feels good to say it. Like a weight is lifted. "Nothing is fun anymore. It's your fault. Thanksgiving and Christmas suck now."

"Good. What else?"

"I'm mad at you for fucking up Mom and Dad's marriage. I have to worry every day that your death will split them apart. They're totally different people now. I want my parents back."

"What else?" Mike puts a balloon in my hand.

"I hate you for leaving me." My fingers tighten around the balloon so hard it's about to pop in my hand. "How the hell am I supposed to get through high school without you? I hate that you won't be there when I get married. When I have kids. I fucking hate you for that, Tonya." I throw the balloon as hard as I can. It splatters on the tombstone.

"Have another drink, Tonya!" Mike throws another. "Fuck another guy. Do whatever feels good in the moment so you don't have to stop and think about how fucked up your life is!"

I pick up another. "I hate you for sleeping with Jason. You were like a fucking spider, tangling him in your web." I toss it. This one misses. That pisses me off. I pick up another. "I hate that you fucked him." This one hits. Vodka explodes everywhere. "You knew how much we liked each other, and you fucked him to feed your ego." I pick up the last three. "Because you were a shallow," it hits, "selfish," it hits again, "bitch!" The final balloon explodes on her tombstone.

Mike turns me to face him. A sob escapes my lips. We cling to each other. "Kira, it's okay for you to be mad at her. You can be mad at her and still love her and miss her at the same time. Okay?"

I can't talk. I'm crying too hard. I nod my head yes.

"I love her, miss her, and feel angry at her at the same time, too." He hugs me tighter. We stand still for a while, hugging and crying. Finally, Mike says, "I want you to go off the antidepressants. They are blocking you from feeling anything. You can't go through life feeling nothing."

"What about my eyes?"

He sighs. "It's been almost a year since Tonya died. Everyone says the first year is the hardest. I have a feeling that after tonight, you'll need to cry less." He pulls a tissue out of his pocket and hands it to me.

I wipe my eyes and blow my nose.

"I researched your eye disease," Mike says. "I think it's amazing that doctors have a cure for your disease. A lot of people go blind, and doctors can do nothing to help them. Think about all the people who can't walk after accidents because doctors don't yet have the means to heal their spines. You are so lucky, Kira."

I never really thought about it that way. "Yeah, I guess you're right."

He smiles. "Let's go home." He goes over to Tonya's tombstone and cleans up all the balloon fragments. Then he picks up a small bundle of flowers from the bottom of the box and sets them on her grave. "We still love you, Tonya. We're pissed off, but we still love you."

We walk back to the car in silence. We hop back over the low stone fence.

"Where did you get the vodka?" I ask when we get close to the car.

"Your parents' freezer," Mike says. "Don't worry. They won't miss it. I only used a tiny amount in each balloon and then filled the rest with water." He puts the box full of popped balloon fragments in the back seat and gets into the car.

I slide into the passenger seat and lean my head back. I'm exhausted.

"That first night, when Jason came to the party with us, I saw Tonya lead him upstairs, and I knew it was going to be a disaster," Mike says.

I turn and look at him, surprised.

"I knew you and Jason were such a good match. Tonya and Jason were totally wrong for each other. Although to be fair, I don't think Tonya would have been right with anyone until she got sober."

"Yeah," I agree.

He starts the car engine and turns off the radio. He sighs and then looks at me with so much guilt on his face. "I saw Tonya experiment with more than alcohol at those parties, Kira."

I look at him shocked.

"I saw her take whatever prescription drugs the kids brought to the party. I saw her do a line of coke, once. She would've done more if she'd had the chance. I was so mad at myself for not doing anything. I should have told your parents sooner." His eyes are watering. "I tried to put all the blame on Kimber to hide how much I hated myself."

I lean over and pull my cousin into a hug. "It wasn't your fault, Mike."

He hugs me tightly. "I know. She was an addict, Kira. She would do anything or anyone that felt good in the moment. She'd get obsessed with guys for short periods and then quickly move on to the next obsession. You and Jason didn't do anything to end her life."

My eyes water. I let go of him and open the center compartment for another tissue.

"You forgave Kimber, but you're punishing yourself by giving up on everything important to you." Mike turns my face towards him, so our eyes meet. "Go back to art class. Tell Jason you're in love with him and ask him to stay."

My jaw drops. "No way. I can't do that." I fidget with my seat belt. "He has a chance to be with his mother's family in Ireland. I won't ask him to give that up and stay here with me."

Mike puts his belt on. "Why not?"

"Because I want him to be happy."

"Because you love him."

I don't answer. I have too many mixed emotions to know how I feel about anything.

"Whatever you decide, do it fast." Mike pulls the car out onto the road. "Last I checked, Jason was searching for flights. He might even skip the engagement party tonight and go to the airport."

I turn and look out the window. We drive home in silence. All I want to do is sleep. I'm going to sleep until noon. If I can.

My mom wakes me up at eleven thirty to tell me that Ginny dropped off a dress and a pair of heels for me to wear to the party tonight.

I grumble and reach for my glasses. I put them on to see my mother standing over my bed holding a gift bag.

"Apparently, Ginny wants all her bridesmaids dressed alike at the engagement party for the photos." Mom pulls out a purple chiffon cocktail dress and matching purple heels. "It's a bit skimpy."

"Skimpy. I've never worn a dress that short before. And those heels. I've never walked in heels that high before."

"If you don't feel comfortable wearing it after you try it on, you don't have to wear it," Mom insists. "I'll tell Ginny and deal with the fallout. I'm sure it will be one of many things we'll end up fighting about tonight."

I roll out of bed at noon. I reach for my antidepressants. I usually take one as soon as I wake up. Today is going to be a huge pain in the ass. I really need these pills. Then I remember that Mike asked me to consider going off of them. *I'll go off of them tomorrow. I'm going to need all the help I can get to get through this party.*

I open the lid and drop one into my hand. Then I remember what Mike said about Tonya. How she'd do anything and anyone for a short-term high. I don't want to be like her. I don't want to have to take a drug to get through the day. I put the pill back in the jar and stand up to get ready for this party.

Chapter Twenty Two

Saturday, August 10, 2024

Aunt Ginny's engagement party is in a banquet hall at a local restaurant in Salem. There are about sixty people here, and most of them are Rick's family and friends. My parents and I haven't been introduced to the guy yet. Ginny has avoided my mom the whole night. She assigned us to a table in the far corner, away from the happy couple. Mike and Seth are seated with Ginny, her fiancé Rick, and his little girl Lily. I have nobody my age to talk to.

"I can't believe I was the last to know," my mother complains and sips on her white wine. "Ginny and Rick sent out invitations to his friends and family members weeks ago. All of Ginny's friends got invitations weeks ago, too."

"Maybe Ginny invited us last because she didn't want to listen to your disapproving remarks," Dad says. "That's why we're sitting in Siberia right now."

Mom looks at him, offended.

"I'm just saying, you can be really judgmental about your sister," Dad says.

"Because she's immature and irresponsible." Mom gulps down the last of the wine in her glass.

I sigh and look at my phone. Thirty minutes down. Three and a half hours to go.

"I agree with Mom. This whole situation is ridiculous." I nibble on my dinner. "I can't believe I had to wear this stupid dress to match the bridal party. If I'd known I was going to be seated this far away from everyone, I would have worn something comfortable," I complain, poking my food with my fork.

I have a knot in my stomach because I don't know if Jason is here tonight or already across the Atlantic Ocean. I didn't see him when we came in. I didn't see him in the buffet line when I was getting my food. I should feel relieved if he's gone, but it makes me feel sad. I'm thinking maybe not taking that antidepressant this morning was a mistake.

"Mimi," Dad calls out and waves her over. I think he wants another adult to talk to so he and Mom won't have another argument.

She comes closer to the table. I slouch down in my chair. I haven't seen her since Jason's birthday. I don't know how much of the fight she heard. I only know that she woke up to the sound of me yelling at her nephew.

"How have you been?" Dad asks.

"Sad. My baby is about to fly the coop," Mimi says.

"Right. Mike told us Jason's leaving for Ireland. How exciting for him," Dad says.

I suck down my soda to help settle my stomach.

"He's all packed up and ready to cross the pond," Mimi says. "It makes me so sad. Although I'm glad he'll finally get a chance to get to know his mother's family."

He's all packed up. Does that mean he came here tonight, or is he home taking care of last-minute details?

"How long will he be gone for?" Mom asks.

"I don't know," Mimi says. "He's young and going off for an adventure." She looks at me for a reaction. "Hi, sweetie." She pats my shoulder.

"Hello." I try to keep my face as blank as possible.

"I haven't seen you around since Jason's birthday." It's an obvious attempt to ask what happened between us.

"Sorry about that. Excuse me." I get up to get another drink.

My anxiety spikes. There are a ton of blurry people between our table and the bar. I do what my therapist told me to do when my social anxiety acts up. I remind myself of all the ways I am safe.

Most people on the planet are good people. I look around the room at all the blurry people moving about. *Everyone here tonight is probably a good person.* That is a hard thing to force myself to believe when I can't see far enough to get a read on anyone's expressions.

I imagine happy smiling faces. *I look really pretty tonight.* I adjust the spaghetti strap on my purple cocktail dress, making sure it stays up. I have my contacts in, and my hair and makeup look great. *Nobody is going to judge me for looking or acting like a freak.* I look down at my feet and pray I don't trip on anything on the way to get a soda.

I wait in line at the bar. A loud, drunk woman almost backs up into me. I side-step to avoid her. "My younger brother already beat me to the altar. Now he's about to tie the knot again, and I'm still single," she complains.

I take it she's Rick's sister. She's so drunk she doesn't even notice she almost spilled her wine on me. "I swear, I'm gonna screw somebody tonight. I don't care who. Anybody."

I roll my eyes and pray I'm never this desperate.

"Did you see that stunning guy?" her friend asks. "The one with the green eyes and the face chiseled by Michelangelo?"

My heart races. Jason's here tonight.

"You should go for him," the friend says.

"I'd love to. You know what they say," Rick's sister says, "if they're young enough to have come out, they're welcome to cum in."

The two drunk women giggle like idiots.

Listening to them objectify him makes me sick. "His name is Jason," I say loud enough to interrupt them. "And he has way too much depth to sleep with one of you shallow drunks."

Rick's sister's smile drops.

I move to another part of the bar. The DJ switches the music from slow elevator music to a loud hip hop song, I don't know. I take it dinner is over, and it's time to party.

I take a deep breath and try not to let myself feel overstimulated from the sound. *I'm safe. My dad is here. I know where the exits are. I can call an Uber and leave whenever I want to. If I need a breather from all the noise, I know where to go.* My family arrived early. I walked around the building until I found a small, single bathroom one floor down. It's the perfect place to hide.

I finally get the bartender's attention. He gives me a soda, and I move through a crowd of people back to my table. It's

235

empty. I have no idea where my parents went. At least my table is so far away from the speakers that I can hear myself think.

Seth walks up to me. "My dad came." He looks really shaken up. They haven't spoken face-to-face since his father kicked him out.

"Really?" I ask, surprised.

"He's over there talking to Mimi," Seth says and motions in their direction.

"Well, that's a good thing that he's here. Maybe you guys can finally patch things up."

"I hope so, but I doubt it. He hasn't spoken a word to me or Mike in months. He's probably going to tell me how unnatural I am again." Seth looks terrified.

"It'll be okay."

"Can you go over there and hear what he's saying to Mimi?"

"Seth, I'm avoiding Mimi. I get the feeling she wants to talk to me about Jason. I don't want…"

"Please. Just go over and listen to what they are talking about. Tell me if he seems like he's in a chill mood. If he's had a few drinks and he's relaxed, maybe I'll approach him. If he's tense, we'll have another argument."

He looks so stressed out, I can't say no. "Fine, but if Mimi tries to talk about Jason, I'm getting the hell out of there." I pull my phone out of my clutch and step in their direction. I pretend to be interested in something on my screen as I listen to what they are saying.

"So, you're a nurse?" Seth's dad asks.

"Yes," Mimi says.

"Good for you, that's a really important job." He sounds nervous.

"Thanks." Mimi sips her drink.

"So, do you like to dance? I don't usually, uh, dance, but you know what they say. When in Rome, act like the Romans. When at a party, dance." He sounds like a schoolboy crushing on a classmate.

I cringe with the worst secondhand embarrassment.

"Sergeant Karlson, do you know how many sick children I help treat?"

He looks taken aback by her question. "I imagine it must be a lot, you being a nurse and all. Like I said, you have a really important job."

"I've helped dozens of sick kids over the years. Kids with cancer. Kids with cystic fibrosis. Most of them won't make it to their twenty-fifth birthday."

"That's terrible."

"I've seen a lot of parents sick with grief when they lost their children. It's one of the most painful experiences a person can have. Losing a child."

"Well, yes. I imagine it would be."

"Doug and Cindy have been in absolute hell this year. They would give anything for one more second with Tonya."

"Yes, I imagine they would."

"Your son is right over there," Mimi points at Seth. "He's perfectly healthy. He's a great kid, and you threw him away like a piece of garbage."

I can't pretend to look at my phone anymore. I'm staring at them.

"So no, Sergeant Karlson. I don't want to dance with you tonight. Ask me again after you grow up and learn how to act like a father." She walks away from him.

My jaw drops. Mimi is so badass. I put my phone away and walk back to Seth.

"Well?" he asks.

"Mimi told him off for abandoning you. He asked her if she wanted to dance, and she shot him down."

"Oh." Seth's shoulders drop. "He's gonna be in an awful mood. I should probably avoid him tonight."

Jason's nearby. I don't know how, but I can sense it. I look up and see Mike and Jason's familiar blurry outlines walking towards me.

"Kira's right there," Jason tells someone. He points in my direction. I feel his eyes on me, checking me out in this skimpy dress. His eyes travel up my legs and land on my pushed-up and padded B cups. I wish I was in an overcoat or a muumuu.

"Kira." A sweet little voice cries out my name. A little girl comes up to me and wraps her arms around my waist.

"Kira, this is Lily," Mike says. "She's been dying to meet you."

I look down. "Hi." All I want to do is run away, but I can't because I'm being held in place by an adorable anchor. I look down and see two big blue eyes looking up at me.

"Hi, I'm Lily. You're even prettier than they all said."

"Thank you," I say awkwardly.

"Agreed, you look stunning tonight," Jason says. He sounds annoyed. Like, he resents me for looking good when he can't have me.

My eyes travel up to him for a split second. He looks gorgeous in his black suit and green button-down. His woody-herbal scent brings back memories of his fingers and lips on me. "Thanks," I say, sounding way too breathy. *Don't look at him.*

My eyes drop back down to Lily. She's in a purple dress, the exact same shade as mine.

"Are we gonna be cousins?" She looks so happy and excited.

This whole situation is ridiculous. Aunt Ginny still hasn't bothered to introduce me or my parents to her fiancé. "I guess so. I don't know," is all I can think to say. "I mean, we'll have to see if they actually make it to the wedding."

"Kira!" Mike frowns at me.

Lily looks confused. "Why wouldn't they make it?" She lets go of me and backs up.

Everyone's looking at me like I'm an asshole. I need to get the hell out of here. "Would you excuse me, Lily? I have to go to the bathroom." I walk towards the stairs.

"The bathrooms are over there," Seth points at the communal bathroom.

I ignore him and take the stairs one floor down. Someone is following me. It's probably Mike coming to yell at me for being rude to Lily. I'll deal with him later. I rush inside the single bathroom and lock the door behind me.

This damn engagement party is a nightmare. Everyone here is miserable. Everyone but Aunt Ginny. She's strutting around like a proud peacock, showing everyone her engagement ring.

I pull my phone out of my clutch. I lean back against the wall and play a few games of solitaire as I make a strategic plan for the rest of the night.

I'll go back upstairs and get my jacket from the coat check. Then I won't feel so exposed when Jason looks at me. I'll avoid him for the rest of the night. I'll find an old lady to sit with. Rick must have a grandmother or great-grandmother. Old ladies love to chat endlessly. I'll look preoccupied, instead of antisocial.

I'll wait until Ginny works up the courage to finally introduce Rick to my mom. I'll greet him with a forced smile. I'll apologize to Lily for being rude. I'll smile for the stupid wedding party photos. Then I'll take an Uber home. If I can somehow avoid bumping into Jason again, the rest of this night should be drama-free.

I put my phone back in my purse, take a deep breath, and prepare to go back to this stupid party. I open the door.

Jason's eyes are glaring at me. He's blocking the doorway. "It's good to know I'm not the only person you're pushing away. Lily's only seven. That was so rude. What the hell is wrong with you?"

I frown at him. "Did you wait out here the entire time I was in the bathroom just to tell me that?"

"Did you stay in the bathroom forever just to avoid me? Don't change the subject. She's seven, and what you did was messed up."

"I did Lily a favor." I have to squeeze past Jason to get into the hall. "My aunt isn't gonna marry her dad! Ginny's relationships never last. She's already married to her own father." I try to walk away.

He steps in front of me and takes me by the shoulders. "You're so bitter." He looks into my eyes. "What the hell happened to you? It's like you're a totally different person?"

I refuse to react to his close proximity, the warmth radiating off of him, or the feeling of his warm hands on my shoulders. I push his hands away. "Maybe you just never knew me that well."

His eyes darken. That hit a nerve. "Bullshit. It's the fucking antidepressants you're on. They're making you apathetic."

"How the hell do you know what medication I'm taking?"

He inhales sharply and looks down. He knows he's said too much.

"Why the hell are you using my cousin and Seth to get information about me?"

"I didn't use them. They tell me things because they're worried about you. We all are. You dropped out of art class. You're not working on your portfolio. You never leave the house. Not even for your friend's birthdays. You and your mom have become shut-ins. As long as you're trapped in the house with her, she doesn't have to worry about you dying out in the big, scary world. You're sleepwalking through life, Kira."

I hate that he's right. I hate that he has such a bad opinion of me. I look away from him. "None of that is any of your business," I say, trying to hold onto a shred of dignity. "You don't need to worry about me, I'm not your anything. Don't you have a plane to catch?" I storm off.

He follows me. I can't outrun him in these heels. His arms slide around my waist. He pulls me back against his chest.

"What are you doing?"

"Waking you the hell up." He hugs me close.

"Are you insane?"

"Are you alive?" he whispers in my ear.

"Why are you doing this?"

"Why aren't you pushing me off of you?"

Because I've missed him. His arms feel so good around me. I sink into his embrace. I feel his breath on the back of my neck.

"Your hair still smells of lavender," he whispers in my ear.

Heat rushes to my face. "I told you to forget about me."

"I haven't been trying to forget you for all these months. I've been giving you time to sort out your trauma."

"You're leaving." I close my eyes and savor the feeling of his arms around me.

"Ask me to stay."

"What? I can't do that."

The feeling of his hand sliding from my waist to my hips brings back memories of being in his bedroom, leaning back against his door as his fingers explored my skin.

His fingers find the hem of my dress. "You're in love with me, Kira. You always have been." He slides his hand up my inner thigh.

"Jesus Christ, Jason." My whole body trembles.

"We both know I'm gonna be your first." His fingertip moves over my panties to my clit.

I gasp.

He keeps his hand still. "This is where we left off. Have you missed my hands on you?"

I whimper and drop my head back against him.

"I'll take that as a yes. Ask me to stay. If I leave, this throbbing between your legs will ache for years." He kisses the side of my neck. "Come home with me tonight."

"What?" My legs shake.

"Come home," a soft kiss on my neck. "with me," on the back of my ear, "tonight. I'll undress you, lay you down on my bed, and kiss you everywhere. I'll tease you with my fingers," he circles his hand slowly.

"Oh, God," I whimper.

"I'll tease you with my tongue and lips until you're aching for me. When you finally feel my tip against you, your whole body will shake against mine. I'll make you wait for it." He stills his finger.

I whimper when he stops. The throbbing between my legs is so intense it hurts.

He slides his hand inside my panties. "You're so wet."

I gasp for air.

His fingertip runs over my slit. "You're so wet and ready for me, Kira." He presses his erection into me from behind and moves his finger back to my clit. He moves his finger in slow circles.

"Jason. God." A moan escapes my lips. "You're gonna make me cum right here?" I look around the empty hallway, terrified someone will see.

"When I finally slide inside of you, you'll be so wet and turned on, it won't hurt. You'll cry out my name again and again as I slide in and out of you slowly." He kisses the back of my ear. "So slowly and so gently, it will be impossible for you to cum," he stills his finger against me. "Until I decide it's time to go faster." He removes his hand, leaving me with an intense throbbing between my legs.

I whimper.

"What? Do you need something from me, Kira? If you want more, turn around and kiss me."

I take a deep breath to compose myself. I turn around, and my lips find his. I kiss him like I'm starving for him. His fingers thread through the back of my hair. My arms wrap around his shoulders and hold him close.

He breaks the kiss, takes my arm, and pulls me into the small bathroom. He shuts and locks the door behind me. It's pitch black. He presses me back against the door and kisses me until I'm starving for him. He reaches for my panties again. This time, he pulls them down.

I whimper. *Oh, God. What's going to happen?*

They reach my feet.

"Step out of them," he orders.

I do what he says.

He takes my hands and puts them on his belt.

I hesitate. This is insane.

"I know you're inexperienced, but I assume you know how to undo a belt buckle."

I gasp.

He kisses my forehead. "Kira, I promise, I'm not going to take your virginity in a bathroom."

My hands shake so hard I can barely undo his buckle. Getting it unlatched seems like an accomplishment.

"Button and zipper," he whispers.

I inhale sharply. Then I do what he says.

He pushes his pants down. He leans into me.

"Jesus Christ.' I had no idea he took his boxers off, too. His tips at my entrance. "Jason, I can't do this in here." I shake uncontrollably.

He holds still against me. "Shh. Don't be scared. I promise, I'm not going to slide inside of you." He moves slowly, teasing me on the outside only. His tip strokes my clit again and again.

It's too intense. It's too much of a tease. "Oh, God. What are you doing to me?" I have to wrap my arms around his shoulders to stay standing.

"You're in love with me, Kira," he whispers.

My heart flutters in my chest.

He holds his tip at my entrance. "That's why you're letting me do this."

"Jason." He could slide inside right now. I want him to.

"Say it."

"I'm in love with you." It feels so good to tell the truth.

He wraps me in a tight hug. "Then come home with me tonight."

I nod my head.

"Give me your hand." He wraps my hand around his shaft. We both gasp at the contact. He places his hand over mine. Showing me how to stroke him. "There you go." His other hand slides between my legs. His finger enters me for the first time.

I jump.

"You're so tight, Kira." He moves his finger inside of me. His thumb circles me on the outside. He holds his ear over my mouth so he can listen to my gasps and moans. He increases his speed and pressure.

"Oh, God. Jason." I cry out. My whole body shakes. My free hand clings onto him for dear life.

The most intense feeling builds inside of me. "Jason, Jason." Moisture gathers between my legs. My hand squeezes him tighter. "Oh, god, Jason."

"I love you," he whispers and ejaculates next to me.

A sound I didn't know I could make escapes my lips. Then I go limp in his arms.

He kisses my forehead and holds me until I stop shaking.

He switches on the light. He looks me in the eyes. "I suggest you go tell your parents we're together, or I'm getting on a plane at seven a.m."

"You want me to tell them right now? There's a ton of drama going on out there. My mom is really stressed out."

Jason frowns. "It will always be something, Kira. Do you want to come home with me tonight?"

"Yes."

"Do you want me to make love to you tonight?"

I blush. "Yes."

"Then go tell your parents we're together."

"But—I"

"Seven a.m. flight, Kira," he reminds me.

"Did you buy your ticket yet?"

"No. I showed up here tonight hoping to—"

"Finger me in a bathroom."

He smiles and kisses me. "Get you to admit you're in love with me. I've waited for you long enough. I'm not gonna live in limbo anymore. If you don't tell your parents tonight, I will."

I really don't want my parents to hear it from Jason, and I can't bear the idea of him leaving me now. "Okay. I'll go tell them. I'll find you after I talk to them."

He smiles, "Good." He steps back, picks up my panties, and hands them to me.

I take them from him. "This is nuts." I clean up the mess between my legs with a paper towel and put my underwear back on. "You pulled me into an alternate dimension. I can't believe I have to go back to the normal world after what just happened."

He laughs.

I fix my hair and smudged eye makeup in the mirror. "I can do this," I say to myself. Then I look at him. "I should go out first. Wait a minute before you come out, so nobody will know that we, um…what we were doing in here."

He smiles. "Okay." He kisses me one more time. "Go, tell them you're in love with me." He opens the door.

I take a deep breath and exit the bathroom.

Chapter Twenty Three

Saturday, August 10, 2024

I drift back to the party as though in a dream. I glide effortlessly over the floor in my heels. It's not like me to walk with so much confidence.

I pass Seth and his father talking in the corner of the room. They look deep in conversation.

"Look, son, I'm sorry," Seth's father says.

I smile at Seth. There might be some hope for a reconciliation between him and his father.

"And that's when I knew I was gonna marry this woman." A man's voice is magnified through the sound system. "I asked her to marry me."

I guess I missed the start of Ginny and Rick's wedding announcement. I go to my family's table, but I don't see anyone in their seats. I scan the room, but I can't see anything except blurry outlines. I walk around the room trying to find them.

Aunt Ginny takes the mic, "And I said yes. I knew as soon as I saw him that I wanted to marry him. I'm so glad he finally got around to asking me."

A bunch of "aws" and other coos come from the crowd.

I bump into Mimi. "Do you know where my parents are?"

"Yes. I just saw them over there." She points to the other side of the room by the bar.

"Thanks," I tell her.

"So, thank you, everyone, for being here tonight to celebrate with us," Ginny says. "And now our first official dance as an engaged couple."

People clap.

I roll my eyes. First dances are supposed to happen at weddings. I've never heard of them happening at engagement parties. God, Ginny, and her fiancé are laying it on thick.

I walk past the dance floor to get to the bar. My parents turn to look at me.

"Mom, Dad, I have to tell you something."

Ed Sheeran's "Perfect" starts playing. Ginny and Rick start their official engagement dance together.

"What is it, sweetie?" Mom asks.

"I…well, for the past few months I've been wrestling with having to tell you something. It's about me and Tonya."

Dad looks concerned. "What about Tonya? Did you find out something else about the night she died?"

"No, Dad. It's nothing like that. Tonya and I both—"

Other couples are joining Ginny and Rick. People walk between me and my parents on their way to the dance floor. I have to wait for them to pass before I can finish

"Tonya and I both—" I sigh. "We both had feelings for—"

Jason takes my hand. "Would you excuse us, Mr. and Mrs. Conway. We'll be back." He pulls me onto the dance floor.

"What are you doing? You said you wanted me to tell them."

He takes my hands and puts them on his shoulders. He wraps his arms around my waist and pulls me close. "We are telling them."

I gasp. *Oh my god, he's so sneaky.* I wrap my arms around his shoulders. I turn my head into his neck and let him lead. Jason breathes a sigh of what seems to be relief. He finally has me in his arms. I relax against him. "Sorry, I ruined your travel plans."

"I have a gift card. I can leave whenever I want. I'll wait until you can come with me," he assures me.

I pull back and look into Jason's intense green eyes. "To Ireland?"

He smiles and touches the side of my face.

"What about my eyes? I don't know if I can fly because of the air pressure. What if I can't go until—"

He kisses me in front of everyone. My boyfriend's lips are full and perfect. Everything about him is perfect.

I have a feeling Mike and Mimi are smiling. My parents' jaws are probably on the floor. I don't care. Jason's mine. If anybody has a problem with that, I guess they are going to have to work out those feelings on their own.

Jason finally pulls back. "Then we'll travel by ship. I'll wait until you can come with me."

I smile and hold him close.

"Are you insane?" my mother yells from across the room. Jason and I look in her direction. We can't see her because there are too many people in the way.

A cold draft fills the room. It feels like the temperature outside dropped to below freezing, and somebody left the front door wide open.

"I'm glad that wasn't directed at us," Jason says, relieved. I cuddle closer to him to keep warm.

"How could you invite him? There's a child here tonight!" my mother yells.

"I thought this would be a good opportunity for the family to finally come back together," Ginny says.

"This man will never be a part of our family," Dad says.

The music stops. The DJ didn't want to compete with the yelling.

Jason and I step closer to see what's going on. Some people brush past us on the way to the exits. Nobody wants to stick around for this.

"Cindy, you're an unstable lunatic!"

His voice sends a chill down my spine. I turn and cling to Jason.

"Ginny, if I've told you once, I've told you a thousand times, your sister is an unstable lunatic," my grandfather says.

Every muscle in my body tenses up. The weirdest sensation of déjà vu washes over me.

"That's why my granddaughter drank herself into an early grave! With a mother like you, who could blame her!"

He did not just say that to my mother.

My mother charges forward. She is going to rip out her father's throat. Dad has to hold her back.

"It's your fault I never saw my granddaughter grow up. It's your fault she died before I got a chance to reconnect with her."

Mike rushes to get between my grandfather and mother. "You fucking piece of shit! Tonya never mentioned you. Not

247

one time in eighteen years did she ever say she missed you. She only talked about you when I complained to her about what an asshole you are. So don't call her your granddaughter. You don't have any grandchildren."

"That's not true. Tonya's dead, and you're a lost cause," my grandfather spits out. He looks around the room. "But there's one left."

I turn my head into Jason's shoulder so the monster won't see me.

"Kira, it's okay," Jason whispers. He doesn't understand why I'm so terrified.

"Where's the little crossed-eyed one?"

"There's the little crossed-eyed one?" My grandfather's face wrinkles up when he sees me. Like he's looking at something gross.

"Don't call her that," my father says as he steps into my grandfather's house. My parents took my eyepatch off in the car. They never let me wear it when we visit here.

"Why not?" my grandfather says. "Her eyes are crossed. Is she always gonna look like that?" He leans over and gets in my face.

I turn my head away from him.

"Vince, stop talking about her like she's not in the room," Daddy warns. He places me down on the couch next to him and starts taking off my jacket.

I don't want to stay here. I hate Grandpa's house. He's mean, and this place stinks of cigarettes.

"Grandpa," Tonya says, coming into the house. "Look. Mommy let me get my ears pierced."

"Wow, look at you. You must be the most beautiful girl in the world." Grandpa picks my sister up, swings her around, and sits down with her at the table.

My mother comes inside, wheeling in our suitcase and carrying an overnight bag. "Merry Christmas, Dad."

Grandpa doesn't get up to help her carry anything in. "Merry Christmas, your sister is in the kitchen cooking dinner. Go help her."

"Sure, as soon as I unpack the car." She takes the suitcase upstairs to the bedroom where we're all sleeping tonight.

Daddy tries again to take off my coat. I keep my arms crossed. "I wanna go home."

"It's okay, Kira, Santa knows where to deliver all our presents tonight." I let him take off my coat. "Here sweetie. Play with this." He takes my crayons and coloring book out of our bag and places them on the coffee table. I stand next to the coffee table and turn the pages in the book. I chose a picture of a cat.

Mike comes over to me. "Merry Christmas, cutie." He hugs me.

"Merry Christmas."

"Can I help you color?" Mike asks.

"Yes, please." I smile. Mike is so cool. He can do anything. He can jump off a swing when it is all the way in the air. He can ride a bike super-fast. He's never scared of spiders. He can crush a creepy-crawly in a second flat. I slide my crayons over to him. If he helps me with this page, it will come out perfect.

My parents rush to get the rest of the stuff out of the car. Then my mother goes into the kitchen to help Aunt Ginny. Daddy sits down on the couch. "So, Mike, what'd you ask Santa for?"

"An Xbox 360," Mike says.

"Wow, that's a big gift. Have you been a good boy this year?"

"Yes," Mike says. "Mostly."

Daddy chuckles.

"What'd you ask Santa for, Kira?" Mike asks.

"Holiday Barbie." I smile. "The one in the red dress with the silver sparkles."

"Doug," my mother calls from the kitchen. "Come help us with the roast. It's heavy."

Daddy stands up.

I grab hold of his pants and cling on. I don't want him to leave the room.

"It's okay, Kira. I'll be right back. Color your picture." He leaves.

Grandpa picks Tonya up and swings her around. "Look. The most beautiful girl in the world can fly." She giggles.

I'm sad. He never does that for me.

Grandpa sits in his armchair. I keep my eyes on the page I'm coloring.

"So, kids, who'd like some early Christmas presents?"

"Oh, yes, please," Tonya says.

Grandpa gets up and gets a pillowcase out of the coat closet. Then he picks up his wine glass and sits back down in his chair.

"What are you drinking?" Tonya asks.

"It's wine, sweetheart. Would any of you like some?" *Grandpa waves the glass around.*

"No, thanks," Mike says.

"I do," Tonya says.

Grandpa hands my sister his wine glass. She needs two hands to hold it. She takes a sip. "It's good." She sips it again.

"I don't think you should be drinking that," Mike tells her.

"Don't be so uptight, Mike," Grandpa says. "So, who wants presents?"

"I do," Tonya says and sips more wine.

Grandpa smiles. He looks like the Grinch.

I look back at the page I'm working on because I hate his face.

"Well," Grandpa says, "since Santa isn't real—"

My hand stops coloring the cat's fur. Did Grandpa really say that? That's not true. I look at Mike for an answer. He looks as shocked as I am.

"—and none of your parents make enough money to buy you great gifts, I thought you guys should get some extra gifts this year." *He puts his hand inside the pillowcase.* "Let's see what I have for the most beautiful girl in the world." *He pulls out the new Holiday Barbie doll. It's the same one I told Daddy I wanted.*

Tonya puts down the empty wine glass. She squeaks with delight. "Oh, Grandpa. She's beautiful."

"One condition." *He pulls the doll back.* "This is a very special, very expensive Barbie." *He turns the box over.* "It says right here, ages seven and up. Don't let your little sister touch it. She's too young."

"Okay, Grandpa," *Tonya says and takes the doll. She sits next to me.*

250

He gets up to refill his wine glass.

"You can play with her whenever you want," Tonya whispers and kisses my cheek.

I still feel like I'm going to cry.

Grandpa comes back with the bottle of wine. He refills his glass and drinks half of it. "Now, let's see what else I have in here." He reaches into the bag. "Oh, yes. This feels like another doll for another special girl."

I look up and smile. Did he get me the same Barbie? He must have been teasing me before.

He reaches into the bag and pulls out the ugliest doll I've ever seen. It has a huge head, a wrinkled face, and two huge brown eyes. Brown hair sticks up from its head. "This reminds me of you." He sets it down on the coffee table in front of me.

"That's a troll doll," Mike says, horrified.

"And it looks like Kira," Grandpa says.

I stare at the ugly thing. Do I really look like that? I start to cry. I want my Daddy. I want to go home. I try to hide my tears. I hide behind my sister.

"Kira's way prettier than that thing," Tonya snaps.

"Oh, relax. It's just a joke." Grandpa drinks some more.

"I don't think it's funny," Mike says.

"I said relax," Grandpa orders. He shoves his hand into the bag. He pulls out a magazine and tosses it at Mike. "Here, this is for you."

It lands on the couch next to my cousin.

"There's a naked lady on it," Tonya says, shocked.

"Calm down. I was half Mike's age the first time I saw a photo of a naked chick. Pick it up, Mike."

"I don't think I want to," Mike says.

"It's good for boys to start young. Your future girlfriends will thank me. Pick it up and look at it."

"No. Mom wouldn't want me to."

"Don't be a fag! Pick it up!"

I start crying hard. I need to get away from him. I crawl to the other side of the room and sit on the hardwood floor.

"When I was your age, I looked at these all the time." He pours more wine and gulps it down. "Did I ever tell you about my dad?"

251

"No," Mike says.

"My dad was in the army, a war hero, did you know?"

"No," Mike says again.

I don't want to know about his dad. I want my Mommy and Daddy. I want to go home. I keep crying. I want my parents to hear me and come out of the kitchen.

"I was born in 1953. My dad was a World War Two vet. Guess how many people he killed?"

"Daddy!" I yell. I don't want to hear anymore.

"Shut up!" Grandpa snaps at me. "Guess," he says to Mike.

"A billion," Mike says like a badass.

"You little smart ass," Grandpa grins. "Good guess," He finishes his wine. He pours the rest of the bottle into his glass and guzzles it down. "My dad was the tail gunner. He sat in the back of the aircraft underneath the plane in a space tighter than Tojo's asshole. My dad had to squat on a bicycle seat for the whole mission. Does that sound comfortable?"

"No," Mike whispers

"Do you know how cold it was in that tail area of the plane?"

Mike shakes his head. He's about to cry.

"Cold enough to get frostbite. Do you think you could be a tail gunner, Mike? How'd you like to shoot some Jap and German enemies?"

"Daddy!" I scream. He's scaring me. I don't want to hear any more. "Daddy!"

"Shut up, you cross-eyed freak!" Grandpa throws his wine glass at me.

I put my arms up to cover my face. The glass smashes into a million pieces right next to me. I lose my balance and fall on the glass. Blood pours out of my hand.

"You can't do that!" Tonya screams and rushes over to me.

Our parents rush into the room. Mommy picks me up. Daddy is screaming at Grandpa. Aunt Ginny is crying. Mike goes over to comfort her. The adults yell and scream for a long time. Dad insists that Mike has to leave with us. We leave without our toys, bags, or coats. We rush out to the car. My parents take me to the hospital.

I come back to the present. Jason's eyes are huge and worried. "Kira, breathe. What's wrong? You're scaring me."

I pull a sharp breath into my lungs. I don't think I took a breath once the whole time I was trapped in the memory.

I look over at the monster.

"Don't look at him, look at me." Jason turns my face.

I look into his green eyes. They're gorgeous.

I take a deep breath.

"That's it, breathe," Jason says.

I'll never get enough air into my lungs again.

Seth steps next to me. "What's wrong with her?"

"She's having a panic attack." Mimi rushes towards me. She places one hand on my belly and her other hand on my chest. "Take a deep breath through your nose," she whispers. "Breathe out through pursed lips." She has me repeat this several times until my breath stabilizes.

Seth's father has been watching the whole event from a few feet away. He steps closer. The big guy is glaring at my grandfather, like he's ready to pounce.

"This is Cindy's influence," my grandfather announces. He looks at Ginny. "How could you let your sister turn your son against me?"

"You're the one who gave me dirty magazines when I was seven," Mike yells.

"It was good for you," my grandfather says.

I finally find my voice. "He also gave Tonya wine," I say loud enough to get everyone's attention. I cling to Jason's hand, and I step closer to my grandfather.

My grandfather looks at me like an object he doesn't know how to use yet. Am I a servant he can exploit? A person he can manipulate? He looks me up and down like a pervert. A young girl he can seduce? "Who are you?"

I look at him like he's dirt. "The other one."

The gears turn in his mind, like a robot, computing who I am. "Well, well. The ugly duckling turned into a swan. You're almost as beautiful as your sister was."

"You gave Tonya wine. She was seven years old. You knew her biological father was an alcoholic, and you let her drink a whole glass of wine."

253

"She liked it," my grandfather snaps.

"Then you gave Mike pornography and ordered him to look at it. He was seven years old, too."

My grandfather knows he has lost the sympathy of everyone in the room. He can't play the victim anymore. "And maybe if Mike had spent more time looking at my magazines, then he wouldn't have turned out to be a fag."

Seth's dad steps up. "Sir, do you admit that you gave minor children alcohol and pornography?"

"Yeah, so what? Who the fuck are you?"

Sergeant Karlson steps in close enough to invade Grandpa's personal space.

"Back off, pal. This is between me and my family." Grandpa tries to shove him back.

The huge cop doesn't move an inch. Sergeant Karlson turns my grandfather around and pins him to the bar. He wrestles the old man's arms back and cuffs them. "You're under arrest. For assaulting a police officer and giving minor children alcohol and pornography."

Mimi looks at Sergeant Karlson like he's the most impressive thing she has ever seen. "Does your dad always carry cuffs on him?" Mimi asks Seth.

Seth shrugs.

"That's so hot," Mimi says and looks at Seth's dad like she's ready to do way more than dance with him.

Jason cringes.

"You have the right to remain silent. Anything you say can and will be used against you in a court of law. You have the right to an attorney. If you cannot afford an attorney, one will be appointed for you."

"This is bullshit! Ginny! Call my lawyer!" Grandpa yells.

Aunt Ginny doesn't move. She looks frozen, like a statue.

"Seth, my police car is parked out back." Sergeant Karlson tosses his son the keys. "Can you please go ahead of me and open the car door for this gentleman?"

"Gladly," Seth says and rushes outside.

I look at my mother. She looks relieved. Like this is the moment she's been waiting for her entire life.

My grandfather is dragged off, yelling about how he has the best lawyer in the world. How Sergeant Karlson is going to be fired. We hear his bullshit until he's finally dragged downstairs out of the building. The downstairs door slams shut. The room feels warm again.

"I wonder if I can get him to arrest any of my ex-family members, too," Mimi says with stars in her eyes.

My mother wraps her arms around me. "Are you okay?"

"I'm much better now. I think things are gonna be much better now," I tell her.

"What the fuck is wrong with you?" Mike screams at Aunt Ginny.

I spoke too soon.

"Why would you invite him here?" Mike asks.

Ginny looks as white as a sheet. "I thought that maybe the whole family would heal once we were all together."

"How can we heal with a psychopath in the room?" Mike screams. He looks at Rick. "This is what you're getting yourself into. My grandfather treats my mother like gold and the rest of us like shit. Is this what you want for your daughter?" Mike points at me. "Do you want Lily to have panic attacks when repressed memories of abuse resurface in ten years?"

Seth comes back inside and rushes over to Mike's side.

Ginny starts sobbing. "Mike, please."

"Shut up! You let that son of a bitch abuse me for years. He called me a fag! He said homophobic things to me every time he saw me! He tried to make me feel like shit for loving Seth. The only reason I'm not more fucked up is because Aunt Cindy always told me not to listen to a word that came out of the bastard's mouth!"

"Let's go home," Seth says to Mike, trying to calm his boyfriend down.

"That's a great idea," Mike says. "I'm going home with Seth, and I'm not coming back until you cut your father out of your life."

Seth pulls him towards the door.

"You know what I find hilarious about all of this?" Mike says, walking back towards his mom. "You pride yourself on being a psychic, someone who is so fucking intuitive. Yet

255

you've watched your father abuse all of us, and you made excuses for all of it. I don't need a set of tarot cards to see that your father will never stop being a psycho. If I find out you visited him in prison, called a lawyer for him, or sent him any money to bail him out, I will never talk to you again. You can have a father, or you can have a son. Pick one!"

"Let's go home," Seth pulls him towards the door.

"Excellent idea. Moving into my aunt's basement. I should've done it years ago," Mike says.

Rick takes Ginny by the arm, "We need to talk, now." He pulls her out of the room. "Lily, stay with your grandmother." He points at his little girl.

Mike takes one look at Lily, who is crying on her grandmother's lap. All his anger melts away. He goes over to her. "I don't know what these idiot adults are gonna decide, but I'll still be a part of your life, even if nobody gets married."

She hops off her grandmother's lap and hugs him.

Oh, my god. That was so cute.

Seth and Mike ask me if I'm okay. I assure them I'm fine, and they leave together.

I go over to Lily. "I think I owe you an apology. I'm sorry if I was rude to you. I was freaked out over a lot of different things. Can we start again?"

Lily smiles at me and shakes her head yes.

I hold my hand out. "I'm Kira. It's nice to meet you."

"I'm Lily." She shakes my hand and smiles at me.

"I'll see you again soon," I tell her.

"I'm sorry about all this," I say to the grandmother.

"Young lady, you seem more mature than the rest of your family," the old woman says.

I take Jason's hand and walk him over to my parents. "Mom, Dad, I have to talk to you. I've made a decision. I'm going off the antidepressants."

Dad sighs, "Kira, I don't think—"

"My mind is made up, Dad. I'll get the surgery when I need it. If I need it in six months or a year, that's okay. I'm not gonna waste my life in an apathetic fog, worrying about a low-risk surgery. We should all be grateful that the doctors know how to perform a surgery that can help my eyes. I wanna focus on that."

Dad looks at me like he's impressed. "Okay."

I look at Mom. "I'm leaving."

"I understand, sweetie, but I think I need to be here for my sister right now," Mom says. "We'll leave as soon as I know she's okay."

"No, you don't understand. I'm going home with Jason. I'll be home sometime tomorrow."

Dad inhales a sharp breath.

"I'm not like my sister. I'm not gonna do anything irresponsible. I'm not gonna drink, or do drugs, or get pregnant. I'll be safe. But I'm going home with Jason."

Mom looks worried. "Kira, you're only seventeen."

"I'll be eighteen in a few months. Please don't make us sneak around until then. We've all had enough drama lately."

"I still don't think it's a good idea," my mother says.

"Mom. I know you want me to stay home with you all the time. But I can't stay in the house with you day in and day out anymore. It's not healthy for either of us. I'm going home with Jason. I'll text you tonight before I go to bed, so you know I'm safe. And I will see you sometime tomorrow."

My mother sighs. "Okay."

I smile and I hug her.

I move over to my dad, who looks like he's trying to come up with a reason for me not to leave with Jason. I hug him and say, "Just so you know, I didn't steal Tonya's boyfriend. She stole mine. I'll see you tomorrow, Dad." I kiss him on the cheek and walk away.

I take Jason's hand. We turn to leave.

"Jason," Dad says. "Stop at our house and get Kira's eyedrops and dark glasses in case she wakes up with a headache."

"Sure. No problem."

"And don't get her in trouble," Dad warns.

"No, sir. No way," Jason says.

We leave together.

Chapter Twenty Four

Saturday, August 10, 2024

We walk into Jason and Mimi's apartment. Mimi has an overnight shift at the hospital tonight. I'm relieved knowing we'll have total privacy.

I take a shower and take my contacts out. I exit the bathroom in my nightgown and robe.

Jason's putting the last of his unpacked clothes away. "I got you a glass of water in case you wake up with a headache." He points to his nightstand. He gives me a quick kiss and exits the room to take a shower.

I text my mom. I tell her that I'm perfectly safe and I'm going to bed.

I take off my glasses. I take off my robe and drape it over the end of his bed. I get in and pull the covers over me. His mattress is big and comfortable. His sheets smell of his woody herbal scent.

He comes into the bedroom. He walks by his nightstand. "I love the way you look in my bed."

I smile.

He separates a condom from the box we bought at the drugstore earlier.

He lights a candle and places it on the other side of the room on his desk. "I got this red candle at your aunt's store before it closed. I was told it was for love and passion. It seems like a good night to try lighting it."

I look at him, surprised. "You don't actually believe in all that stuff, do you?"

"I'm not sure yet. Let's see how good the sex is tonight," he teases. He turns off the light. The room glows in the soft red light of the candle. He takes off his boxers and places them next to my robe at the foot of his bed. He pulls the covers down and slides into bed next to me. I roll towards him. He pulls me into his arms and exhales a deep breath. I cuddle closer and hold him tighter. Smooth skin over hard muscle. He holds me close until my breath slows.

He rolls me on my back and looks at me. I can't believe how gorgeous he is. He kisses me gently. His lips are warm and soft. My hands and arms pull him closer. I can't believe I almost lost him. If he went to Ireland, how many years would have passed before I saw him again? I cling to him and kiss him out of desperation.

He pulls back. "Kira, slow down." He strokes my cheek. "Relax, I'm not going anywhere."

I take a deep breath to calm myself.

I get a kiss on the side of my neck. My collarbone. His hands slide the straps of my nightgown down over my shoulders. My breath catches again. I close my eyes and let him undress me. I gasp when his lips reach my nipple. His fingertips caress my other breast. He lingers on my breasts for a long time. Any fears that they might be too small to turn him on melt away.

He moves my nightgown down and kisses my stomach. My hips rise as he pulls my nightgown and panties off. The sheets and blankets fall away. I have an instinct to reach for the top sheet and cover myself.

"No, Kira," Jason whispers. "Lie back and stay relaxed." He kisses me until I calm down. He places my hands back on my pillow.

"Keep your hands there," Jason whispers. "Please don't reach for the blankets or cover yourself." He moves away from me.

I'm totally exposed. "What are you doing?"

"Looking at you." His fingertip runs along my lower stomach.

I gasp.

"Beautiful." He gently pulls my legs apart. "I'll paint this one day. You naked in my bed." He runs his finger between my legs, and my whole body shakes. "Wet and ready for me, with your legs spread. I'll paint this if I ever have the talent."

His hand runs along my inner thigh.

I whimper.

Over my stomach again. Down my other thigh.

"Jason?"

On my inner thigh.

"Oh, god, Jason." I jump and sit up a little.

He stops. "Lie back, Kira."

I lie back down. He does nothing. Until I return my hands to the pillow.

He kisses my inner thigh again.

He kisses a path up my leg, but stops before he reaches my most sensitive area. He kisses my lower stomach, but stops again. He does the same with his fingers.

"Jason, God." I cry out.

I feel his warm breath on my clit. He moves his head lower like he is about to kiss it. Instead, he blows on it.

"Jason, please."

He kisses it softly.

I tremble.

He licks it slowly.

"Jason." I sound scared.

"What's wrong?"

"You're too far away. You're too far away from me."

He laughs softly. He kisses back up my body so his mouth is over my ear. "That was the cutest fucking thing I've ever heard." He kisses me. "We'll save that for another night, then."

His fingertips move up my legs, over my stomach. Up to my breasts. He caresses them gently and then circles my nipples. I close my eyes and get lost in the feeling of his hands on me. He moves his fingertip to my clit and circles it slowly.

I gasp and shake against him.

"Go slowly, section by section," he whispers in my ear. "Pay attention to every little detail. Isn't that what you taught me, Kira?"

My hands grip the pillow. "Oh, God."

He keeps rubbing me slowly until I'm on the brink of orgasm. Then he stops. I lift my hips to try to get him to finish me. He kisses me to muffle my protests. I cry out when he slides a finger inside of me. His thumb returns to tease my clit. "I told you I was going to tease you," he whispers in my ear. "I

261

wanted you since the second you fell into my arms. You made me wait, and wait, and wait." His fingers work me slowly.

I cry out. I gasp for air. I try to lift my hips to get him to move faster.

He stills his hand until I relax. Then he continues his slow pace until my orgasm builds again.

"It's just my finger, Kira. How good is it gonna feel when I'm really inside of you?" He presses his erection into my leg.

I squeeze the pillow in my hands. I gasp. I cry out. I shake everywhere. All the tension in my body drains away.

He removes his hand from between my legs. He opens the condom wrapper and slides the condom on. He positions my legs around his waist. My hands grip his arms. His tip is at my entrance again. He strokes it back and forth on the outside until the throbbing between my legs intensifies. Then he holds it still at my entrance.

"Jason?"

"Kira." He kisses me gently. He teases my clit with his tip and then holds it at my entrance again.

My whole body trembles. What is he waiting for? I try to pull him close, but he backs up slightly. He turns my face so our eyes meet.

"I love you," I finally say.

"Good." He lowers himself into me.

"Oh, god. Yes."

He enters me halfway and then pulls out slowly. He enters again, deeper this time. "You're mine now, Kira." He slides into me fully. "All mine."

I gasp and cling to him for comfort. Part of me is pushed open for the first time. It hurts a little. I gasp and whimper.

"You're so tight." He holds still inside of me and kisses me gently on the lips. He waits until I'm silent before he moves again.

I whimper as he slides back in. He fits me perfectly. Like he's made for me. I close my eyes and get lost in the feeling of him moving slowly in and out of me. "Yes, Jason." It feels so good. How can anything feel this good? I love the sound of his heavy breathing in my ear. I love the way the muscles in his arms feel as I cling to him. "Oh, god, Jason, Jason."

He slows his pace slightly.

"Jason."

"Shh. I need to make this last."

He moves so slowly and so gently that I start aching for more. "Oh, god, please," I whimper.

"Kira." He turns my head so our eyes meet again.

I can see traces of green in the dim light. He's so gorgeous. Why does he have to be so fucking beautiful? "I love you." I cry out. "I love you. I love you so much. Jason."

He increases his speed.

Oh, fuck yes. I had no idea sex could be this intense. It's overwhelming. I cry out, gasp, and then cry out again. My hands grip him hard. He's mine. I love him.

"Kira," he whispers in my ear. He's close.

I climax with him. "Oh, god, Jason." The sensation of him pushing through me washes over my entire body. *How long can this last?* "Oh, God. Yes. Oh, God."

He collapses on top of me. He rolls over onto his back and pulls me close. We cling to each other.

"You're mine, too," I tell him.

He laughs and kisses my forehead. "I've always been yours, Kira."

The candle goes out on its own.

`

Chapter Twenty Five

Sunday, August 11, 2024

Jason drives me home. He's nervous to see my parents. "I'm the pervert who deflowered their little girl."

I laugh. "You have to get used to being with them. Come on."

We step inside my house. A thumping comes up the basement stairs. Seth appears, dragging his suitcase behind him.

"What's going on?" I ask.

"My dad asked me to move back home," Seth says. "He's taking me and Mike out to dinner tonight. He's trying hard to be okay with 'the whole gay thing,' as he calls it."

I hug Seth. "That's great."

"Mike's gonna stay in your basement for a while," Seth says. "He and his mom need some space."

Seth takes his stuff out to his car and then comes back inside to thank my parents. They come into the living room and hug him goodbye. They tell him that he is welcome back anytime.

Jason sits on our couch, looking so nervous. I sit down next to him.

Alma jumps on my lap and looks me in the eye. I smile and kiss the top of her head. She knows it's me. The real me. I pet her and cuddle her, and tell her she is the cutest cat in the world.

Jason laughs and pets her, too.

My parents sit down across from us. Dad looks as nervous about this conversation as Jason. "Kira, your mother has made a doctor's appointment for you to discuss birth control options."

This is a nightmare. "Okay."

"There will be no pregnancy scares." Dad insists.

Jason and I sink deeper into the couch.

"During the summer, you're allowed to spend nights at Jason's. You can also sleep there on the weekends after school starts," Mom says.

I smile.

"But until you graduate high school, you'll spend school nights sleeping in your room, alone," Dad adds.

"I understand," I say.

Dad looks at Jason. "When Kira's grandfather showed up at the party last night, I knew it was going to be a disaster. I couldn't get to Kira when she had her panic attack because I had to make sure Cindy didn't murder the guy. I was glad to see you step up and be there for her. I know my daughter is safe with you. That is the only reason I'm allowing Kira to sleep at your house."

"Thank you, sir," Jason says.

"Don't make me regret my decision."

"No, sir."

"And stop calling me sir. Call me Doug."

"Okay, sir." Jason cringes after his mistake.

Dad gets up. "I'll be in my office." He rushes away.

Jason and I both exhale. "I'm gonna go," he says. "I've gotta go beg my boss for my job back and find another one if he says no. I'll be back tonight to pick you up for a date." He kisses my forehead.

"Okay," I agree. I want a real kiss, but my mom is in the room, and it doesn't seem like the right moment.

"Bye, Cindy," he says.

"See you later," she says.

He shuts the front door behind him.

"Did you have sex?" Mom asks.

I nod my head.

"Did you use protection?"

"Yes, Mom. A condom with spermicide. Two birth control methods in one."

She moves from her chair and sits next to me on the couch. "How was it?"

I smile and blush.

"Did you enjoy it?"

I nod and blush harder.

266

"A great first time is rare, you know?"

"Yeah, well, my boyfriend has skills."

She laughs. "I'm happy for you. I'm glad you finally got together. I suspected Jason had feelings for you when he showed up here with that photo collage. I was worried he and Tonya moved way too fast, and they weren't right for each other."

"I know."

"You must have been dealing with confusing emotions since your sister died. I'm sorry I haven't been able to help you."

"It's okay, Mom."

"No, it's not. I was so overwhelmed by my own grief that I let everything in my life fall apart. I ignored you when you needed help. It won't happen again."

"Thanks, Mom. So, what happened with Rick and Ginny?"

Her face drops. "Rick decided to call off the wedding. After what Mike said to his mother, Rick got scared. He said that he couldn't marry a woman who let her son be abused. He said he couldn't let her raise Lily. Ginny's devastated. I was up all night with her. She sobbed all night long. I think my sister finally opened her eyes. She finally owned up to all the abuse she witnessed. My sister actually apologized to me and agreed to start therapy."

"I can't believe it."

"Neither can I. I think Hell froze over last night." Mom pauses.

"It seemed like Rick and Ginny were more in love with the idea of marriage than they were with each other," I say. "Maybe Ginny will find someone she loves after she works out her problems in therapy."

Mom hugs me. "How are you like this? So optimistic? I've been a pessimist my whole life."

"It's understandable. Your father was a raging asshole. I don't think any of us have to deal with him anymore."

Mom's eyes water. "Kira, I'm so sorry I left you, Tonya, and Mike alone in the room with him that Christmas. He was a verbally abusive bastard, but he never threw things at me when I was a little girl. The older he got, the meaner he got." Mom strokes my hair. "It only takes a minute for a monster to teach a

267

child the world is a horrible, scary place." She hugs me tightly. "You're special and beautiful, Kira. You have so much creative talent. You can do anything you want. An artist, a cook or baker, an art teacher, an interior decorator. Anything. Do you understand me?"

I nod my head.

"The money your father and I set aside for Tonya's education is yours now. You can study anything you want. I'll support you no matter what you decide."

"Thank you."

"Does Jason make you feel beautiful and special?"

"Yes."

"Then you picked a good one."

I call my best friend. I have a lot to apologize for.

Liz picks up. "Hey, Kira. What's up?"

I pace around my bedroom. "I have to tell you something. I, uh, well…I'm sorry."

"For what?"

"For being in a daze for a while. For acting like a zombie since Tonya died. For missing your birthday."

"Kira, it's okay. Your sister died. You're allowed to fall apart sometimes."

"I know, but lately, I've been putting myself back together. Mike's been helping me get in touch with my anger. My therapist has been helping me come to terms with my trauma, and I, um, I slept with Jason."

"What? Really?"

I pull my phone away from my ear to muffle the sounds of her excited squeals.

"Are you serious?"

"Yes, Liz."

"It's about damn time. Are you guys a couple now?"

"Well, yeah."

She squeals like a five-year-old, tells me to hold on so she can text Will the news, and then starts planning a million double dates. Then she makes me tell her every detail about my first time. I stay on the phone with her for hours. Until Jason comes to pick me up for dinner.

Chapter Twenty Six

Monday, September 16, 2024

South Middlesex Correctional Center smells like an odd combination of body odor, stale air, and cleaning supplies. The minimum-security allows visitors to hug inmates once before we sit down and once when we say goodbye.

Kimber looks so nervous to see me. Nervous but also relieved. "You came. You really came." She hugs me tightly.

"I promised you I would." I hug her back.

We sit across a metal table. I tell her all about my junior year at Marblehead High. How I hate gym class. How I still have to take the bus because I can't drive. She hangs on every word like she's watching a movie she loves. A movie about a high school girl living the life she lost.

I tell her how I've started a YouTube channel teaching people how to draw. How I already have three thousand subscribers and a ton of grateful comments. How it was Jason's idea. How he taught me to edit videos.

"How are your parents?"

I tell her they are doing so much better.

"I'm so glad they're okay," Kimber says. "I think about your family every day. I think about your sister every day."

"I know. Me too."

"I'm gonna do what you told me to do. The prison is letting me take my GED in here."

"That's great."

"After I get my GED, I plan on studying to be a substance abuse counselor. If I can prevent anyone else from dying the way Tonya did, I might actually get to do something useful with my life."

"I'm sure you're gonna do many useful things in your life, Kimber."

She smiles at me. "You saved my life, you know," she says. "The day you visited me in the hospital. You saved my life, Kira."

Our time is up. We stand and hug. "I'll see you next year, Kimber," I promise her.

It is really late. I should be getting ready for bed, but I'm too wired to sleep. I use my ring finger to blend the pastel colors as I draw Jason's lips and cheekbones. I followed him back on Instagram and scrolled through photos until I found a clear image of his face. I grab my flesh-colored pastel stick and blend it in with a pink stick to recreate lip color. Then I blend with my fingertips.

Tonya steps into my bedroom. "Did you have fun today? Was it a good birthday?"

"Yes. It was a great sweet sixteen."

"So, Jason is a hottie, isn't he?"

"Yes, he's the most gorgeous person I've ever seen in my life."

Tonya laughs at me. "He's so hot, you blushed every time he looked at you."

I hate my sister and her perfect vision. "I did not."

"And when he broke your fall, you stayed in his arms way longer than you needed to. And the two of you were alone in that tiny gallery room forever. What happened in there?"

"We talked about art."

"Just art, huh?" She asks doubtfully. "Did he do anything to make your heart race?"

"Yes, Tonya, but don't ask for specifics because you're not gonna get them."

She comes around and looks at my drawing. I make no attempt to hide what I'm working on. "Wow. You're crushing on him big time. Let's figure out how you can get him."

"He's not an object you can pick up at the store." I don't like hearing him objectified. "I already invited him over to

draw. We'll have to see what happens when we spend time together."

"I'm happy for you. He's gorgeous. Mom and Dad like him. Mike and Aunt Ginny adore him. He saved you from falling on your ass, offered to help pay for your birthday dinner, and bought you an awesome gift. Most guys our age are major assholes. I think you found a great one, Kira." She hugs me. "Can you do me a favor and tell Mom she should go back to school."

I pull back and look at her, confused. "Mom's never mentioned anything about that."

"She will. When she does, tell her she should definitely go back to college."

"Okay," I say, confused.

"Do you know how many people pass away every day? There are so many guys for me to chase in the afterlife. I assure you. I'm totally over Jason. We were never right for each other. He was always supposed to be with you." She takes my face in her hands. "We don't have much time left. The living always wake up too soon.

"Jason was right about how selfish I was. When you remember all the good things I did. Letting you sleep with me when you were scared. Doing your hair and makeup. Helping you with your Halloween costumes. That was the real me. Drinking while you were in the car with me. Sleeping with the guy I knew you wanted. Checking out of rehab. That was all my addiction."

"Okay," I agree. My eyes water.

"Don't cry. You'll wake up." She touches my face. "You kept your promise. You visited Kimber today."

"Of course I did."

Tonya smiles at me. "Kimber is going to help so many people stay clean and sober. And all the people she helps will help others to. Hundreds of people will be better off because of Kimber and you. Because you saved Kimber's life when you visited her in the hospital."

I hug my sister tightly.

"Tonya, come on," someone says behind me in an Irish accent. "Let's go make sure your grandfather stays behind bars."

I turn and see Jason's mom standing in my doorway.

She looks at me and smiles. "Do me a favor. Tell my son he'll never be like his father. Mimi saw to that. Thank her for me."

Tonya and her exit my room together.

I turn and look at my drawing of Jason.

I open my eyes and see him sleeping soundly next to me. I move closer to him. He wraps his arms around me.

Chapter Twenty Seven

Thursday, November 28, 2024

Aunt Ginny and Mom help me prepare this year's feast. For once, there's no sisterly bickering.

"How are you holding up?" Ginny asks Mom.

"I'm sure I'll need to cry later because Tonya isn't here with us," Mom says, "but I'm still going to let myself be happy today that all of you are here with me."

I smile and go back to stuffing mushrooms.

Aunt Ginny goes into the living room to see if any of our guests need anything.

"Kira, I have something else to tell you," Mom whispers. "I'm not ready to tell anybody else. It's kind of embarrassing."

I lower the spoon I'm using. "What is it?"

I've decided to do something kind of crazy for a person my age."

I remember the dream I had a few months back. I never told my mom about it, because the moment never seemed right. I didn't want to bring it up and make her cry.

"I've decided—"

"To go back to school."

She looks at me stunned. "How'd you know? I haven't told anybody yet, not even your father. I've been looking into it online when I'm alone in my room because the idea of going back at my age is a bit embarrassing. How'd you know?"

"Tonya told me."

Mom looks confused.

"In a dream," I explain. "I had a dream about her, and she said you should definitely go back to college."

Mom's eyes look big and glassy.

"She's with Jason's mother," I explain. "I saw them together. Tonya seems healthy again, wherever she is."

A look of relief sweeps across my mother's face. She pulls me into a hug. "Thank you for telling me." She pulls back and grabs a paper towel to fix her face. "No. I am not crying today. I'll cry later on tonight after the holiday. I'm going to enjoy today."

"What are you doing to study?" I ask.

"Psychology. I want to be a grief counselor. I want to help people the way my counselor helped me."

"I think it's a great idea, Mom."

She smiles. "You do? You don't think it's crazy? Someone my age going back to school? I think it's embarrassing."

"You have nothing to be embarrassed about."

"I love the idea of an online school. That way, I don't look like the old fart on campus. I got the idea when Mike and Seth were talking about taking classes online. I'm going to tell your father I'll be working with him part-time and going to school part-time. It might take me forever to get my degree. And after I do, I will need even more training before I can counsel people."

"You'll get there eventually," I assure her. "I'm really proud of you."

Jason comes into the kitchen. "Everything looks amazing." He wraps his arms around me from behind. "This is the best Thanksgiving I've ever had. Thank you for inviting us."

"You're welcome." I turn around and kiss him. "I think it helps, having so many people here this year. It still feels like Tonya's missing, but it helps having so many loved ones here." I slide the stuffed mushrooms into the oven.

Mimi comes into the kitchen and asks what she can do to help. Mom asks her to help set the table.

"It smells delicious," Mimi says to Seth's Dad as she places the plates down. "I'm so excited. This is the first year Jason and I have had a home-cooked Thanksgiving. I'm a terrible cook. I order. For years, it has been the two of us at my kitchen table."

Seth's dad smiles at her. "I know how you feel. It was just me and Seth for many years, too." He looks at Seth and Mike, playing video games in our living room. "We should've started coming here years ago."

When all the food is placed on the table, we sit. I look at my mom. She's dressed up in a nice outfit. She looks happy.

Dad carves the turkey.

"Cheers to the cooks," Mimi raises her glass. "I'm a disaster in the kitchen. I'm glad my future daughter-in-law is such a good cook."

Jason squeezes my hand under the table.

Dad stops carving and looks at Mimi.

Mike and Seth laugh at Dad's shocked expression.

"I don't think we need to have this conversation yet," I assure my dad. My parents have been really cool about letting me spend the weekends sleeping at Jason's. They even let Jason spend the night in my room with me on the anniversary of Tonya's death because I was sad. I had to swear that all Jason and I were going to do that night was sleep. The last thing I need is them flipping out and laying down annoying ground rules. "Not for about a decade," I add, hoping to ease the tension.

"Agreed," Dad says and goes back to carving.

"Sorry about that," Jason whispers. "My aunt gets overly excited about things sometimes." He squeezes my hand again. "She knows how much I love you."

"I love you, too. But how about we don't give my dad a heart attack," I tease.

Jason smiles at me and kisses me on the cheek.

Chapter Twenty Eight

Friday, March 10, 2028

I sit in my room in one of Montserrat College of Art's apartments. I have my own room. I share a bathroom, a kitchen, and a common room with three other girls.

My art teacher told me to take a risk. To do something provocative. I work on a drawing of Jason and me naked, wrapped in each other's arms. This is definitely provocative. I use charcoal to draw the muscles in his back, and then blend it with a paintbrush. One of my teachers taught me that. It creates a softer blend than using my fingers.

The blur in my peripheral vision has worsened slowly over the years. I have a small section of clear visibility in the center of my eyes. The rest of my vision has blurred to the point that glasses can't help me function easily anymore. My dad wanted me to take a semester off from school to recover from the operation. I refused. I've been living with this disease for so long that I know how to function around it. I'll take two weeks off after spring break ends to recover from my surgery. I'm going to work on my assignments until the second my father picks me up to take me to the hospital. It helps me feel normal.

Dad texts me that he and Mom are here. I sigh and put my charcoal stick down. I wash my hands and pick up my suitcase. I'll be back in my apartment in three weeks. I need to stay with my parents as I recover.

Dad hugs me and helps me with my suitcase. I get in his car. He talks about how safe my procedure is the whole way to Jason's apartment. "About seventy-five percent of corneas stay clear for at least five years after surgery. The success rate of corneal transplants is about ninety-five percent."

"I know, Doug. She'll be fine," Mom assures him.

Jason is waiting outside for us. He gets in the back seat with me and holds my hand the whole way to the hospital in Boston. "Are you scared?"

"A little," I whisper so my parents can't hear me. "I'm glad I'm getting general anesthesia. I want to be unconscious as they cut sections of my eyes out and replace them with a dead person's eye."

"Don't think about that," Jason says. "Think about our trip to Ireland this summer. All the things you're gonna see once your eyes heal. Rolling lush green hills. The Cliffs of Moher."

"You would've seen that all already if it wasn't for me."

"Yeah, but it'll be better with you. Everything's better with you." He kisses my forehead. "Think about all the places we'll see. All the drawings and paintings you'll create."

"All the writing you'll get done as we relax at your grandmother's house," I add.

"Yeah. If you get scared at all, keep your mind focused on our trip."

I check into the hospital. I change into a gown. A nurse comes in to insert an IV drip into my arm. They give me a shot to help me relax. I look at Jason.

I come out of anesthesia. I can't see anything. I'm too weak to talk. *Am I blind? Did they mess up the operation? Why can't I see?*

"Kira, it's okay," Jason says. The bed moves as he sits next to me. He takes my hands and holds them up to my face. "The doctors said your operation was a success. You have to wear eye patches. That's why you can't see."

I touch the plastic shields over my eyes and relax.

"They'll come off tomorrow," Jason assures me. "Go back to sleep."

I refuse to lie back and relax. I reach for his hands and pull him closer.

He lies down next to me. "This is probably gonna get me in trouble, but I don't care." He wraps his arms around me.

I drop my head on his chest and relax.

"Pretend we're home. At my place. Your eyes are closed because you're falling asleep. That's not scary, is it?"

I shake my head no. *I'm going to marry this guy.* I fall back to sleep.

Saturday, March 11, 2028

My eye shield comes off. I blink my eyes and try to focus on the doctor in front of me.

"Everything looks blurry," I say, scared.

"That will go away in time," the doctor assures me. "It's going to take some time for the swelling to go down."

I'm given dark glasses and wheeled out of the hospital in a wheelchair. I get in my dad's car. I'm so groggy.

My parents take me home.

If I get water in my eyes, it might be disastrous. Jason helps me shower carefully with the detachable shower head. Normally, this would be a good opportunity to get kinky, but I'm not allowed to have sex for three weeks. We're too exhausted to do anything anyway. Last night, he stayed up next to my bed in a chair in case I woke up. He barely slept.

I crawl into my old bed. Jason crawls into my bed next to me. Alma jumps on my bed and curls up with both of us.

I cuddle close to Jason. "I'm going to marry you someday," I whisper.

"I know." He kisses me gently. We fall asleep.

Friday, March 31, 2028

Jason drives me back to my apartment. It's been three weeks since the surgery. My eyes are slowly getting better. I can see five feet ahead of me, the way I could when I was sixteen. Mom and Dad keep insisting that my sight will improve with time. I'm tired of waiting for that to happen. I want to get back to my normal life.

Jason helps me up to my room. I take off my sunglasses, go over to my easel, and look at the drawing I was working on. I can't wait to get started again.

Jason goes down to the car to get my bags. I look at him as he comes back and places my bags down on the floor of my bedroom, ten feet away. He notices that I'm staring at him. "What?"

"You're so hot." I look him up and down. I always knew he was gorgeous, but I've only ever seen him close up. I can't believe how stunning he looks. He goes to the gym and works as a waiter. He's in such good shape. His chest is broad. His arms are way more sculpted than they were when he was a teenager. His hair is thick, and it begs to be grabbed. His eyes are so green I can see the vivid color from ten feet away.

He smiles at me. "You can see me from all the way over there?"

"Yeah. You're beautiful."

He smiles and rushes towards me. He kisses me and lays me down on my bed. "I'm gonna be slow and gentle, just to be safe," he whispers.

I reach for his shirt and pull it off. Three weeks without him inside of me has been torture.

Saturday, May 27, 2028

We pull up to the international departures curb at Logan Airport.

"Make sure you text me as soon as the plane lands," Mom says from the front seat.

"Cindy, you do know we can track the plane's entire flight online," Dad reminds her.

Mom turns around and looks at us, "I don't care. Text me anyway. The idea of anything happening to either of you makes me so nervous."

"I will text you as soon as the plane lands," Jason assures her. "And again, when we get to my grandmother's house."

"Thank you," Mom says.

Dad pulls up to the curb, and we all get out of the car. Jason takes our suitcases out of the trunk and hugs my parents goodbye.

Dad smiles and hugs me. "Go. Have a wonderful time."

Mom is more dramatic. "I can't believe my baby is leaving."

"Cindy, let her go," Dad says. "You're being a drama queen."

"I know. My baby is leaving. I'm allowed to be a drama queen."

"Mom, I'll be back in two months," I assure her.

Mom sighs, "I know." She had the same look on her face the day she dropped me off at college. Excited for me, but sad that my childhood is over. "I'm happy for you. Go."

Jason takes my hand and we walk into the airport.

The flight takes off on time. Jason sits next to me, working on his novel. It's about his mother in the afterlife. She fights to help abused women on Earth flee from their abusive relationships. I pull out my tablet and work on the illustration for his novel's cover. I draw his mother's round green eyes and thick red hair.

Jason is squirming like crazy. He gets up to use the restroom and to stretch his legs. He sits back down and tries to go back to work, but he can't sit still.

"What's wrong?" I ask.

"Nothing. I'm fine."

"You're nervous to finally meet your mom's family."

He looks at me, surprised.

I lower my stylus and look at him. "You've imagined this moment so many times, you're worried it's not gonna live up to all your expectations. When you didn't get to make this trip four years ago, part of you was relieved that you didn't have to meet them. They could keep being the perfect family in your imagination."

"Sometimes it's annoying how well you know me."

I laugh at his grumpy expression. "You don't need to worry about any of that, Jason. You're a very lovable person. They are all gonna love you."

He smiles at me.

I pick my stylus back up. "So relax and stop squirming. It's hard enough to draw with occasional turbulence. I don't need you fidgeting like a lunatic."

He tickles my waist. "Who's squirming now?"

I squirm and giggle like crazy.

The lady sitting across the aisle gives us a dirty look.

We laugh at her grumpy face.

"Sorry," I tell her, and we sit still.

"I love you," Jason says.

"I love you, too."

The plane lands. We text my parents and Mimi immediately and let them know we arrived safely.

The airport is full of intense sounds and smells. People all around us rush in all different directions. Everyone is talking on their phones.

"Are you okay?" Jason asks, making sure I'm not feeling overstimulated.

I smile at him. "I'm great." I'm too excited to be nervous. I can't believe how clear and sharp the world looks. A girl several paces ahead of me has a beautiful floral dress on. I catch up to her to ask her where she got it. Then I smile at the cute little boy and his father walking next to me. They smile back. I look at everyone we pass. Some people look tired, others look excited. Nobody looks scary.

My boyfriend is so nervous to meet his relatives; he is in a bit of a daze. I'm the one reading signs and figuring out where to go. I lead him to the baggage claim, where his aunt and grandmother said they'd be waiting for us.

Jason freezes in his tracks when he sees his aunt. The woman looks so much like his mother, there's no doubt she's Niamh's sister. She has the same round eyes, lips, and thick red hair.

The older woman recognizes Jason as soon as she sees him. Her red hair is peppered with grey strands. She smiles. Tears fill her eyes.

Jason's hand tightens on mine.

"They're going to love you," I assure him. I have the best feeling about this. Jason is going to have two families, on two different continents.

ABOUT THE AUTHOR

Isis Chandler

When I'm not writing, I upload YouTube videos about spirituality and recovering from an abusive family. I also teach children language arts, history, and English as a second language. I love drawing, painting, and spending time with my husband and two cats.

isischandler.com